Suitable for Framing

Lori Roberts Herbst

Editor: Lisa Mathews, Kill Your Darlings Editing Services
Cover Designer: Molly Burton, Cozy Cover Designs

ISBN-13: 978-1-7362593-1-3
First printing: January 2021

Electronic edition:
ISBN-13: 978-1-7362593-0-6

For my amazing husband Paul, who gently but firmly nagged me into making this happen.

Acknowledgements

I've never been an athlete (as anyone who knows me will attest), but I have been lucky to have an enthusiastic and talented squad of cheerleaders to urge me onward. Many thanks to the following people:

Lisa Mathews, editor extraordinaire. Finding her at Kill Your Darlings Editing Services took my writing to the next level. I hope we have a long and mutually satisfying alliance.

Cover designer Molly Burton of Cozy Cover Designs. Her talent brought my vision to life in living color.

My fabulous beta readers, including Lisa B., Rodger, Melanie, and Mandy. (I've been through so many drafts of this book that I worry I've left someone off the list. If so, I'll double up the appreciation on the next book.)

My first critique group: Catherine, Margie, Elizabeth. Your encouragement kept me going when I thought about giving up.

Kendel Lynn, whose in-depth edit of the book's first chapter was the equivalent of a master's class.

Anna Castle, fellow Sisters in Crime Guppy, who provided more self-publishing guidance than I had any right to expect.

My daughters Jenny and Katie, who read the book in its early stages and boosted my confidence with their kind words.

Marilyn Herbst for her proofreading skills, not to mention her love and patience as my mother-in-law these past decades.

Nicki Huntsman Smith, who jumpstarted my writing journey and encouraged me every step of the way. "…it is by standing on the shoulders of giants."

And finally, Sisters in Crime, especially the Guppies. I wish I'd found this group earlier in the process. I can't say enough about their support and the resources they provide. Swimming with the Guppies makes me a better writer.

Suitable for Framing

1

The tires on my mother's Jeep crunched across the Creekside Event Center's gravel lot as she pulled into a spot near the entrance. In front of us, at the edge of the ravine, a family of bighorn sheep perched atop a pile of tumbled rocks. The setting sun melted a pink and orange radiance across the Colorado Rockies behind the sheep.

"I'm doing this under duress," I said.

"Yes, sweetheart, you've made that clear."

The silence stretched between us, broken only by the soft hum of the Jeep's heater. I turned my gaze toward the town. Sodium streetlights spread a hazy aura over the village shops, a mixture of Adirondack and Victorian architecture.

Everything looked exactly as it had when I'd left twenty-five years ago. It was as if I'd stepped into a time capsule, and I was the only thing that had changed.

I chewed my bottom lip, tasting lipstick for the first time in weeks. "I just wanted it on the record."

She picked up an invisible pen and mimed writing. "There. I have noted it. But I must remind you again that we have been unable to locate our original photographer. You're the obvious replacement."

I heard her growing irritation but didn't care. She'd guilted me into photographing the annual Snowflake Swirl winter ball, so I was irritated too. My mother had plucked me from my cozy cabin and wrenched me from my ever-present box of wine. Worst of all, now I was going to have to see *people.*

At that thought, I flipped down the sun visor and studied myself in the mirror, prodding the wrinkles on my forehead. "I still can't believe you're making me do this."

"You look lovely, Callie," she said, her voice tight. "You're going to be fine."

I snorted. Lovely was a stretch. Despite a layer of makeup, my face appeared pale and blotchy. The skin beneath my green eyes was puffy and shadowed. My hair, usually dark brown with auburn highlights, now hung limp and faded around my shoulders. My stylist back in D.C. would tsk at the sight.

"Humph," I said. "Next thing I know, you'll sign me up for speed dating. I'm sure I'd generate a lot of interest."

Mom took a deep, meditative breath and locked her eyes onto mine. When I tried to turn away, she cupped my chin in a firm hand. "Listen to me, Angelface."

The childhood endearment conjured memories of rocking and singing and soothing. Hearing it now brought a surge of tears to my eyes.

"The minute you were born, I knew you would always be my pride and joy. And for the past forty-three years, I've never stopped feeling that way. You have not once disappointed me." She paused and dropped her hand. "But right now, you are on the verge."

I blinked. She raised her teacher's eyebrow. "I've been patient for over a month. But time is up. You need to call an end to your pity party. It's quite unbecoming. You are an excellent journalist and a stupendous photographer. Even more important, you are a good person."

I shook my head. "Mom, an innocent man went to jail because of my mistake and my stupid arrogance. I don't consider that being an excellent journalist. Or a good person."

"As soon as you realized your error, didn't you do what you could to repair it?"

I hesitated, then nodded. The man—boy, really, just twenty-one—was still in prison, but word had it his release was imminent. "Well, yes. I mean, I took the fresh evidence to the prosecutor."

"And you wrote a retraction. That's what good people do. Sweetheart, you're not perfect. Welcome to the real world. It's time to forgive yourself."

My mother gazed at me across the center console. At sixty-seven, gray hair framed her face, and her porcelain skin glowed. She looked regal in her floor-length silver brocade gown and her faux-fur coat. If Princess Diana had lived to this age, she would have looked exactly like Maggie Cassidy.

I sniffled and forced a smile. "I can't tell if I've just been adored or scolded."

She smiled and wiped my tears with her thumbs. "Both, I think. At least, that was my intent."

"I'll do my best to take it to heart." I gave my hair one last pat and glanced in the mirror to check my lipstick. "But now, if I'm to dazzle your Chamber of Commerce cronies, I need to get inside. Fetch Dad and hurry back so I can shoot a portrait of my favorite couple all gussied up in their winter finery. You may not have heard of me, but word is I'm a pretty decent photographer."

I slid my camera strap over my head, grabbed my equipment bag, and stepped from the warm Jeep into the chilly January air. Mom blew me a kiss. "Back in ten." I wiggled my fingers as she drove away.

She was right. It was time to give the real world another go.

I skipped around puddles of slush as if avoiding land mines, holding a hand over my Nikon DSLR to protect it from errant splashes. When I reached the Event Center portico, I stripped the gloves from my shaking hands, feeling as nervous as if this were my first job. I took a moment to gaze at the majestic mountains and the bucolic shopping village. The pleasant Norman Rockwell aura filled me with a sense of warmth I rarely experienced when I craned my neck to view big city skyscrapers. I lifted my camera and snapped a few images. For the first time in a month, I felt glad to be home.

I took one last deep breath and entered the ballroom.

It was dazzling. Metallic blue and silver snowflakes, suspended by silken threads, swayed and spun overhead. Swirled, one might say. As in Snowflake Swirl. Wasn't someone oh-so-clever? Soft light trickled from the faux candles in the chandeliers, shooting colorful prisms through dangling crystals. Floor-to-ceiling windows comprised the left wall, and the view of the mountains in the waning rays of sunlight created the effect of a vast mural.

With only an hour to showtime, an energetic group of servers bustled about, straightening the plump couches and polishing the silver coffee tables. Behind an elaborate audio station, the DJ arranged the evening's music. A hefty man in a light gray button down and black slacks stood at the bar, polishing glasses in anticipation of alcohol-laden merrymaking.

As I approached, hoping he could direct me to the person in charge, a dull metal door behind him swung open, and a man emerged from the kitchen. Not just any man, mind you, but a blond-haired, blue-eyed, Hollywood-icon type who made me suck in my breath.

And my stomach.

Like the bartender, he wore a gray button-down shirt and black slacks, but in his case, the clothes fit his tall, lean body in a—to be understated—physically pleasing manner. His hands were rough yet tender, his lips soft yet firm. All the usual clichés.

And I should know. Those hands and lips had once been quite familiar to me, some twenty-five years ago.

4

2

The man I'd just spotted preparing for the Snowflake Swirl was Sam Petrie, my high school sweetheart and the boy I once expected to marry. Though I hadn't seen him in a quarter of a century, my heart still pitter patted at the sight of him.

Sam carried a Saran-wrapped tray to the buffet table. After nestling it among the cutlery and plates, he rested his fists on the table, shoulders slumped. It looked as if he carried a heavy weight on those shoulders. After a long moment, he straightened, sucked in a breath, and surveyed the room.

When his eyes landed on me, they widened as if he'd seen a ghost. Three seconds passed. Four. Five. Then his lips curved into a hesitant smile.

He didn't make a move toward me, so I went to him and hugged him clumsily. The breadth of the years wedged between us. Still, the physical contact soothed my nerves. His too, apparently. When we pulled apart, his smile had turned genuine.

"Callie. I can't believe it. I mean, I knew you were in town, so I can believe it. But here you are, in the flesh."

He stepped back to inspect me, and a rush of self-consciousness hit me—the gray in my hair and the lines on my face—but Sam didn't appear to notice any of that. He looked at me the same way he had when I was his eighteen-year-old prom date.

I grinned like that same high school girl and studied him back. Sandy blond hair swept back from his forehead and fell to his collar, shorter than he'd worn it in high school but still as thick. A few lines had etched themselves around his eyes and mouth, giving his face a character and depth it had not yet developed when I'd last seen him. There was no denying it. The man had aged beautifully.

"You look great." We spoke at the same time and chuckled awkwardly. Then, in unison, we said, "Go ahead." More nervous laughter. I reached out and touched his arm. "It's nice to see you," I said.

He paused. Just as I began to wonder if the feeling was mutual, he pulled me into another hug. This one felt more natural, as if it hadn't been more than half our lives since we'd last embraced. I breathed in the smell of him: a spicy, earthy scent I remembered well.

Nostalgia threatened to sweep me away, but before it could, the kitchen door swung open and slammed against the wall. A tall, lithe teenager emerged, her long blond ponytail swinging across her shoulder. When she caught sight of us, her face registered confusion.

"Dad?" she said in a squeaky voice.

I pulled away from him. "*Dad?*" I repeated, my own voice rising an octave.

He beamed and slung an arm around the girl's shoulder. "Elyse, I want you to meet a dear friend from the old days. Callie Cassidy, allow me to introduce my darling daughter."

I snapped my gaping mouth shut. Sam was a father? How was that possible?

Really, though, what had I expected? The town might look the same, but time had marched onward in Rock Creek Village, unconcerned with my absence.

But still. Why hadn't my parents mentioned Sam's daughter? Or my lifelong best friend Tonya, for that matter? Why wouldn't anyone tell me my old boyfriend had a child?

That led to another jarring realization. This girl hadn't

sprung fully formed from Sam's head, like Athena from Zeus. She must have a mother. I took a surreptitious glimpse at Sam's ring finger, noting its nakedness. Then I turned my gaze to Elyse, her face a mask of simmering irritation. She looked familiar—the eyes, maybe, the pouty mouth… Recognition tickled the edge of my memory, just out of reach. From the corner of my eye, I saw Sam watching me expectantly. I reached out to shake his daughter's hand. "So nice to meet you."

The girl looked at my outstretched hand as if I were offering her a dirty diaper, but after an elbowed nudge from her father, she touched her fingers to mine. "Hey," she mumbled, then turned to her father. "Dad, doors open soon. We still have a lot to do."

"Then you'd better go get the tarts plated." He pointed at various spots on the table. "We'll put them next to the cookies. The sandwiches can go on the left side of the table, vegetable tray on the right."

Elyse shot me a sidelong glare and didn't budge. Sam snapped his fingers. "No time like the present."

She huffed, then stomped into the kitchen. He grinned. "Teenagers," he said, his voice infused with affection. "As you've no doubt guessed, my cafe is catering tonight's event." He nodded at the camera hanging around my neck. "From the looks of it, you're not here as a guest either."

"Photographer of record," I said. "Sophie Demler was supposed to do the honors, but apparently no one has seen her for a couple of days."

He snorted. "No surprise. Remember how ditzy she was back in high school? Not much has changed. Now, though, she fancies herself the next…well, Callie Cassidy, I suppose, casting herself into the role of Rock Creek Village's lead investigative journalist. She's disappeared before, chasing leads, as she says. She always pops up."

"Got it," I said, then glanced at my watch. "Well, this particular disappearance of hers has thrust me into a job for which I haven't done due diligence. I don't even know who

I'm supposed to report to."

He lifted his eyebrows. "Your mother didn't warn you?"

A cacophony of alarm bells clanged in my head. "Noooo. Mom only came to me this morning, in pure emergency mode. Said she was in charge of Snowflake Swirl photography, and Sophie was missing. She claimed the Chamber of Commerce would have her hide if no one showed up. You know how she is—she eroded my resistance, shoved me into a dress, and dropped me off at the door."

"Good old Maggie." His eyes darkened. "Guess I have to be the bearer of bad news then. Your boss for the evening is Victoria Ratliff."

It took me a second to process the name. Victoria Ratliff? The only Victoria I'd known in Rock Creek Village was... "Wait a minute. Are you referring to Victoria Dunleavy? As in, Vile Victoria?"

"The one and only."

"My mother is going to pay for this," I muttered.

One side of Sam's mouth twisted up in a smirk—an expression I recognized from the past. "Well, you're stuck now. But a lot of time has passed. Who knows? Maybe you two can bury the hatchet."

"I doubt she's gone through that drastic of a personality change." My mind flashed back to our high school days, with images of a teenaged bully surrounded by her clique of like-minded girls. Last time I'd seen Victoria was graduation day, when she'd embarrassed one of our shy classmates so much that the girl hadn't even made it through the ceremony.

And this was the woman from whom I'd get my marching orders. I grimaced. In my career, I had come into contact with raging lunatics, serial killers, and lying politicians—the dregs of society. Vile Victoria eclipsed them all.

When I looked at Sam, his jaw was clenched. "Let's just say that if you do bury the hatchet, there are a lot of villagers who wouldn't be upset if it ended up in her skull."

I cocked my head. This vitriol didn't sound like the Sam I remembered, the boy who plumbed even the worst personalities searching for that glimmer of goodness. Maybe even Sam's long-suffering patience had reached an end.

He read my expression. "Yeah, she hasn't exactly mellowed with time."

My lips fell into a frown. But as my mother had taught me, better to face the devil than to let him—or her—set up housekeeping in your head. "Guess I'd better get this over with. Feel like joining me? You could be my bodyguard…"

He laughed. "Not on your life. You've always been much braver than me." He pointed to an archway carved out of the ballroom's mirrored back wall. "Her office is at the end of the hall. If I don't see you after the party starts, I'll send the cavalry."

"Thanks a lot." I smiled at him. "Seriously, though, it's been so good to see you—"

A metallic crash interrupted the thought. Over Sam's shoulder, I saw Elyse peering through the kitchen door's round window. Sam rubbed his eyes. A dark smear on the cuff of his shirt caught my eye, and I touched his sleeve. "You have a little stain there."

He twisted his hand and frowned at the spot. "Well, that won't do." He rolled up his sleeves to hide the blotch, revealing tanned, muscular forearms. But who noticed?

Another clash of metal on metal. "Listen, I do need to go," he said. "Let's get together soon. Catch up, as they say."

"It's a date," I said, and felt myself blush at the word choice. "I'll look forward to it."

He headed toward the kitchen, favoring me with one last glance over his shoulder before disappearing through the door.

Leaving me all alone to face the lion in the Colosseum.

On my way to Victoria's office, I paused in front of the

mirrored wall to assess my appearance. I tugged at the hem of my dress, snugger than the last time I'd worn it, and ran my fingers through my hair. Unless Victoria had made a dramatic metamorphosis, she would be slender and fit. Probably even a boob job. Despite her foul insides, her outside had always been beautiful.

Whatever. I wasn't here to win a beauty pageant.

Reflected behind me, my mother walked through the front door, her arm laced through my father's. I scurried off before she could catch me preening.

I trudged down the hallway, past a restroom, a small conference room, and a couple of unmarked doors. At the end of the hall, a red exit sign glowed above a thick metal emergency door. Beside the last door, a brass plate announced Victoria Dunleavy Ratliff's office.

The door was open a crack, and a moaning sound filtered through. I tilted my head closer, trying to decipher the noise. Chanting, perhaps? Was Victoria meditating? Was she sitting cross-legged on the floor in a yoga pose?

Then my nose caught a coppery scent, one I recognized from the crime scenes I had worked. Blood.

I held my breath and slowly nudged the door. One inch. Two inches. And then I saw a slender, tan length of leg that ended in a bare foot, its painted silver toenails sparkling in the light.

3

I shoved the door open. A woman I recognized as a grown-up version of Vile Victoria lay on her back, body twisted like a viper, eyes open but unseeing. She wore a form-fitting, low-cut powder blue gown. A sapphire pendant rested between breasts that, as I had predicted, suggested the intervention of a plastic surgeon. Her body was as perfect as a marble sculpture.

Except for the oozing crimson slash mark above the left breast.

The tip of a sleek brass letter opener dripped blood as it hovered in the air above the gash. It was clutched in the fingers of a woman in a gold sequined gown, crouching beside Victoria's prone body. "Help her," she murmured. The chanting I'd heard from the hallway. The woman lifted beseeching eyes to mine, and I realized I was looking at another girl from my past. She'd changed her hair from blond to red, but I was looking at Kimberly Wainwright, Victoria's high school best friend and Princess to her Queen of Mean.

Kimberly unclenched her fingers, and the letter opener clattered to the floor. She leapt to her feet and rushed toward me, grasping my shoulder and leaving a bloody print on my dress.

"This is not what it looks like." Her voice was shrill, and her face looked so gaunt that I immediately thought *eating disorder.* "I didn't kill her. I swear I didn't. It wasn't me..."

The sound of humming floated down the hallway. Kimberly froze, her grip tightening on my shoulder. Then she shuttled past me and bolted to the exit door, flinging it open and disappearing outside.

The humming ceased abruptly. I turned toward its source and saw Elyse midway down the hall, a tray of goodies perched atop one upturned palm. She stared at the exit door and shifted accusing eyes toward me. "What's going on?"

The vexed tilt of her mouth, the haughty posture...recognition clicked. The girl resembled a teenaged Kimberly. Elyse must be her daughter.

With Sam? My mind reeled, but they were thoughts for another time. Right now, I needed to protect the girl—and the scene. I lifted my hands. "Don't come any closer. Go get your father."

But as Sam had alluded, teenagers weren't especially obedient. Elyse barreled down the hall, sugary treats bouncing precariously on the tray. I stood spreadeagled in the doorway. She couldn't get past me, but she did manage to peer over my shoulder. Elyse's hands flew to her cheeks, and the tray clattered to the floor, scattering tarts and cookies across the carpet.

Then she screamed. A piercing, blood-curdling scream that presaged a future in horror movies.

The girl's cheeks had gone pale. Her cornflower blue eyes moved from the body in the office to the exit door, widening as comprehension dawned. When her body seemed to deflate like a balloon, I feared she might faint. I reached out to support her, but she pulled away.

Footsteps pounded down the hall. Sam sprinted toward us, trailed by my father. Relief rushed through me. Elyse's father would handle her, and my father, Rock Creek Village's police chief until his retirement a year ago, would deal with the rest of it.

Sam took Elyse in his arms, and she buried her face into his chest. He craned his head toward the office. When he glimpsed Victoria's body, his arm tightened protectively around his daughter.

My father took in the office scene with a quick glance. He put a hand on Sam's arm, still wrapped around Elyse, and nudged the two of them away from the door. He gestured to my mother, who stood a few yards away. "Butch? Is it bad?" she said. She read the unspoken message on his face and nodded.

"Maggie, can you see to them?" he asked. She quickly guided Sam and Elyse away from the office and through a group of staff members gathered at the end of the hall.

"Dad," I said, keeping my voice low, "I found Kimberly Wainwright crouched over the body holding what appeared to be the murder weapon. She dropped it and ran out the back door."

Dad glanced at the exit door but made no move toward it. His priority was the woman lying on the floor. Stepping carefully into the office, he bent over Victoria and placed a finger to her neck. After a moment, he shook his head and pulled his phone from his pocket. I knew he was summoning emergency responders.

I also knew they wouldn't need to hurry.

As Dad spoke to dispatch, his eyes examined the wound and scanned the floor around Victoria's body. After he disconnected the call, he turned to me. His eyes narrowed when he spotted the bloody smear on my shoulder. "You okay, Sundance?"

My lips curved up slightly at the nickname that had been attached to me since birth. I was Sundance to his Butch. Right now, I found it oddly comforting. "I'm fine. Kimberly grabbed my shoulder with her bloody hand before she escaped. Shouldn't one of us go after her?"

He shook his head. "We'll let the police track her down. You and I need to keep the scene secure."

He glanced toward the looky loos at the end of the hall and pointed at the bartender. "Dan, lock all the entrance doors. Don't let anyone in except emergency personnel. Put a sign on the front door telling people the party is canceled. Don't give any specifics. Just say we'll provide details as soon as we can."

Dan gave him a salute. "Will do, Chief." Villagers apparently still thought of Charlie Cassidy, who had acquired the nickname Butch back when Paul Newman made it famous, in his former professional capacity. After thirty years on the job, I imagined they always would.

"The rest of you, go on back into the ballroom. No need to stand around here gawking—I'm not going to let you in. You'll need to remain on the premises until officers question and release you." He raised a hand at the grumbling that ensued. "Sorry, folks. That's how it is. We have a serious situation, and that's all I'm going to say about it right now."

After he finished issuing his commands and the group dispersed, he returned to the doorway and leaned toward me. "Body's still warm," he said. "No rigor. Blood pool isn't tacky yet, but the flow has stopped."

"Meaning, she died within a couple of hours. But not necessarily minutes ago."

"That'd be my guess. You say you actually witnessed Kimberly Wainwright holding the murder weapon?"

I nodded. "Before I came in, I heard her wailing *Help her* over and over. When she saw me, she immediately denied killing Victoria. I have to tell you, though, she sounded sincere."

He shot me a cynical look. "We'll figure all that out later. Right now, I have a question for you. The coroner and crime scene techs will have to come here from Pine Haven, and it'll take at least an hour. But I want the scene photographed before the EMTs trample everything. Would you find it too disturbing to take pictures?"

"Disturbing? Dad, do you remember how I made my living the past quarter of a century? I've written about and photographed all sorts of violent crimes."

"I know. But this isn't some random victim. It's someone

you were acquainted with. I don't want to put you in a tough position."

I shrugged. "It won't bother me. No more than any other crime scene I photographed. Anything in particular you want me to focus on?"

He gave a slight shake of his head. "I noticed an oddity, that's all. I don't want to influence your observations. Let's see if you pick up on the same thing I did. Mostly I just want the scene documented. For the detectives, of course."

"Of course." My father had investigated crimes for many years. As much as he enjoyed running the ski lodge resort property he and my mom had purchased when he retired, I could only imagine how much the siren song of police work still called to him.

I knew the feeling well. As depleted and empty as my job as an investigative photojournalist had left me, studying the crime scene in this office triggered muscle memory I didn't know I had. It was like an itch on an amputated limb. And now Dad had given me permission to scratch.

4

Dad headed to the ballroom to await the first responders. My hand tightened around my camera. *Action time.*

I paused for a moment and dropped my eyes, as I always did at a murder scene, to pay my respects. No matter who the victims were, what they had done, they were human beings. None of them deserved to die a violent death. I may have disliked—all right, hated—Victoria in high school, but that was twenty-five years ago. My mind and heart filled with compassion for her.

Now I was in the right frame of mind to start the process. First step: observing the scene. Victoria's body stretched across the white tile floor. I stood near the door and snapped the camera's shutter a few times. Then I moved around her, careful not to touch anything. Stepping over the displaced stiletto, I examined her wound. Sprays of red had splashed across the gown's shimmery blue bodice, which was sliced open above her left breast. Beneath the fissure, a three-inch maw in Victoria's chest gaped like a screaming mouth. I leaned in and shot a close-up of the wound. Then I turned my attention to the weapon lying next to her torso, its brass length tipped with crimson. A cell phone lay near her outstretched hand, and I took another close-up. I was in my element now: not thinking, not analyzing, just shooting.

When I stepped back for a wide angle shot, I spotted the oddity Dad had alluded to. A small wildflower about the size of my thumbnail lay near Victoria's face. Five bright blue petals encircled a yellow center, like the sun in the Colorado sky. A pretty little flower—I'd seen it a thousand times on clear spring days along mountain trails.

But this was the dead of winter. Surely the first frost had exterminated all the wildflowers months ago. I lifted the camera and zoomed in. Then I glanced around the room, searching for a bouquet or vase from which the flower might have fallen. Nothing.

After one last scan of the room, I felt satisfied I'd gotten all the pictures Dad needed. I glanced at Victoria's ego wall, adorned with photos of ribbon cuttings and ground breakings. A studio shot with a muscle-bound man I assumed was her husband and twin boys who had to be her sons. There was a shot from our high school prom: teenaged Victoria and Kimberly flanked by three other girls, all dressed up in fancy clothes, arms draped around one another. Vile Victoria's Vixens. I glanced at Victoria's body on the floor, her gown not much different than the one in that long-ago picture. A shudder coursed through me.

Next, I turned to Victoria's workspace. Pure nosiness led me across the office to have a look.

It was a sleek, modern setup—white leather chair tucked into a white lacquered desk. Invoices, unopened mail, and a copy of *The Rock Creek Gazette* littered the surface. To one side, a crystal wine glass held a quarter inch of coral liquid. Some fancy zinfandel, I assumed. Probably not from a box.

It all appeared routine—until I noticed a stack of four slender books near the right edge. I moved behind the desk and looked at the spines: Rock Creek High School yearbooks spanning our shared years there. Why would Victoria have our old yearbooks on her desk? Taking a step back, I snapped a picture of the desktop. That's when I spied a lavender notecard tucked inside the top book.

I knew I shouldn't look. It was none of my business. But

when had that stopped me?

Not wanting to contaminate the scene, I extracted a tissue from a brushed nickel box on the desk and wrapped it around my finger. I reached toward the yearbook, looping the protected finger beneath the corner of the cover, and slowly lifted…

"What do you think you're doing?"

The baritone voice rattled the windows. I jumped like the proverbial kid with her hand in the cookie jar. I stared at the man, willing myself to calm down. Mid-thirties, I guessed, with smooth, olive skin and black gelled hair curling around his ears. In his burgundy dress shirt, tightly creased black slacks, and shiny wingtip shoes, there was no mistaking that he was a detective. Even his ramrod straight posture transmitted energy and adrenaline. Definitely a take-charge kind of guy.

But then again, I was a take-charge kind of woman.

Before I could dazzle the detective with my professionalism, my take-charge father entered the office and stole my thunder. "Evening, Sanchez. This is my daughter Callie. She's a journalist. I asked her to shoot a few pictures before the EMTs arrived. You know how it goes— they can trample a scene." He smiled and held out his hand. Sanchez grasped it, but I saw the muscles in his jaw tense.

A third man, this one vaguely familiar, entered. Despite his laid-back demeanor, he exuded authority. "It'll be all right, Raul. Ms. Callahan is a professional. I'm sure she hasn't disturbed any evidence."

The three men looked at my tissue-covered finger. A flush crept up my neck.

Dad cleared his throat diplomatically. "Callie, you remember Frank Laramie?"

Ah yes. Frank Laramie, a longtime Rock Creek Village detective who had worked with Dad for decades. He was older now, of course, with gray at his temples and deep lines grooved in his weathered forehead. His lanky form was clad in a plaid flannel shirt, dark jeans, and boots.

"Of course. Hello, Detective Laramie. I'd say it's nice to see you, but…"

"*Chief* Laramie," my father interjected. "Frank took over when I retired."

I should have known that, I realized with shame, but I'd been *too busy* to attend my father's retirement celebration. *Too busy* for a lot of family events and milestones over the years. But my pity party would have to wait until I was in proximity to my wine box.

"Sorry," I said. "*Chief* Laramie. Congratulations."

He grinned. "Thanks. Call me Frank. When someone says 'Chief,' I look around for your dad."

Sanchez bounced on his heels, eager to be done with the niceties. "Ms. Callahan, since you've wandered around in here, we'll need your fingerprints. When the officers take your statement, let them know what you touched."

Frank lifted his eyebrows but didn't speak. Dad crossed his arms, also silent. I looked at the three of them and understood the dynamic. Sanchez was the young pup with something to prove. Frank was his boss and mentor. And Dad was the wise elder who'd handed over the reins.

"You can take my fingerprints, but I assure you I didn't touch anything," I said. "I've been a journalist for a long time. Actually, I'm a convergence media specialist. That means I investigate, write, and photograph my own stories…" I realized I was babbling now. "The point is, I've covered more crime scenes than I care to remember. I know not to touch anything." I stared at Sanchez, daring him to challenge me.

"Good to know." The condescension in his tone rankled me. "Thank you for your…help. You can wait in the ballroom with everyone else. We'll handle it from here."

I understood I was being dismissed. I geared up to argue. Maybe he'd like to hear about some of the crimes I'd helped solve. Perhaps I'd tell him about the prestigious Felden Prize for Excellence in Journalism I'd won. But Frank caught my eye and smiled tactfully. "We appreciate your assistance, Callie. I expect your photos will be a great help to the investigation."

"Thank you, Chief Laramie. *Frank*." I emphasized for Sanchez's benefit. But he'd already turned his back to me as he studied Victoria's body.

Dismissal complete.

I paused at the office door, watching the detective and the chief pace the room as my father observed. My fingers tingled with the need to take more pictures, to thrust myself into the investigation. But I couldn't get involved.

For one thing, Sanchez had made it clear my talents weren't needed. But more importantly, I'd returned to the village to escape just such wrenching emotional quandaries. I wanted to go home to my little cabin, bury myself under the quilt, pet my dog, drink some wine, and disappear into the pages of a book. Maybe I'd even forgo my usual mystery and sink into a romance. These days, I preferred my adventures fictional.

As I wrested my eyes from the murder scene, a sliver of light and a draft of cold air pulled my attention to the steel exit door. Instead of being tightly latched, it was cracked open. I reached toward the aluminum handle, intending to pull the door shut, but then hesitated. Kimberly had escaped through this door. Crime scene techs were probably going to examine it for fingerprints.

Still, these emergency doors were installed to glide shut automatically after someone exited. Why had this one refused to latch?

I leaned forward to look more closely and immediately determined the problem. Someone had shoved a folded piece of paper inside the strike plate, meaning the bolt couldn't catch.

The wad of paper could mean nothing. People jimmied latches all the time. There was a staff parking lot right outside the door. Maybe a delivery man didn't want to wait for someone to open the door while he transported multiple loads. Perhaps a staffer needed to make a couple of trips to her car and simply forgot to remove the paper afterwards.

Or maybe someone had rigged the latch earlier in the day so he—or she—could sneak in the back way to commit murder.

That person might be Kimberly. Or it could have been another intruder. In that case, Kimberly had ended up in the wrong place at the wrong time.

One thing was certain. Dad needed to see this. But first, I did what I'd been trained to do. I lifted my camera and documented the scene.

Then I reached inside the office and grabbed Dad's arm, pulling him to the exit door. I pointed at the latch. "Huh," he said. "Have you touched this?"

From Sanchez, the question would have evoked a defensive response. But from Dad, I treated it as routine and shook my head.

He rubbed a hand across his chin. "Could be a coincidence. Seems unlikely, though. We'll—they'll—need to dust the door for prints."

"If someone did this on purpose, I doubt he'd be stupid enough to leave prints."

"One thing you and I have learned in our careers, Sundance: criminals often get caught because of their own stupid mistakes. It's worth pursuing. You head into the ballroom. I'll get Frank and Raul."

"Sure you don't want me to wait here? Maybe I could help…"

He looked at me, his green eyes gentle. "This was a good catch. But you've done your part." He sighed. "I have too. We need to let the current team handle this. Go join your mother. I'll be with you in a minute."

I nodded, fighting the sinking feeling in my chest that I knew my dad was experiencing too. It was hard to let go.

5

C louds shrouded the moon. A light snow drifted from the sky, leaving tiny wet trails along the window. Buckled into the backseat of the Jeep, I listened idly to Mom and Dad's soft chatter as we drove the short distance from the Creekside to the Knotty Pine Resort. My teeth chattered in the cold, and my breath exhaled in a cloud of frost. At least my rear end was toasty, though. Whoever invented the seat warmer had my tush's undying gratitude.

I watched the dark shapes of the shops slide past as I replayed the evening's events in my mind. Soon after I'd joined Mom in the ballroom, emergency responders had arrived. As they rolled an empty stretcher into the hallway, Dad made his way toward us. Three uniformed officers documented staffers' contact information and released them. One of the officers took Elyse and Sam aside and recorded their statements. Afterward, Elyse rushed out the front door so fast her father had to jog to keep up. I wondered if she was on her way to find her mother.

The same officer then took my statement, jotting notes and extracting my promise to appear at the station tomorrow to formalize it. At Sanchez's direction, the officer took possession of my camera. I was prepared to put up a fight, but Dad intervened, so I reluctantly agreed.

Then the EMTs rolled the gurney back through the

room. This time, though, it bore Victoria's unmoving, blanketed form. A swatch of blue silk flapped out from beneath the cover. A tress of blond hair snaked over the edge of the thin mattress.

Back in the present, I wiped away a tear as Dad parked the Jeep. He glanced at me in the rearview mirror. "You okay, Sundance?"

"Just tired. Ready to pick up Woody, change into my pj's, and curl up in bed with a book."

Mom bobbed her head. "I'm ready for bed myself."

The three of us exited the vehicle. Dad draped an arm around Mom, and she looped her arm through mine as we slogged across the sidewalk to the Knotty Pine's entrance. As the glass doors slid open, I braced myself for Woody's traditional greeting: a furry missile launching himself at my shoulders.

Instead, I was met with a slight wafting of warm air.

Jamal, the college kid who worked the evening shift, smiled at my silent query and tilted his head toward the Great Room. With a glance, I understood the snub. My not-so-loyal dog was stretched out on the couch, his head snug in Tonya's lap.

Traitorous creature.

Mom and Dad greeted Tonya warmly and excused themselves. I plopped onto the couch and patted Woody's haunches. He responded with a doggie grin and a single swish of his tail as he snuggled an inch closer to Tonya.

I turned my gaze to her. "Hey, what are you doing here?" I asked, though I already knew the answer. As my best friend, she'd come to check on me. And as editor of the local newspaper, she'd come to get the scoop.

She smiled and lifted her mug. "Just came for the alcohol."

"Sounds good to me. Let's go to my cabin, so I can get out of this ridiculous dress. I have wine there."

She wrinkled her nose. "That boxed junk you poison yourself with will never pass my lips. Your cabin isn't nearly as appealing as this anyway."

I looked around the Knotty Pine Great Room. Oversized brown leather couches faced an immense stone fireplace. A massive window wall overlooked Mt. O'Connell, the village's ski slope. In the moonlight, fat snowflakes drifted downward against the mountain's silhouette. Tonya was right. The ambience here beat my tiny cabin, no contest.

"You win," I said. "Just let me grab a mug of wine."

"I'll join you, dearheart. I'm ready for a refill."

Except for Jamal, we had the room to ourselves. Recent lack of substantive snowfall had slowed tourism, and tonight's tiny bit of precipitation was unlikely to help much. Business owners throughout the village were on the verge of organizing native rain dance ceremonies.

Despite the dearth of guests, my parents insisted on maintaining an evening buffet, complete with hors d'oeuvres, coffee, and the mulled wine for which the Knotty Pine had a reputation. Tonya and I took turns holding mugs under the urn's spigot, adding cinnamon sticks and orange slices to the hot wine. She set her drink on the table and dotted a small plate with a selection of goodies. "No sense letting this yummy food go to waste."

I hesitated, knowing the yummy food would definitely go to waist—mine. But I succumbed to temptation, piling a plate with cubes of gouda and gorgonzola, black pepper crackers, green grapes, and the pièce de résistance: a pair of chocolate raspberry truffles.

I'd deal with the guilt later. In my elastic-waisted pajamas.

Tucked onto the couch, I munched on snacks and sipped wine as I studied my best friend. Flames leapt inside the hearth, creating a soft strobe effect across her face. She still wore the dress intended for the Snowflake Swirl—a long-sleeved chartreuse ankle-length maxi with an open back and fluttering flounce. Not many women could pull off such an ensemble, but Tonya made it look classy. From the corner of my eye, I saw Jamal pretending to restock the buffet, but I knew he was mostly sneaking peeks at Tonya. He was clearly smitten. And why not? She was stunning. Exquisite, graceful, sensuous.

A red-lipsticked grin widened her mouth, and her teeth shone white against a canvas of mahogany skin. Brown eyes sparkling, she lifted a hand to her hair, currently pulled into a knot at her neck. I sighed, slightly infatuated myself.

She nibbled at a cheese covered cracker. "Your first foray back into the real world and you stumble across a murder."

"Hey. It wasn't my first foray. I'm not a total hermit."

"I don't count your tri-weekly visits to the Quicker Liquor as social events."

I rolled my eyes. "Now you sound like my mother. For your information, Woody and I take daily hikes. I also do odd jobs around the resort. I earn my keep."

"Whatever. All I'm saying is, you know how to spice things up in our sleepy little village." She leaned forward. "Now tell me all about it."

After extracting a promise that I wouldn't be quoted in *The Gazette*, I regaled her with the details: Victoria's body lying on the ground, Kimberly poised above her with the letter opener. The photos I snapped of the crime scene, the flower, the yearbooks. That arrogant detective throwing me out of the office. I finished with Elyse hightailing it out of the Creekside.

"That reminds me," I added, narrowing my eyes. "I'm a little mad at you."

She sat back and raised a perfectly plucked eyebrow. "Do tell."

"You never mentioned that Sam had a daughter. With Kimberly, no less. That information merited a conversation."

She took a long, slow drink of wine, staring at me over the rim of her mug. When she finally spoke, her tone was matter-of-fact. "My darling friend, heart of my heart, soul of my soul. Please recall that you wanted nothing to do with this place. Remember that I was the one to initiate whatever contact occurred between us. Whenever I attempted to entertain you with village news, I was politely but instantly rebuffed. Our conversations revolved around *your* career, *your* life, *your* travels. And I was perfectly happy to hear about your adventures. But tell me, exactly when was I was supposed to have offered you these little updates you're now resentful of not getting?"

Ouch. Though she colored it with affection, Tonya painted a portrait of me I had been reluctantly visualizing for the past few months: Callie Cassidy as a self-centered, overly-ambitious person whose quest for the award-winning photo, the top breaking story, superseded everything else.

"Besides," she added, "it was Sam's news to tell, not mine."

I snuffled. Woody, a dog filled to the pads of his paws with compassion, twisted toward me and jabbed his long doggie tongue between my lips. I pushed his snout away and wiped my lips.

"Tonya, I'm sorry—" Tears welled in my eyes.

"Water under the bridge, sweet girl. I love you anyway." She reached across Woody's back and squeezed my fingers. "Let's start fresh. Ask me whatever you want, and I will enlighten you with twenty-five years' worth of pent-up gossip."

I blotted my eyes with a napkin. "Well, I *would* like to hear about Sam and Kimberly…"

She snickered. "Near as I can tell, a night of drunken debauchery resulted in quite the surprise. You know Sam—he'll always do the right thing. So they got married. Of course it didn't last. Before Elyse turned one, they called it quits. The marriage was a mistake, I guess, but Sam considers Elyse a gift. He adores that child, despite her current teenage angst."

I shook my head. "Kimberly. Of all people."

Tonya's lips curved in an ironic smile. "Well, my friend, there has been some speculation that she was his rebound relationship."

"From me? Elyse has to be seventeen years old. I'd been

gone, what, seven years by the time she was born."

"He always said you were the love of his life."

A fresh wave of guilt washed through me. I'd dumped Sam for college in the big city and a chance at my dream job. "There's been no one else since Kimberly?"

"A few dates here and there, but nothing ever sticks." She tapped a fingernail against her chin. "It occurs to me that you've never maintained a long-term relationship either. All these years, you and Sam have pined for each other..." She sighed in mock sadness.

I backhanded her arm. "Knock it off." I pictured Sam, then and now, and felt a rush of warmth. "I will say, he's as good-looking as ever. It was nice to see him again, in spite of the circumstances." She smirked, and I flushed. Time to change the subject. "Speaking of circumstances, I just can't understand this murder. I mean, Victoria and Kimberly were so tight back in the day. Why would Kimberly kill her best friend?"

"It's simple." She crossed her legs, much to young Jamal's delight. "For the past few months, Victoria has been engaged in a steamy, not-so-secret affair with Kimberly's husband, Parker Lyon. I'm surprised you hadn't heard, what with all those trips to the liquor store."

I frowned. Fran, the owner of Quicker Liquor, was notorious for her loose lips, but she'd never mentioned the affair. "Why would Victoria do that?" I asked. "I thought she and Kimberly were inseparable. Mom told me they co-own some swanky boutique."

Tonya's eyes brightened as she warmed to the story. "V&K's Fine Fashions. Even the name foreshadows the problem. Victoria's initial comes first. Since high school, she's always been first. Over the years, Kimberly has grown increasingly tired of playing second fiddle. She and Victoria stopped going out together. Glares passed between them like daggers. They say love and hate are opposite sides of the same coin. Somewhere along the line, the coin flipped."

"So, you think Kimberly murdered Victoria?"

"Don't you?"

I stared toward the fire, thinking. "Seems likely, I guess. Maybe too likely. But unless Victoria changed dramatically since I knew her, there must be other suspects."

"Ha." Tonya swirled the dregs in her mug. "Victoria inspired murderous rage the way Mother Teresa inspired altruism. She didn't have any real friends—just hangers-on who were afraid to cross her." She tapped her fingers against the leather armrest. "But of all the people who might have wished her ill, there's one I keep coming back to."

"Who's that?" I leaned forward, my adrenaline pulsing.

She looked at me as if I were a particularly dense student. "Kimberly, you dolt. You found the woman with the murder weapon in her hand, leaning over the victim's body. Sometimes a cigar is just a cigar."

I fell back against the couch cushion and sighed. Tonya was right, of course. But wrong too. As I well knew from recent experience, appearances could be deceiving.

6

Moonlight pierced the branches of the pine trees as Woody and I made the short walk from the lodge to my cabin. Tilting my head back, I inhaled the clear, brisk mountain air, tinged with the scent of evergreen. A yawn overtook me, and Woody followed suit with one of his own. It had been a long day, filled with drama. All I wanted was to change into pajamas, light a fire, and get to that book. And maybe indulge in another glass of wine. Just one.

But as we drew near the cabin, Woody stiffened, and I stopped in my tracks. A figure was huddled on the wooden porch—a woman, I thought, based on the stature. Her hood-covered head rested on her knees, which she'd drawn to her chest.

When she heard us, the woman raised her head, her face still shadowed beneath the hood. As she clambered to her high-heeled feet, I caught a glimpse of gold sequins and realized I was in the presence of Kimberly Wainwright Lyon. *Correction.* Kimberly Wainwright *Petrie* Lyon.

I looked at Woody. "Guess bedtime will have to wait, big guy." He grinned up at me and trotted off to greet our uninvited guest. I trudged along behind him, not nearly as enthusiastic.

Kimberly reached down to stroke Woody's thick fur, which earned her a few brownie points from me. But still.

A probable murderer had come calling. I wasn't sure how to handle it.

"Callie, I know what you must think," she said, as I mounted the steps. "How it looked in the office. But I swear to you, I didn't kill Victoria."

"You mentioned that earlier. But it's a conversation you need to have with the police."

She gave Woody one last pat on the head. He emitted a little whimper and nudged her hand with his wet nose. "I will. But please, just hear me out first. I need your help."

Bathed in the yellow porch light, her face appeared haggard, almost ancient. Streaks of black mascara stained her cheeks. She shivered and wrapped her spindly arms around her torso. Though fancy and fashionable, the thin, rose-colored duster she wore provided little insulation against the arctic temperatures.

I bit my bottom lip and made a decision, one I'm sure my father would say was ill-advised. Opening the cabin door, I herded Kimberly into the heat. "Let's get you warmed up."

She gave me a grateful look, but I held up a finger. "Then we call the police."

Her face fell, but she didn't speak. Instead, she wriggled out of her damp coat and hung it on the hook beside the door. Her hand flew to her hair, patting the wild red curls. "I must look frightful. May I use your bathroom?"

I pointed to the cubicle in the back wall of the room, and she scurried inside, shutting the door with a thud. At the fireplace, I busied myself with logs and matches. Just a month into my inauspicious return to Rock Creek Village and I'd already rekindled my fire-making skills. Flames crackled, and I went to the kitchenette, placed a filter into the coffee maker, and scooped in sufficient grounds to brew two cups. I wouldn't allow myself to offer a fugitive more than a single cup.

I knew my actions would draw ire from Detective Sanchez—as well as my parents. But every instinct in me screamed to hear Kimberly's story. One thing I'd learned in my career: follow my instincts.

The coffee dripped rhythmically into the carafe. Kimberly emerged from the bathroom, her face glistening and her hair tamed. I pointed her to the only armchair in the cabin, and I sat cross-legged on the bed facing her. Woody leapt up beside me, curling into a ball against my thigh.

Kimberly gazed at the fire. The popping of the flames and the trickle of the coffee created a hypnotic effect. Against that backdrop, my voice sounded harsh. "Tell me why you're here."

She held her breath for a moment and exhaled. "I need your help. No one else in this town is likely to believe I'm innocent."

"What makes you think I believe it? I'm the one who caught you in a compromising position, you know."

"I promise, I can explain. Just hear me out."

"Get a lawyer, Kimberly. That's who needs to hear you out."

"I know, and I will. But you're a big-time, important journalist. People here respect you. I need you to find out who really killed Victoria."

I shook my head. "I'm sure you've heard the story of my downfall. I doubt anyone respects me these days. As for being a journalist, I'm not in the field. Not anymore."

"You have to try. At least once more. For me." She locked her eyes into mine. "We're family, after all."

I broke her gaze with a roll of my own eyes. Family? Pish. My grandmother's cousin was Kimberly's step grandfather or something along those lines. We didn't share a drop of blood in common. "That's a stretch," I said.

She stared into the fire again. A nostalgic smile played on her lips. "Remember when we were little? We'd play together for hours at your grandmother's house, building pillow forts and telling spooky stories. Your grandma taught us how to bake Snickerdoodles, remember? I haven't made those in years…"

Her voice trailed off. I flashed back in time, letting the

childhood memories wrap themselves around me. Kimberly and I had been thick as thieves back then, playing in the woods behind Grandma Cassidy's house. I'd been the pirate, and she'd been the princess. The giggles, the hugs, the little girl secrets. I hadn't thought of those days in a long time.

The coffee maker beeped. I climbed across Woody and went to the kitchen. My mind fast forwarded to middle school, when things had changed between Kimberly and me. First, her father ran off and left the family. She reacted by withdrawing, and I took it as rejection. In hindsight, I understood she'd been dealing with emotional upheaval. But back then, my already pinballing pre-teen feelings had been hurt. So I quit trying, immersing myself instead in my new hobbies: writing and photography. Then I met Tonya, and pirates and princesses seemed childish.

In the meantime, a new girl moved into the village and quickly declared herself alpha dog of our school. Victoria Dunleavy was knock 'em-dead beautiful, and as a transplant from the big city, she exuded self-assurance. But it wasn't just her beauty and confidence that wove the magic. From the beginning, Victoria was a force of nature, radiating a gravitational pull destined to attract a lonely, lost girl like Kimberly into her orbit. A few other girls joined the pack, and the group soon gained power through humiliation, intimidation, and ridicule. Thus Vile Victoria's Vixens was born.

As I poured steaming coffee into two mugs, a question flitted through my mind: if I'd been more attentive to Kimberly, would she have turned out differently? Could this murder have been prevented? I brushed the thought away. Ego talking, my mother would say. As if I had the power to change the course of history.

"I wish we'd stayed close," Kimberly murmured, looking at me with doe eyes as I passed her a mug.

"Me too," I said softly. I could feel my resolve crumbling. I yearned to help that little girl I'd run hand-in-hand with through the wildflowers in the meadow.

Still, I resisted the urge. For one thing, I wasn't entirely sure either of those little girls still existed within our present selves. As a teenager, Kimberly had turned mean and vindictive. From what I'd heard, adulthood hadn't mellowed her much. Villagers detested her almost as much as they had Victoria. Who knew how long I'd be here in Rock Creek Village? I didn't want to alienate the entire community by aiding and abetting one of their icons of evil.

Also, I wasn't in top-notch emotional shape myself. My career had ended, my self-doubt had descended to epic depths, and I had no idea what the future held. Did I even have the fortitude to take on someone else's cause?

On the other hand, maybe helping Kimberly could restore my sense of self-worth, my belief that I was, after all, a good person.

"If you won't do it for me, do it for my daughter," she said, her eyes pleading. "For Sam's daughter. She doesn't deserve the embarrassment and pain of having her mother in jail for murder." She clasped her hands as if praying. "Please help her. Help us."

An image of the girl who used to be my friend drifted across Kimberly's face. I felt myself creeping closer to the precipice. I knew I shouldn't get involved. It was none of my business—I'd told myself that a dozen times already. Sanchez had told me as much. And Tonya. My parents would also confirm it, I was certain.

But Kimberly deserved an advocate. Even one of the Vile Vixens should be treated as innocent until proven guilty.

I took a deep breath and stepped into the abyss. "Tell me what you've got."

7

Kimberly squealed and clapped her hands. "You're going to help me!"

"Don't get carried away. First, we need to talk. Walk me through the series of events. How did you end up at the scene?"

"Well, the first thing you should know"—she paused to toss a wave of red hair over her shoulder— "is that I was framed."

My eyebrows lifted, and I twirled my finger in a circle, indicating she should continue.

"This afternoon, I received a text from Victoria's phone."

I held out my hand. "Let me see the text."

"I can't. I dropped my cell in Victoria's office. I was hysterical when I saw her lying there, all bloody…Then you came in, and I rushed out without giving it a second thought."

Ah. The phone I'd seen beside the body. I'd assumed it was Victoria's. And now it was in police custody. "All right, then. Tell me about the text."

"Like I said, it was from Victoria's phone. But I believe someone else wrote it. The real killer. Setting me up."

I half expected *dun dun dun* music to play in the background. "Just tell me what it said."

"That she wanted to meet with me at the event center to discuss…a certain issue."

"What issue?"

"There were no specifics."

"But you have an inkling, right?"

Kimberly averted her eyes. "I can't say."

"Then I can't help you." I leaned against the headboard. "If you're not going to be honest, I'm of no use to you."

Her eyes flicked to my face and back to her lap. "All right. I'll tell you." She fidgeted, rotating her wedding ring around her finger. "It seems...Victoria and Parker—Parker is my husband, you know—it seems they were having...a bit of an affair."

A bit of an affair. Rather like being a bit pregnant? For heaven's sake. Was Kimberly truly oblivious to the fact that Victoria and Parker's dalliance was common knowledge throughout the village?

"You're not surprised."

"I've heard rumors." I studied her face. Years as an investigative journalist had honed my deception detector, and now it tolled wildly. There was more to the story than she was divulging. "So, Victoria and Parker were involved in some extramarital activity. I think there's more to the story."

She set her mug on the nightstand and walked over to the fireplace, picking up the poker and stabbing at the logs. Buying time to think, I figured. "My husband and my best friend having an affair. I was humiliated. Isn't that enough?" She dropped the poker and buried her face in her hands.

I fought off a wave of irritation. Histrionics never held much sway with me. But I decided whatever secret she was keeping didn't matter, at least not right now. The affair would provide Sanchez reason enough to warrant Kimberly's arrest. Any additional secrets would eventually be revealed during the investigation, gravy on the top of an already meaty motive. A sense of doom permeated the room.

I heaved a sigh. "All right. Let's put motive aside for now and talk about opportunity. With my own eyes, I saw you crouching over Victoria's body with the murder weapon in your hand. How do you explain that?"

Tears trickled from her eyes, but her voice didn't quaver. "I panicked when I saw her on the floor with that thing sticking out of her. I thought she might be okay if I could just get it out of her. So I yanked it from her chest. There was this horrible sucking sound…" She shuddered. "Then you came in."

The blood had drained from her face. Then a tremble raced through her limbs, and just like that, I believed her. I stood up and rested a hand on her shoulder as she began to sob. "It's okay, Kimberly. It'll be all right."

Woody jumped off the bed and stood beside us, offering himself for comfort. Kimberly stroked his back and hiccupped as she began to calm down. Then she reached up and took my hand in hers. "Thank you, Callie. You've given me a ray of hope."

I squeezed her fingers. "Just don't make me regret it."

We headed into the kitchen. I was wavering between making more coffee and pulling out the wine box. Kimberly rubbed at her wet cheeks and offered up the brightest smile she could manage. "What do we do now, partner?"

Partner? I decided I needed the wine. Grabbing a couple of tumblers from the cabinet, I contemplated my next move. In my opinion, there was really only one way to proceed. "You're not going to like this, but you have to turn yourself in."

In warp speed, her smile morphed into a frown. She shook her head with a force that sent her hair whipping across her face. "No way. I'm not going to jail. They'll make me wear one of those terrible jumpsuits." When I stared at her, she looked at me as if I was clueless. "Callie, you must have seen prison jumpsuits on TV. They're orange." She shuddered. "I'm a redhead."

As I considered the horrible fate of red hair and orange

prison clothes, my eyes drifted to her gown. Gold sequins reflected the firelight, sending sparkles across the walls. I noticed a smear of dried blood near her hip and realized she hadn't changed since she'd fled Victoria's office, probably hadn't even been home. Without access to her phone, she might not have let her husband know she was safe. Or her daughter.

I opened my mouth to ask her but was interrupted by Woody's yip and a simultaneous rap at the door. My father's voice followed. "Callie? I'm here with Frank and Raul. We need to talk to you."

Kimberly's eyes flew open so wide that her fake eyelashes tickled her eyebrows. She glanced desperately around the room like a cornered deer looking for an escape. "I'll hide in the bathroom," she whispered. "You get rid of them."

An insistent banging shook the door, and Sanchez's voice boomed. "Ms. Cassidy, we know Kimberly Lyon is with you. Open up."

I looked at Kimberly. "Too late," I told her.

She dashed into the bathroom anyway and shut herself inside. I walked over to the front door and unlocked it, barely stepping aside before it slammed open and Sanchez barreled inside. Dad followed, and Frank ambled in after them.

Jerking a thumb over my shoulder, I gestured to the bathroom. Raul strode to the door and jiggled the knob. Locked. With a clenched fist, he pounded three times on the thin wood. "Kimberly Lyon, come out here immediately."

No response. I ignored Sanchez's drama and turned to Dad. "How did you know she was here?"

"Her car is in the parking lot. Couldn't think where else she might have gone."

The woman had no future as a fugitive. Sanchez lifted his fist again. "Excuse me," I said to him. "Kimberly is distressed. You might be better served with a gentler approach. You know, flies and honey and all that. Just a suggestion."

He shot me a dark look but lowered his fist. When he spoke, his tone was more subdued. "Ms. Lyon, we're not going to leave until you come out. Don't make this any harder than it has to be."

A few seconds passed. "Are you going to arrest me?"

Sanchez pursed his lips and glanced at Frank, who lifted his palms in a "your call" gesture. "It's a possibility," Sanchez said. "But I can promise you'll be treated fairly and respectfully."

"Will I have to wear an orange jumpsuit?"

The detective's brow furrowed. "What?"

I tried hard to conceal my grin. "I think she'll come out if you tell her she doesn't have to," I said in a low voice.

Frank chuckled. "We don't even have orange jumpsuits. Tell her no worries on that count, Sanchez."

Sanchez leaned toward the door. "No orange jumpsuit. You have my word."

After a pause, we heard the lock turn. The door opened, and Sanchez took a step back to let Kimberly pass. She held her shoulders back and her chin up, like a member of royalty meeting with the peasants. Bravado at its finest. I felt a stir of admiration.

Sanchez did not appear to share my sentiment. He put a hand on Kimberly's arm and tugged. "Let's go."

Kimberly twisted from his grasp and narrowed her eyes. "Don't touch me."

I walked over and stood beside her. Her bottom lip quivered. "It's going to be okay," I said again, the words sounding hollow even to my own ears. "The best thing you can do now is go with them. But I advise you not to talk to them until your lawyer arrives."

Sanchez shot me a death glare, but I met it with one of my own. Kimberly took a deep breath, straining the low neckline of her gown. Her voice shook. "Can I…can I change clothes? Callie, do you have something I could wear? I don't want to go to the police station dressed like this."

I glanced at Frank, figuring he'd be more likely to allow

it than Sanchez. But the chief shook his head. "Afraid not. The dress will need to be tested, so we'll need you to change at the station. We have clothes you can wear." Kimberly stiffened, and Frank hurried to reassure her. "No orange, I promise. Gray sweatpants and shirt, if memory serves. Nothing fancy, but you'll be comfortable."

"It's probably only for one night," I added, not sure why we were all placating the woman. "You'll likely be able to get bail tomorrow."

She nodded. Head high, she walked to the door and retrieved her thin coat from the hook. Dad held it as she wriggled her arms into the sleeves. "I'm ready now," she said to Sanchez.

Dad opened the door, and a gust of frigid wind swept inside. Kimberly looked over her shoulder, catching my eye. "Will you call Parker? Tell him to contact my lawyer?"

I nodded. "Of course."

"And…will you let Elyse know what's happening? Tell her everything is going to be all right."

"I will."

Kimberly squared her shoulders and strode down the path, not once tottering on her six-inch heels. The woman had gumption.

Good thing, I thought. She was going to need it.

When everyone had departed and Woody and I had the place to ourselves, I grabbed my cell phone and called Tonya. She began to scold me for calling so late, but held her tongue when I told her about Kimberly.

"You *what?*" she squealed. "Little girl, you are crazier than I even imagined. Did the two of you stab your fingertips and become blood sisters too?"

I snickered, remembering Tonya and I completing that ritual as kids.

"Only you, sister," I said.

"Well, that's a relief." She sighed. "Listen, Callie.

Everyone, myself included, would warn you to stay out of this. But I know that won't happen. There's no stopping you when you get your nose to the ground. You are your father's daughter, stubborn to the core. So I have only one request."

"What's that?"

"Whatever comes of this, *The Gazette* gets the story first."

I laughed. "Speaking of leopards who don't change their spots…"

"Yeah, yeah. Keep me posted. And Callie?"

"Yes?"

"Lock your door and keep your phone by the bed."

8

F ollowing Tonya's subtle safety message, which I interpreted as only semi-joking, I hadn't expected to get much sleep. So I was startled to be yanked out of a deep slumber by the pealing of my phone. Without opening my eyes, I grabbed it from the nightstand and delivered what I hoped was a coherent greeting.

"Callie, I was just about to give up," an amused male voice responded.

It belonged to Preston Garrison, my boss. Former boss, I reminded myself.

I hadn't talked to him in weeks and didn't really want to now, either. He just reminded me of everything I'd lost. But Preston had stood by me throughout the ordeal, so the least I could do was have a conversation with the man.

I tried to put a smile in my voice. "No, you weren't. If I hadn't answered, you'd have pressed redial every ten minutes until you eroded my resistance."

He chuckled. "You don't ascend to my lofty position without tenacity."

"Tenacity. Is that the word you're using these days? I'd have chosen obnoxiousness."

"Hey, now. Play nice." I heard him tapping on a keyboard and knew he spent Sunday multi-tasking. Some things about the journalist's life I didn't miss.

A yawn threatened as I waited for him to finish his task.

"Sounds like you're busy, Preston. What can I help you with?"

The tapping stopped, and he cleared his throat. "I heard there was a murder last night in your supposedly sleepy little village."

My yawn disappeared. "How on earth did you know that? You're fifteen hundred miles away. And Rock Creek Village isn't exactly a booming news hub."

"I have sources," he said cryptically. "I also hear you're intent on getting yourself involved."

I glanced around the room, searching for evidence of a hidden camera. "I'm just asking a few questions. No big deal."

A deep sigh rumbled through the phone. "Tread carefully, Callie. Small-town murder investigations are often the most volatile kind."

I returned the sigh. "I appreciate your concern, but I'm already getting all the advice I can handle from my nearest and dearest. As you remember, Careful is my middle name."

I waited a few seconds, but he didn't respond. "Well, if that's all, I need to run," I said. "Places to go, people to see—"

"Wait, Callie. Your little murder story isn't the only reason I'm calling. I have some news of my own."

He paused, waiting for me to prod him. I decided to play along. "You have an insufferable flair for drama, Preston, but I'll bite. What's your news?"

"The judge overturned the verdict. Your frat boy will be released from jail tomorrow."

I felt as if the air had been sucked from the room. A war of emotions erupted—joy grappling with pain, relief jousting with guilt. A sudden burst of hot tears spurted from my eyes, and Woody licked them off my cheeks. It took me a moment to compose myself enough to respond. "I...I don't know what to say. Or how to feel. I'm just glad it's over."

"It may not be completely over. Our lawyers tell me

Jarrett could sue us—and you—in civil court, but there's little chance he'd win. First Amendment and all."

"I'll cross that bridge if I come to it," I said. "I'm just glad he's getting out."

Preston drew a breath. "There's something else you should know. A message we found in your email inbox."

"My work email? It hasn't been shut down? I just figured when I resigned…"

"Well, I haven't exactly gotten around to signing your termination paperwork. I keep hoping you'll change your mind. I still want you back, you know."

I winced at his choice of words. Preston and I had a complicated relationship. He'd been my editor, yes, but occasionally more. We never exactly dated, but we were sometimes closer than boss-employee.

When in doubt, pretend you didn't hear what was clearly said. I moved past the statement as if it had never been uttered. "So anyway, you've been monitoring my email. What turned up that has you in a tizzy?"

"It's supposedly from Jarrett, though we haven't verified its authenticity. It purports to be a letter of forgiveness."

My heart rate accelerated. "Can you read it to me?"

"It's long and fairly convoluted. Lots of references to ways in which Jameson Jarrett has been wronged and his life irrevocably damaged. But he says now he's found religion. Wants you to know he's forgiven you for your sins against him. I'll send a copy to your personal email address. But I find it more than a little creepy and concerning."

Well, that didn't seem so bad. Forgiveness was a good thing, right? I'd received a number of threats throughout my career, so I didn't understand why Preston was getting so worked up. "Geez, Preston, the man has been in jail for months and wants to forgive me for putting him there. I think your concern may be misguided."

"Don't blow this off, Callie." His voice was tight. "A wronged man can be a powder keg, and you never know when a powder keg will explode." He sighed. "I'd feel a lot better if we could keep an eye on you here in D.C. Your desk is waiting for you."

The man wasn't going to let me ignore his request. At least I could address it at the professional level and leave aside the personal aspect. "It's not as if I'm on vacation, Preston. I resigned. Even if I wanted to work at *The Sentinel* again, I doubt the powers-that-be would have me. I've put a black mark on the face of their precious publication."

"The powers-that-be, as you call them, have dealt with black marks before. Keep in mind, you also covered them in glory on more than one occasion. It's easy to overlook a black mark made by someone who has a Felden Prize in her pocket. You're the best convergence journalist on the team. No one photographs a crime scene like the Queen of the Dead. We need you. The world needs you."

Heat bloomed in my cheeks. The moniker Preston had bestowed upon me years ago used to fill me with pride. Now it just felt dark and dreary. Sundance was more to my liking.

"You're laying it on a little thick, don't you think? No doubt a new wunderkind waits in the lobby even as we speak. Hire her, Preston. I won't be back."

"Callie, please. At least consider it."

My grip tightened around the phone. I had to admit the attraction of my old life tugged at me. I'd been admired and competent in my career. Until the end of it, anyway. Could life in this sleepy village compete with the adrenaline rush of big-time journalism?

I wasn't quite ready to close the door on the past. "I'll think about it, Preston. I promise."

"Thank you for that, Callie. How about if I call you in a couple of days?"

"I'd rather call you," I said. "But if that hungry young journalist comes along in the meantime, don't hesitate to give her my desk."

When we hung up, I noticed a missed text from Dad. It

took me a minute to read through it, since my father had not yet mastered the art of brevity in messaging.

Callie, I thought I'd drive you to the police station, if that's okay. Meet me at the truck at 8:40. We don't want to keep Raul and Frank waiting. If you want to come by the lodge a little early, we have donuts.

He followed the words with three emojis: an alarm clock, a chocolate covered donut, and a yummy face. Given that he still typed with one index finger, this epic must have taken him ten minutes to compose.

I smiled and texted back a thumbs up emoji. We were too cute.

After a quick shower, I threw on jeans and a flannel button up shirt. My monkey mind bounced from one thought to another. Jameson Jarrett's release. His letter of forgiveness and the threat Preston seemed to attach to it. Preston's desire to rehire me.

After five minutes of non-stop obsession, I turned my attention to my most immediate concern: my impending visit to the police station. That's where I needed to focus my mental energies.

Figuring Sanchez was just the type to keep me waiting, I tossed my Kindle into my oversized purse. As I squirmed into my coat, Woody issued a pitiful whine.

"What is it, big guy?" He looked up at me with wet brown eyes, and I dropped to my knees. He licked my neck and rested his chin on my shoulder.

Then I understood. He wasn't used to being alone. The two of us had been together practically twenty-four seven for more than a month. And before that, when we lived in D.C., I'd take him to doggie daycare when I worked so he could frolic with a group of furry friends.

"Poor lonely boy. How about if I drop you off at the lodge? Mom can spoil you all morning. Would that make you happy?"

His back end shimmied in delight, and he leapt across my knees toward the door. Apparently, the plan met with his approval.

9

W oody and I emerged from the cabin into a picture-perfect day. The blue sky filtered through the evergreen branches, and the sun glinted off a thin layer of snow. I just wished we'd gotten more precipitation yesterday--for the skiers' sake. I'd heard predictions of a storm in the forecast, but the only sign so far was a flat layer of clouds to the west. Mountain-covering snowfall might be coming, but not today.

Faithful dog at my heel—though in truth he bounced ahead, to the side, and everywhere but at my heel—I traipsed the short path leading to the lodge.

I examined the property with my photographer's eye, wishing I had my Nikon. Morning light gleamed across the landscape, highlighting the mountain backdrop as well as the lodge's architectural charm. The resort spread across the foot of Mt. O'Connell in the southern section of the Rocky Mountains.

In my youth, the lodge had been called Mt. O'Connell Inn, but when my parents purchased it, they renamed it Knotty Pine Resort. The three-story Swiss chalet contained my parents' condo-style home, along with eight rooms on the second floor and four luxurious suites on the third. Jutting out on either side of the lodge were eight free-standing cabins: five ski-in abodes mountainside and three riverview cottages forest side. I currently occupied the riverview unit closest to the chalet, the smallest of the bunch.

But what could I say? For now, I was living rent-free.

Mom's retired teacher friend and part-time employee Penelope was due to arrive at ten, as she did every Sunday. Until then, Mom occupied the seat behind the registration desk. She lit up when she saw Woody, seeming as happy to see Woody as he was to see her. Well-mannered dog that he was, he graced her with a wag and a grin before turning his attention to the treat tin she kept at hand. I grabbed my own treat in the form of two chocolate covered cake donuts and followed Dad out to his truck.

The drive to the lower village took only ten minutes. During that time, Dad and I managed to dissect every potential weather occurrence, thoroughly assess the Colorado Avalanche's playoff hopes, and come up with options for an anniversary gift for Mom. All the chatter saved me from having to talk about Preston's call. I wasn't ready to tell Dad about Jarrett's note and be subjected to a rush of overprotective sternness.

We pulled into an open spot in front of the town hall, where the police station occupied a wing. All the city's governmental operations took place in this one building— residents could pay the water bill, report a stolen bike, check out a library book, and register a car without having to waste a drop of gasoline. As in most small towns, it was an efficient setup, with the net result that everyone knew everyone else's business.

When we exited the truck, a short blond man hurried by us. After he passed, Dad leaned toward me and whispered in my ear. "That's Parker Lyon, Kimberly's husband. Here to post bail, I bet."

I watched the man walk toward the entrance with a stiff, almost prissy gait. His well-coiffed blond hair looked like something you'd see on the cover of a magazine, and his beige tweed coat, while stylish, wouldn't provide much protection from the elements. He and his wife apparently shared an affinity for fashion over practicality. My first impression was of a self-absorbed social climber. Unfair, sure, but my career had molded me into a decent judge of character. Hard to believe Kimberly had traded Sam in for this guy.

I saw Dad's mouth curl as he watched me watching Parker. "For what it's worth," he said, "I think you have him pegged."

By the time we got inside, Parker was nowhere in sight. We stopped at the reception desk, and every employee we saw greeted Dad with enthusiasm that bordered on hero worship. He responded with a kind word for each of them, asking about family members, sports leagues, and details of their lives that only someone who truly cared would remember. Trailing along in his wake, I beamed with pride.

A receptionist led us to an interview room and asked Dad if she could bring him coffee, water, snacks. He declined, and she shuffled out without sparing me a glance. We draped our coats over the back of aluminum folding chairs and settled in to wait.

Fifteen minutes later, just as I was getting antsy and Dad had begun to snore softly, the door swung open and Frank stepped into the room. "Sorry to keep you waiting," he said. "Busy morning, as you can imagine." He flashed a warm, peace-making smile, diffusing my pent-up frustration at being kept waiting. He laid my camera bag on the table and pushed it in front of me. "Thanks for letting us have this overnight, Callie. The photos we downloaded will be very helpful. I am a great admirer of your talent."

I grinned at his praise. Then I unsnapped the bag and checked my equipment. Everything appeared to be in order. The door thumped open again and Sanchez walked in, placing a folder and a notebook on the table and taking the chair next to Frank's. I tilted my head and watched him. Amidst yesterday's chaos, I hadn't noticed how drop-dead good looking the man was. Thick eyebrows framed eyes so dark they were almost ebony. Full lips, stubble covering his jaw and chin. Tiny diamond studs twinkled from earlobes that peeked out beneath curls of jet black hair.

But his good looks didn't translate to a pleasant demeanor. He stared at me, lips tight. Maybe I was being paranoid, but the detective seemed to hold something against me. Pish. I'd dealt with worse. I turned my attention to Frank. "Did you arrest Kimberly Wainwright?"

Frank opened his mouth and shut it, gesturing toward Sanchez to give the younger man the lead in what was probably his first homicide. I sighed. I'd worked with rookies before, and they were usually a pain in the patootie—so busy trying to prove themselves that they often overlooked the obvious. Then they got their feathers ruffled when someone—like me, for instance—pointed out what they had missed.

But I'd give him a chance. I looked at him, waiting for a response. "We don't discuss ongoing cases," he said finally.

So much for his chance. My irritation returned, on steroids.

"And yet here I sit, at your request, waiting oh-so-patiently for…" I glanced at my watch, "…almost thirty minutes. I assumed I was summoned regarding Kimberly Wainwright. Or that maybe you wanted to get some facts straight about the murder scene. Perhaps I was mistaken. Would you prefer to discuss the weather? Seems a storm is brewing."

Dad reached beneath the table and put a hand on my leg, squeezing. I sat back and crossed my arms.

Sanchez paused. "It's Kimberly Wainwright Petrie Lyon. As long as we're getting our facts straight."

Had the man just made a joke? His expression was inscrutable, but I spotted a twinkle in his eye. Maybe there was more to this man than the by-the-book caricature of a cop I had conjured. I offered up a tentative smile.

He opened the folder and pulled out a stack of photos,

spreading them in front of me. Prints I had taken of the crime scene, including Victoria's body. He slid a pen and a typed document in front of me. "This is an affidavit indicating that these photos are yours, that they are genuine and unaltered. Also that you attest you did not touch or otherwise manipulate the body or the crime scene."

I scanned the paper. Fairly routine. I scribbled my signature across the bottom. Sanchez gathered the pictures, fastened the stack with a paperclip, and put them back in the folder. Then he opened the notebook. "Just a couple of follow up questions."

I waved. "Go ahead."

"Did you speak with Sam and his daughter prior to finding Victoria?"

My forehead creased. "I did. They were setting up the buffet."

"Mm hmm." Sanchez jotted something in his notebook. "Did either of them seem *off* in any way?"

Why would Sanchez be asking about Sam and Elyse? Were they suspects? I remembered the disdain on Sam's face when he'd talked about Victoria. My mind flashed to the stain on his sleeve. After a brief hesitation, I shook my head. "Not that I noticed."

He lifted his eyebrows and waited. When I didn't add anything, he opened the folder again and removed another sheet of paper, sliding it in front of me along with a pen. "All right. Here's a copy of your statement from last night. Please look over it and sign if you find it to be accurate and complete."

Dad leaned forward and peered over my shoulder as I scanned the statement. "It looks fine," I said.

Sanchez nodded. "Go ahead and sign and you can be on your way."

Rather than picking up the pen, I folded my hands on top of the paper and stared at the detective. "I'm not ready to be on my way just yet. I have a few questions of my own." There was Dad's hand on my leg again, and another insistent squeeze. I yanked my leg from his grip. "If I'm going to sign a statement, I have a right to know how it's going to be used."

Though Sanchez's face remained impassive, a quiver of irritation rippled in his voice. "Ms. Cassidy, I'm not sure how they do things in the big city, but here in Rock Creek Village, the police share information when we are ready to do so. Not when it suits the whims of a witness."

"Well, I'm not your run-of-the-mill observer. Not only am I intimately involved in this investigation, but I have a background that warrants additional consideration. I'm just asking for some professional respect, okay?"

He didn't respond and didn't break eye contact. Seconds ticked by as the two of us engaged in a silent stalemate. Finally, Frank cleared his throat and spoke. "Callie, I'm sure you understand that we can't get into details, but yes, we arrested Ms. Lyon. A judge has issued bail, and she should be released within a couple of hours."

Sanchez's face darkened, and the chief turned to him. "It's going to be public knowledge in a few hours, Raul. Callie here has years of experience with police investigations. We can trust her to keep this information to herself. Right, Callie?"

"Of course. But still, I'm wondering if you've considered any other suspects—"

Sanchez scooted his chair back and stood, resting clenched fists on the table. "Ms. Cassidy, do you recall telling us that when you entered Ms. Ratliff's office, you found Ms. Lyon standing over the body?"

"I actually said she was crouching. Says so right here." I pointed at the paper in front of me.

"Do you remember saying that she held a bloody letter opener?"

"Yes, I remember. What's your point?"

"Doesn't it seem evident that arresting her is the right move?"

"I'm not suggesting she shouldn't be a suspect. Probably

even your main suspect. But it sounds as if you're not considering any other possibilities. When I arrived at the scene, Kimberly immediately told me she didn't do it." All three of the men looked at me. "I get it. They all say they didn't do it. But once in a blue moon, they're telling the truth. I want to make sure an innocent woman doesn't go to prison."

Sanchez's jaw tightened. "Thank you for your input, Ms. Cassidy. We will keep an open mind. In the meantime, sign the statement at your leisure. Or don't sign it at all. Ultimately, it makes no difference." He looked at my father and had the grace to appear slightly embarrassed. "Chief Cassidy, thank you for coming." Then he left the room.

I had been dismissed. Again.

10

"All I'm saying is we need to let the detectives do their jobs." Dad looked over his shoulder to check his blind spot and reversed out of the parking space.

"And all I'm saying is that cops sometimes get tunnel vision."

"You do remember who you're talking to, right?" He put on his blinker and turned onto the street. "I'll try not to take offense."

"Obviously, I wasn't talking about you," I said. "Or even Frank. It's that Sanchez. The man is insufferable. His mind is about as open as a clogged toilet."

Dad sighed. "I think he'll turn out to be a top-tier detective, but it's his first homicide. He's eager to make his mark. I remember feeling that way. Don't you? I imagine you were a little insufferable yourself in the beginning."

I flashed back to my early years as a reporter, hungry for the big story, longing for an opportunity to make a name for myself. It seemed so long ago. But I did remember.

"And you know, Sundance, he's not wrong. The facts are self-evident. You can be as open-minded as you want and still be forced to see what's right in front of you."

I stared out the passenger window, visualizing Kimberly huddled over the body, her fingers gripping the murder weapon. Maybe everyone else was right. The simplest answer was often the right one.

Then I thought of Jameson Jarrett. My assumptions about the simplest answer had helped seal his imprisonment. I couldn't let the same thing happen to Kimberly. If she'd killed Victoria, I'd be the first to denounce her. But if she was actually innocent, I was determined to prove it.

When we parked at the resort, Dad headed toward the toolshed, saying he had some repairs to attend to. I went to the lodge to retrieve my dog. Penelope sat behind the front desk, registering a guest. One glance at the newcomer led me to an immediate double take.

At least six feet tall, the woman had the broad-shouldered, muscular build of an Amazon warrior. Her gray hair, streaked with purple, swept across the top of her rectangular glasses. A purple velour jogging suit encased her large frame. Her age was a mystery. Though her hair and attire suggested a woman at the upper end of her sixties, her physique appeared at least fifteen years younger.

Curious, I loped over to introduce myself. "Welcome to the Knotty Pine Resort," I said. "I'm Callie Cassidy, the owners' daughter."

She gazed at me, her fingertips forming a tent on the counter. "Those we have not met are not always strangers." Her deep voice carried a British accent. I thought perhaps I'd misunderstood her.

"I... um, what? I don't..."

The woman slid a sturdy hand into mine and shook it with force. "I'm Mrs. Finney. Pleased to make your acquaintance."

Penelope gave me an amused smirk and nodded toward an adjacent door. "If you're looking for that handsome boy of yours, he's upstairs with Maggie."

"Thanks," I said, still slightly dumbstruck. Mrs. Finney wiggled her fingers in front of my face, shaking me from my stupor. "It's a pleasure to meet you, Mrs. Finney.," I added quickly. "I hope you'll enjoy your stay in Rock Creek Village."

She dipped her head regally. "Enjoyment is a state of mind, unencumbered by external circumstances."

"Ah. Yes, well...I look forward to seeing you around, then."

Still trying to decipher her words, I opened the door and climbed the stairs to my parents' home. They'd renovated the area above the lobby into a two-level habitat worthy of a spread in *Better Homes and Gardens,* including upgraded amenities and huge picture windows overlooking Mt. O'Connell.

I crested the stairs into an empty living room. "Mom? Where are you?" My shout sounded like I was an eight-year-old home from school and in search of a snack.

"Upstairs, dear."

I looked wearily up the next set of stairs to the floor that held my parents' master suite, a guest bedroom, and a small study. Visiting my mother was proving to be the equivalent to a Camp Gladiator workout. If I wasn't careful, I'd find myself back in some semblance of physical fitness.

Woody bounded halfway down the stairs to escort me, displaying an irritating level of energy. When I dragged myself huffing into the study, I stopped short. "Mom! What the heck?"

She was hanging upside down on a black leather contraption that resembled a massage table. Her feet were wedged into harnesses to keep her from falling. Gravity pulled her silver hair toward the floor, giving her the appearance of an upended senior citizen troll doll.

She tugged the side handles and hoisted herself upright, stepping out of the restraints. "Don't you love it? It's my new inversion table. Supposed to increase brain health. Give it a whirl!"

I lifted my hands and backed away as if the padded bench might be contagious. "No, no, no. Another time. Maybe."

She wrinkled her nose. "And to think I pegged you as the risk taker in the family. Want some coffee?"

She fluffed her hair and glided down the steps with an ease that belied her age. I clunked along in her wake, into a modern, white-on-gray kitchen with quartz countertops and stainless steel appliances. Mom slipped Woody a treat and took two coffee mugs from a cabinet.

I had settled myself into a chair at the kitchen table, ready to relax, when an object dropped from above and landed squarely on my chest. My lungs emitted a soft whoosh. A squeal pealed through the air. I realized the sound had come from me.

I looked down to find a golden-colored creature I'd never met making himself at home in my lap.

My mother stifled a laugh. "Oh dear. You should see your face. It's a cat, dear, not a nuclear bomb. The sweet boy turned up outside yesterday. He doesn't seem to belong to anyone, and we simply couldn't leave him to the elements."

"You're taking in a stray cat? Does Dad know about this?"

"He's the one who found the little dear. I'm thinking of naming him Fireball…The cat, not your father."

I swore I saw the cat roll its eyes.

Woody and the cat had clearly already met and become fast friends. The cat batted playfully at the dog's nose, and Woody nuzzled the cat's neck.

"Those two were made for one another," Mom said, carrying two steaming mugs to the table and setting one in front of me. "Look at them—two adorable golden balls of fur. They could be brothers." She narrowed her eyes. "Perhaps Fireball should move in with the two of you."

I lifted my hands, palms out. "Not happening. I don't want one more smidgen of responsibility. Besides, I'm not a cat person."

But still. The creature studied me with intelligent eyes, and a purr vibrated from his throat. I found myself stroking his satiny fur.

Mom sat across from me and propped her elbows on the table, her expression one of motherly concern—all too familiar these days. "How are you holding up, sweetheart?"

I lifted my cup to my nose, inhaling the nutty aroma. "I'm fine."

"Mm hmm. Well, don't forget about your appointment with Dr. Lowell tomorrow."

I dropped my eyes to the cat curled in my lap. "I'm thinking of canceling. I feel fine."

"That's twice you've used that word in ten seconds. Fine doesn't cut the cake, dear. You deserve better than fine. You deserve peace, contentment, joy. A few counseling sessions might help you obtain them. It's about growth. Healing. You keep everything bottled up inside you. It's not healthy."

"That's not true. I talk—"

"Please, Angelface. Do it for me. Just a few sessions. For starters."

I remembered this same conversation every time Mom had signed me up for swimming lessons, cooking class, basketball. Even photography classes, which turned out to be my life's passion. I had always needed to be dragged, pushed, cajoled into any new experience. With the exception of that wretched dance class, I'd always ended up enjoying them.

Maybe she was right about this too.

"All right, all right, I'll go. I'll blubber about my feelings for an hour and spill my deepest, darkest secrets to a stranger. Sounds like a blast."

11

Back in my cabin, I sat at the round wooden dining table and stared at my laptop screen. My goal for the afternoon involved social media research— Victoria's, Kimberly's, and anyone in their circle that might have a motive in the crime. Much as I personally disdained it, social media provided prime real estate in which to uncover murderous intentions.

But I was having trouble concentrating, given the incessant surround-sound of high-pitched whining. Since I'd wrested him away from my mother's newly rescued cat, Woody had stood sentinel by the door, glaring alternately at the knob and at my face while emitting torturous noises I didn't even know he could make.

I tried to ignore him, but it was like working with a constantly blaring fire alarm as background noise. Above the din, I heard the chime of an incoming text and grabbed my phone hopefully, as if the message might contain instructions on how to stop Woody's madness.

Next best thing: a missive from Tonya. *How's the investigation going? Have you and K, aka Holmes and Watson, solved the Case of the Vile Vixen?*

I smirked. *Haha. About to start some online research. Want to come help?*

Three flashing dots, followed by: *Too much work since Sophie's MIA. Tomorrow?*

Sure, I responded. *Stupid counseling appt at 10. After?*

A thumbs-up emoji appeared. *Something to show you.*

What? I asked.

More blinking dots as I awaited her reply. Then: *Can't spoil the surprise, love. Meet me at the Fudge Factory at 11.*

The words *surprise* and *Fudge Factory* seemed to quiver on the screen. My best friend knew which of my buttons to push—curiosity and taste buds. *Temptress*, I typed. *See you then.*

A heart emoji appeared, followed by an angel, and I smiled. Like my father, Tonya had developed a love affair with emojis.

I tossed my phone back on the table and returned to staring at the screen. My brain finally convinced my fingers to tap on the keyboard to pull up Facebook when a piercing howl rattled the windows. Woody was escalating.

"Woodward Cassidy, knock it off!" I said, using my strictest voice, one I'd learned at the hands of the master, Maggie Cassidy. The dog trotted over to me, nudged my leg with his wet nose, and went back to the door. This time, he let out a soft whimper and looked at me as if to say, *I can do this all day, lady.*

I looked at him sternly. "It's not going to happen, Woody. Look at this tiny place." I swept my hand around the cabin's interior. Less than three hundred square feet, the cabin boasted a bedroom-slash-living room, a bathroom sans tub, and a kitchenette, all visible from the front door. Furnished in a traditional cabin-in-the-woods style, the room contained a cedar log bed and armchair that folded out into a futon. Framed portraits of elk, bears, and mountain lions lined the walls. When their daughter wasn't commandeering the place, my parents marketed it to renters as "cozy."

Woody stopped whining and followed my gesture, his eyes inspecting the room. I took it as a sign of acquiescence and softened my tone as if I were trying to persuade a reluctant child that she couldn't have a longed-for toy. "We don't have room for a cat. They come with paraphernalia, you know. Like a litterbox." I wrinkled my nose. "I'm sure you wouldn't be the one cleaning up that mess. Besides, there's nowhere to even put one."

He trotted into the kitchen, straight to a spot in the corner next to the trash can. He sniffed the tile and tucked his furry body into the space.

I snorted and followed him into the kitchen, plopping to the floor beside him. I wrapped my arms around his neck. "It's been the two of us for four years. Has that been so bad?"

His tongue slurped the side of my face. I giggled, and he slurped again. Then he wriggled his seventy-pound frame into my lap. "See? We're good just as we are."

But after a couple of minutes of the mutual lovefest, he launched himself off me and raced to the door, his focus back on the knob. Another whimper.

I heaved myself up from the floor and sighed. "Sorry, Chief. I'm the boss here, and we're not getting a cat."

An hour later, I tucked the litterbox into the corner Woody had selected, grimacing as I filled it with some little pebbly stuff called "clump and seal." Then I watched the two creatures streak around the cabin, bound across the bed, and finally snuggle up together in a big ball of orange fur. They looked at me with self-satisfied expressions. "Point taken," I said. "You're both delirious with happiness." I gestured to the cat. "But I refuse to call this one Fireball."

I opened the refrigerator and glanced longingly at the box of wine. It was only four-thirty, though—too early even for me. I complied with a strict five o'clock rule. At least, most days. Settling on Diet Coke, I filled a plastic cup and stirred the resulting carbonated froth with my index finger. Then I rummaged around the shelves that served as my pantry and grabbed a box of Cheez-its. The low-fat version. I congratulated myself on my healthy choices.

After I placed my bounty on the table, I switched on my Nikon and attached a cord from it to the computer's USB port. I'd decided to put off my social media quest until I could accompany it with alcohol. Instead, I turned my attention to the photos I'd shot at the scene of the crime. When the collage of images appeared on the screen, I uploaded them. Then I used the cursor to surround the collage of images with a dotted line and double clicked. The pictures were now ready for me to scroll through and edit.

I tossed a handful of Cheez-its into my mouth and washed them down with a slug of Diet Coke. As I leaned toward the screen to examine the first photo, an orange ball of fur pounced across my right shoulder. I put a hand to my chest, covering my racing heart. "You nearly scared me to death, Cat."

He sat tall and majestic next to the computer, his tail swishing rhythmically against my forearm. His eyes were fixed on the computer screen and a wide angle shot of the Creekside ballroom, with its swirling blue and silver snowflakes glittering from the ceiling. I'd used a fisheye lens, and the result was an artsy, appealing shot designed to set the scene.

Apparently, the cat found it boring. He meowed, yawned, and tapped my hand with his paw. I narrowed my eyes. Was he urging me to keep scrolling? Focusing on the cat's response, I clicked onto the next picture. He leaned in closer, as if to study the image of the wait staff completing preparations for the ball that never happened. There was Dan the Bartender, polishing a glass. Nearby, the DJ fiddled with his audio mixer. Three young servers huddled together, laughing at something one of them had said.

The orange paw tapped my hand again. I scrolled rapidly through the next few photos, which seemed of little interest to the feline. But when the scene shifted to the office, he moved in so that his nose nearly touched the screen—right at the point of the bloody letter opener on the floor. A small growl rumbled in his throat. When I forwarded to a close-up of the fatal wound in Victoria's chest, the cat put his paw on my hand and turned his green eyes to mine.

A wave of adrenaline flooded through me. Was this creature able to analyze the content of the photos? Was he trying to communicate with me?

Woody rested his head on my leg as he stared affectionately up at his new brother. I forwarded the images again, and the little wildflower filled the screen. The cat meowed with urgency and tapped my hand with his paw. I cocked my head at him. "Are you a fledgling journalist, my friend?"

He swished his tail and continued to stare at me, intelligence gleaming from his eyes. I glanced down at the dog—Woodward—whom I'd named after a hero of mine, one of the most famous journalists in America. I looked back at the cat, and another name popped into my head.

It felt right.

"You seem to have a nose for news, cat. How would you like to be named for Woodward's partner? Bernstein doesn't really suit you, but maybe..." I smiled at him. "Would you like to be called Carl?"

With a sudden screech, he made a long leap from the table to the bed, arching his back as he landed. He pranced across the quilt and held his head high. No rolling of the eyes this time. I might have imagined it, but I thought I saw pride there.

Carl it was.

12

Despite Carl's interest, I discerned no clues from the crime scene photos. After a second pass, even the cat grew weary of the images and curled up on the bed for a snooze. Perhaps I had overestimated his investigative abilities.

I poured myself a glass of wine. Thus fortified, I opened Facebook and pulled up Victoria Dunleavy Ratliff's page, still intact and now filled with RIPs and tributes. I marveled at the halo of goodness that death often bestowed upon people who had been reviled while they were alive.

I skimmed through the condolences, on the off chance her killer had confessed his sins right there on her site. No such luck. I turned to her photo album. Not unexpectedly, Victoria had maintained an active page, plastered with selfies in which she appeared beautiful, glamorous, and happy. The most current shot had been posted on Friday. In it, she posed for the camera as she hung silver and blue snowflakes from the ballroom ceiling in preparation for the ill-fated Snowflake Swirl. Seeing her bright smile, the twinkle in her eyes, and contrasting it in my mind with the image of her body lying bloody and lifeless on the floor just a day later made me shudder.

I moved on to recent images of her family on the slope of Mt. O'Connell, broad grins showing off four sets of straight white teeth gleaming as brightly as the snow. Their dentist and orthodontist should have requested a tag on the photo. Next was a photo designed to appear candid but obviously posed. Victoria and her husband Brian nestled in front of a fireplace, staring lovingly into each other's eyes. A happy couple, picture-perfect family. It was enough to make me gag.

But when I came to a photo taken at a New Year's Eve party, the mood changed.

In the photo, Victoria wore a sparkly headband with the numbers 2021 bouncing atop it. Her clingy red dress stopped at least nine inches above her knees. The neckline was cut low, revealing expansive breasts powdered with golden glitter. Her left hand lifted a flute of champagne in an apparent toast. Her other arm was wrapped around a man whose eyes were locked on her cleavage.

And it wasn't her husband doing the leering—he was nowhere in sight. The lascivious grin belonged to the man I'd seen at the police station this morning: Parker Lyon.

Off to the side, barely even in the photo, stood Kimberly Lyon, hostility practically radiating from her skin as she glared at the pair.

I remembered a quote I learned in a college class: "Photography takes an instant out of time, altering life by holding it still." There was truth in that statement, but maybe it didn't go far enough. In fact, an instant was a long time in the making. A moment of laughter was the outcome of years spent building a sense of humor. A child's surprise at opening an unexpected gift occurred only because of the gift giver's planning. Even a landscape shot—a panorama of the mountains, for example—resulted from eons of earthly momentum.

Years of bitterness and rivalry had climaxed in the scene before me. That didn't bode well for Kimberly's claim of innocence.

My phone rang, and I checked the caller ID. Speak of

the devil. I chugged the last inch of wine from my glass and headed to the kitchen as I answered. Talking to Kimberly required a refill.

"Hello, Kimberly," I said, pulling the box of wine from the refrigerator and pouring myself another glass. I stopped just short of the brim. "Guess they gave you back your phone."

"Yes, and I'm out on bail," she said. Her voice sounded shrill, on the verge of hysteria.

I returned to the table and tried to lighten the mood. "Did they make you wear orange?"

"Not funny, Callahan. I'm calling to find out what progress you've made. I refuse to go back there. And they put this revolting ankle monitor on me. If I leave the village, I'll spontaneously combust or something. Not only that, I had to pay for the privilege. Please tell me you're on the verge of finding the real killer."

I almost felt sorry for her. Then I made my way back to the computer and saw the picture on the screen, the contempt on her face. I wondered, not for the first time, if I was being played.

"It's been less than a day, Kimberly. I don't even have a list of suspects yet. In fact, you can help with that. You must have a theory. If you're right about being framed, someone must have hated you both enough to kill one of you and set up the other."

She responded without hesitation. "Victoria's husband. Brian Ratliff."

Naturally, the victim's husband would land on the suspect list. The spouse was always the first person considered, so that wasn't exactly an earth-shattering leap. Still, she answered so quickly, so unequivocally. There had to be something more. "I'm sure he was enraged with Victoria, what with the affair—"

"And the divorce."

"What? I hadn't heard about a divorce."

"Oh, sure. Victoria filed the papers weeks ago. Their

money is all hers, of course, so he stood to lose everything. That's...what do you call it? Motive. Right?" She sounded pleased with herself.

"It's interesting information, for sure. Did you tell the police?"

She huffed indignantly. "They wouldn't listen to anything I had to say. Anyway, I wasn't supposed to talk without my lawyer present, remember?"

I pulled a yellow legal pad in front of me and wrote down Brian's name. "Okay. Suspect number one: Brian Ratliff. But why would he go to all the trouble of framing you? Is there some animosity between the two of you that I should know about?"

A few moments of silence followed. "Umm...because I was friends with his wife? And married to Parker, who was having an affair with her? I'm an easy target."

The waver in her voice hinted at deception. Something else was definitely going on, but I wasn't going to waste time pursuing it. Instead, I made a mental note to ask Tonya about it tomorrow. And if she didn't know, there was always Fran at Quicker Liquor.

Since Kimberly had brought up her husband's name, I followed that line of questioning. "Speaking of Parker, I'm wondering if he should be a suspect..."

"No, no, no," she said. Too quickly, I thought. She had clearly already considered the possibility. "Parker and I have our issues, just like any other couple. I'm not sure our marriage will survive this. But I simply can't fathom that he would murder Victoria—or anyone. And frame me? He just...he doesn't have it in him." Was that disdain I heard in her voice? Almost as if she'd have more respect for the man if he were capable of murder.

"Mm hmm." I jotted Parker's name on the pad. Kimberly might believe her husband was too weak to have committed the crime, but I'd seen plenty of unlikely murderers over the years. They came in all shapes, sizes, and demeanors. Parker Lyon had strong links to both Victoria and Kimberly, and he warranted investigation.

I tapped my pen on the paper. "Anyone else I should look into?"

She paused, thinking. "Well, Victoria's twins are first-class thugs. I wouldn't put it past them, especially if they're in the will or something."

Wow. Accusing the victim's sons of matricide was not what I'd expected. But I wrote Victoria's sons on the page with a big question mark. I hadn't lived here since before they were born, after all. For all I knew, they could be psychopathic killers. Another question to run by Tonya tomorrow.

Kimberly made a tut tut sound. "Someone else who comes to mind is Sophie Demler, though I don't know if she has the brains it would take."

Another surprise. Back in high school, Sophie had managed to weasel her way into the Vixens. She wasn't exactly their type, in terms of appearance and snottiness, but she'd definitely been one of them. I'd assumed once a Vixen, always a Vixen.

But then again, the two leaders had turned on one another, so why not Sophie?

"Why Sophie? What did she have against you?"

"Just some business dealings," Kimberly said dismissively. "She made a much bigger deal out of it than necessary. Listen, Callahan, I didn't get a wink of sleep in that nasty cell. I'm exhausted. After I take a nice long soak in the hot tub, I'm going to bed. You should have enough to start with. We can touch base tomorrow."

She sounded for all the world like a CEO giving instructions to her lowly assistant before she jetted off to some exotic vacation locale. Gone was the hysteria, the pleading. In its place was the haughty expectation of a Vixen, that I existed only to do her bidding.

I took a moment to remember Kimberly as the little girl I'd played with years ago. I needed to remind her of the dynamics of our current working relationship, the scenario that put me at the helm. But that was a battle for another day. "Yes, well, you just relax and take it easy," I said, knowing my sarcasm would be lost on her. "Be sure not to get too many bubbles on the ankle monitor."

13

I awoke the next morning to a wet dog tongue in my nostril and a furry cat paw in my ear. When I wrenched my eyelids open, a smiling snout rested on the pillow next to my face. I rolled my eyes upward, where Carl peered at me from his perch on my head.

Untangling the cat from my hair, I set him on the bed and swung my feet to the floor, shivering as I pulled off the quilt. After a yawn and stretch, I glanced at the digital clock on the nightstand. The creatures had awakened me at seven, a half hour before my alarm was set to go off. I frowned at the cat. In the B.C. days—Before Carl—Woody had permitted me to sleep until noon if I so desired. I'd have to train the cat. Or, more likely, he would train me.

I checked my phone and was surprised to find a text from Sam, timestamped five a.m. *Just wanted to check on you. Elyse tells me you've agreed to help Kimberly. Guess that's a good thing. If I can help, let me know. Not crazy about the idea of my daughter's mother being convicted of murder.*

A pang of guilt stabbed me. I glanced across the room at the legal pad lying atop the table. The list of suspect names I'd started. Last night, after much hemming and hawing, I'd reluctantly added Sam's name to the list. It was that expression on his face when he'd talked about Victoria. And the stain on his sleeve. I didn't know if he had a motive, but he certainly had means and opportunity. As an investigative journalist, I knew he had to be considered.

Tossing my phone on the bed, I opened the blinds to let the dawn's rays enter the room. I needed some exercise to clear my mind.

"Come on, Woodster," I said. "Let's get up the trail before I have to go see this Dr. Lowell person to get my head shrunk."

I headed to my closet—really just a curtained recess in the wall—and selected a pair of insulated pants and a sweatshirt. After I dressed and pulled on my hiking boots, I called Woody, who sat beside me patiently as I rubbed balm on his paw pads to keep them from being burned by the snow.

"Want to join us, Carl?" He gave me a contemptuous glare and began grooming himself. Message received.

Outside, the thermometer beside the door read twenty-seven degrees. Balmy. I sat in the rocking chair on the porch and secured traction devices to the bottom of my boots. Then I grabbed my walking poles. There wasn't currently a lot of snow on the resort property, but the higher elevations maintained deeper drifts and even slick ice in some areas. I knew enough to be prepared.

The newly risen sun sparkled on the snow-dusted path that led from the back of the property and wove into the tree line. Since tourists were sparse this week, I left Woody off leash. He bounded a few yards ahead of me and paused on the footbridge spanning Rock Creek to wait for me as I trekked across packed dirt and dead grass.

Past the bridge, the trail narrowed and turned steeper. Snowdrifts lined the dirt path, becoming deeper as we ascended. I trudged upward, my mind focused on the exertion, on coordinating my steps with the walking poles, on the beating of my heart and the speed of my breath. Woody took the trail slower than he would have liked, looking over his shoulder at me with patient tolerance. We hiked for twenty minutes, finally arriving at my special place on the precipice of a cliff—not even close to the top of the mountain, but a good height for a stunning view of Mt. O'Connell. My furry companion awaited me, tongue lolling from his mouth, tail sweeping the ground and swirling a cloud of white powder. I scratched behind his ears, brushed snow off a fallen log, and sat down to catch my breath.

On the western slope of the mountain, boulders peeked through the snow like trolls in sparkling tiaras. Evergreens had donned white winter coats. The mountain air seared into my lungs. Mom said the oxygen here contained magical healing powers.

Perhaps it was the magic of the moment that conjured the vivid memory. As I looked toward Mt. O'Connell, I saw Sam and I skiing down its slope, some twenty-five years ago. We'd been the only two people on the mountain that evening, but we'd felt like the only two people in the world. As we neared the end of the run, he'd swooped in behind me, wrapping his arms around me and dropping us both to the ground, skis and all. The snow crunched beneath us as he stared into my eyes, finally touching his lips to mine.

The feeling that welled inside me now was nearly as intense as it had been back then. Why had I let that drift away?

In truth, though, we hadn't drifted apart. I'd severed us. When I went off to college in Austin, I'd been so dazzled by the bustling city life that Rock Creek Village—and Sam—had seemed unsophisticated. Wearisome. Like many teenage romances, ours couldn't survive the distance.

I sighed. My mind flashed to present-day Sam, so handsome and self-assured. I'd seen a wave of pain in his eyes when he'd first spotted me at the event center, and I knew the pain we'd buried at age eighteen hadn't sunk too far beneath the surface. I didn't know how I could make it up to him.

But one thing I did know. Sam was not a killer. I'd been wrong to include him on my list. As soon as we got back to the cabin, I was scratching off his name.

Mom stood on the lodge's front porch, handing a cup of coffee to the purple-parka-clad Mrs. Finney, who sat in one of the rocking chairs. The large woman waved at me with a mittened hand. Mom glanced pointedly at her watch. I rolled my eyes like a teenager. I had fifteen minutes to make the ten-minute walk to Dr. Lowell's office, but like my father, Mom was a firm believer that right on time meant five minutes early.

I lifted a hand to the two of them and hurried past, crossing Evergreen Way with little concern for traffic. With the sparsity of tourists, elk were more likely to lumber along the road than vehicles.

Evergreen Way was one of two main arteries into the upper village. The other principal thoroughfare, situated a mile east and perpendicular, was the aptly monikered Mountain View Road. Early city planners had evidently put their most creative minds in charge of the street-naming business. Shops and restaurants lined the two roads, which formed the northern and eastern borders of the valley. In the basin, neighborhoods and ranches dotted the landscape, along with the more utilitarian shops providing groceries, fast food, and other so-called necessities of modern life. The Rocky Mountains created the western boundary, which lay behind my parents' resort and provided Rock Creek Village's residents and visitors with magnificent sunsets.

Despite my reluctance to rush, my mother's scolding expression lingered in my mind. I speed walked past the empty municipal lot, past the Quicker Liquor, Pearly's Steak and Chop House, and Tabitha's Treasures. I still had a few minutes, so I strolled down the street to Yoga Delight, which sounded to me more like an ice cream shop than an exercise studio. My mother harangued me regularly to join her there—in fact, she wanted me to attend a meditation class this afternoon. I'd forcefully refused, but gazing inside now made me wonder if I should give the place a try.

True to the name, the participants inside appeared

delighted. Expressions ranging from concentration to peace to sheer joy danced across their faces as they contorted their bodies into unnatural positions. Their leader, a tall, slender woman with blond hair cascading down her back, walked from one participant to the next, guiding their movements with gentle touches. I could hear her through the glass. "Picture enlightenment as a serene butterfly that settles gently on your arm."

My knee jerk reaction was an eye roll. But I considered her words and felt a sudden yearning to experience such enlightenment. I wanted that butterfly to land on me.

Maybe my counseling session would serve the purpose.

I retraced my steps. Dr. Lowell's office occupied an upstairs space just above The Fudge Factory, and the rich scent of chocolate wafting from the shop made me salivate. Was this a purposeful location choice on Dr. Lowell's part? Did the aroma of chocolate create a psychologically soothing effect? If so, this was a savvy therapist. She might even be able to teach me a thing or two.

I approached the stairs, distracted by thoughts of fudge and butterflies. As I placed my foot on the bottom step, a muscular hand closed like a vise over my shoulder and dragged me into an alcove beneath the stairs.

Was I being mugged? All those years living in big cities without incident, only to experience assault in the safe little haven where I'd grown up?

Because journalism was sometimes a dangerous career, *The Sentinel* had made us all take self-defense courses, so I was well trained for a situation such as this. As my attacker thrust me toward a stucco wall, I whirled around and rammed the heel of my palm into his nose, savoring the crunch of cartilage.

"Yeowwww." His head jolted backward, and his hands flew to his face. Though I hadn't drawn blood, I knew the punch had hurt. The nose was one of the most sensitive parts of the body—a perfect target, according to my trainer.

When the brute dropped his hands, I saw a face contorted in pain and rage. I searched for an escape route and took a quick step to the side, but the man was built like a flabbier version of the Hulk, and he blocked my path.

I considered my next move. If this guy didn't back down, I'd have to go for the groin.

"How dare you?" he growled.

I decided offense was my best strategy and leaned in, placing a finger on his chest. "I'd advise you to give me some space here."

He put his hand to his nose and took a step back. "How dare you?" he repeated, but a little less belligerently.

I plastered an irritated expression on my face, the kind I might use with a defiant child. "How dare I *what*, for heaven's sake?"

"You're aiding and abetting the woman who murdered my wife."

The tumblers clicked into place. This was the man I'd seen in the photos in Victoria's photos—her husband, Brian Ratliff. How had he known I was helping Kimberly?

"What makes you think that?"

"She posted it on Facebook." He fumbled in his pocket for his phone and pulled up Kimberly's page. Sure enough, her most recent post proclaimed her innocence, followed by the statement: "If prize winning journalist Callahan Cassidy believes me and wants to help me, it should be obvious to everyone I didn't commit this atrocious crime."

Once I got past my surprise that Kimberly had used the word atrocious, I sighed.

Brian leaned in. "What do you have to say for yourself?"

My next words dropped onto my tongue like a gumball, apparently bypassing my brain. "Did you kill your wife?"

His face went slack, eyes blank. "What—?"

"It's a simple question. Did you murder Victoria over her affair? Or maybe the divorce? Or both?"

He shook his head as if confused.

"Where were you Saturday afternoon?" I demanded.

His face turned as purple as an eggplant, and I suddenly remembered that I was alone in an out-of-the-way alcove with a steroid stuffed, rage-filled madman. He roared and raised a fist.

As I lifted my knee to wallop him between the legs, a figure rushed around the staircase and into the alcove. A figure whose hand hovered near the gun on his hip.

"Back off, Ratliff. Now!" The thunderous voice belonged to Detective Sanchez, and any prior irritation I had felt toward him evaporated.

Brian turned toward the detective, who looked at Brian's swollen nose and then glanced at me, with my knee mid-lift. Sanchez moved between us and Victoria's husband appeared to deflate when the detective placed a hand on Brian's chest. Testosterone-fueled rage must carry a brief shelf life.

Sanchez addressed me, though his eyes never left Brian. "Ms. Cassidy, was this man threatening you? Would you like to lodge a complaint?"

I hesitated but shook my head. "We were just chatting. No harm done. But if you gentlemen will excuse me, I'm late for an appointment."

Sanchez kept his hand on Brian but turned toward me as I brushed past him. "Just a minute. We need to talk about this."

"No can do. As I said, I have somewhere to be." I pointed up to Dr. Lowell's office and made my way up the staircase.

When I reached the landing, I looked down at the sidewalk and spotted Brian crossing the street, his head lowered and hands shoved into his pockets. Sanchez stood at the bottom of the stairs, watching me with an appraising eye.

14

The brass plate on the door read: *Dr. Rebecca Lowell, Clinical Psychology.* Before entering, I took my phone from my purse with trembling hands. It wasn't fear that caused the shaking, but a simple adrenaline rush, fueled by anger. Mostly, I was livid at Kimberly. Her Facebook post proved the old saying that no good deed goes unpunished. I sent her a text. *Delete your FB post. Now!*

Three dots flashed on my screen. *Is this Callahan? Which post?*

I resisted the urge to type, "You stupid moron." *The post about me helping you. And you should stay off social media.*

A pause. I tapped my foot until I got her response. *You're making too big a deal, but I deleted it.*

A click back to her page confirmed it, but the damage was done. By lunchtime, our unholy alliance would be fodder for the town's gossip machine.

I took a moment to calm my nerves—but then something else occurred to me.

When word got out that I was looking into Victoria's murder, Brian might not be my only adversary. Whoever the murderer was, he—or she—wouldn't welcome my interference.

After less than a minute in the waiting room, Dr. Lowell

ushered me into her office. I guessed she was a few years older than me. She wore a well-cut turquoise pantsuit that highlighted her slender, athletic physique. Her dark hair was styled in a short shag, and a pair of tortoiseshell glasses rested on the bridge of her nose, framing hazel eyes.

"Make yourself comfortable," she said.

My still-raw nerves vibrated, and I responded to the discomfort in my usual way: sarcasm.

"So how does this go? Do I lie on the couch clutching a box of tissues while you probe my deepest, darkest thoughts?"

Dr. Lowell smiled, unruffled. "This goes how you want it to go. Would you like to lie on the couch? Most clients don't, but a few do. Whatever puts you at ease."

I wrinkled my nose. "Sorry. Anxiety makes me snarky."

She continued to smile indulgently, and I shifted my focus to her office.

The space exuded warmth. A stuffed couch faced two plump armchairs across from a coffee table that sported a small floral arrangement and the obligatory Kleenex. The place even smelled tranquil, with a slight scent of lavender wafting through the air. Dr. Lowell settled into a leather armchair.

Instead of sitting—or lying down—I wandered around the room, studying the framed certificates on the wall. Bachelor's degree in psychology from the University of Minnesota, a master's and a doctorate from UC Berkeley. High honors across the board. Impressive.

Near the certificates, framed photos showed Dr. Lowell participating in various athletic pursuits. In one, she stood on skis atop a gleaming slope I recognized as our own Mt. O'Connell. In another, she was clad in scuba gear, sitting on the edge of a boat ready to tumble backwards into an expanse of cobalt water. Yet another displayed her posed in a martial arts stance, trim and strong, a determined expression on her face.

If my counseling session didn't go well, perhaps I could

hire her as a personal trainer.

On her desk, I saw a framed snapshot of a younger Dr. Lowell dressed in graduation garb, flanked by a beaming woman and a somber girl.

I gestured toward the photo. "Your family?"

Her lips held the gentle smile. "You know, Callie, in all the years I've been seeing clients, I don't recall any of them ever venturing behind my desk."

I felt myself flush as I realized I had trampled across a boundary. "I'm so sorry," I said, hurrying to the couch. "Professional hazard. Former profession, that is. I'm a snoop. I think everyone else's business is mine."

"No worries," she said. "Let's turn our attention to you, Callie. At this point I usually ask a new client what brings her into counseling. But considering the weekend's events, I suspect we already have a topic."

"Whatever do you mean?" I fluttered my eyelashes in mock ignorance before turning serious. "Really, though, I'm fine. Better than you might expect."

"I heard you agreed to help Kimberly Lyon," she said.

I'd speculated that my association with Kimberly would be common knowledge by lunch, but I had clearly underestimated the speed of information dissemination in Rock Creek Village.

"Sort of," I said. "You might say it's just for old time's sake. We were close as children. Almost like family. I need to know if she's actually guilty."

Dr. Lowell raised her eyebrows. "If I'm not mistaken, you found her standing over the body."

"I did, yes. But without going into too much detail, there is a chance she is being framed. It warrants further investigation, anyway, and I'm not sure the police will be doing that. They seem convinced they have their culprit."

She nodded thoughtfully and tented her fingers on her lap. "You believe Kimberly should get the benefit of the doubt."

"Exactly."

Dr. Lowell gave me one of those therapist nods that told me she didn't agree. "All right. Let's leave that aside for the moment. Victoria's death wasn't the reason you made this appointment."

"No, it was my mother," I said, without hesitation. "She's worried that I drink too much. And that I might be depressed."

"Do you? Are you?"

I thought about taking the path of least resistance—denial. But in my heart of hearts, I knew Mom was right. I hadn't talked, really talked, to anyone in a long time. What did I have to lose?

"Maybe," I admitted. "I think the drinking is just situational. A habit I've picked up to pass the time and take the edge off since…" My voice trailed away. "As for depression," I added, "isn't everybody a little depressed these days? I don't see much point in dwelling on it."

"Can you pinpoint a time when the feelings of depression first appeared?"

I bristled. "You're referring to my resignation from the paper. You probably already know the details. Everyone in town probably knows. I'm sure I'm the subject of a lot of gossip."

Even as I said it, I wondered at my own defensiveness. The reason for my return to Rock Creek Village was bound to arise.

Dr. Lowell leaned forward and rested her elbows on her knees. "Callie, I wasn't referencing a particular event. But you're right—I do know about the cause of your resignation. And it still seems raw. I think we should talk about it."

I saw genuine concern in her eyes. Suddenly, it seemed right to talk. Necessary, even, to share with someone the burden I'd been carrying. Yes, everyone knew what happened—what they'd read in the papers, anyway. But I hadn't confided in anyone how it felt to go through the ordeal. Not my parents. Not Tonya. It was time. I took a deep breath and a leap of faith.

"Just so you have some context, I've never had any patience with bullies. They infuriate me. So when a source came to me with a story that essentially involved bullying, I probably wasn't as objective as I should have been." I paused and dropped my eyes to my lap.

"Go on, Callie," Dr. Lowell said gently. "I'm listening."

My head pounded. I rubbed my temples and forced myself to keep talking. "When I heard the allegations of hazing—torture, really—at a D.C. university fraternity, I believed the source. His insistence on anonymity didn't seem strange to me. A lot of sources want to keep their names out of the press. I wrote the story, complete with names and photos of the alleged perpetrators. It was a blazing exposé, another feather in my journalistic cap. The repercussions came swiftly. The fraternity chapter was suspended indefinitely. Even more important, the president of the frat—Jameson Jarrett—was arrested, tried, and found guilty of aggravated assault. Sentenced to five years. All in all, a good day at the office, right?"

I closed my eyes, picturing Jameson's face that day in court—the fear, the tears. "You know what happened then. The man—kid, really, just twenty years old—had served over a year when evidence of his innocence came to light. A witness recanted, said he'd been bribed by my original source. Apparently, my source thought he should have been fraternity president and wanted Jarrett out of the way."

My cheeks were hot with shame. "I was biased. Made assumptions. I did a half-hearted job on my investigation. And that young man lost more than a year of his life."

From beneath my wet lashes, I saw that Dr. Lowell's expression was filled with compassion. Not judgment. Not pity. Not disgust. She wasn't seeing the ogre I imagined myself to be.

After a moment, she said, "Callie, I understand your sense of responsibility. But it was the police who arrested the young man. It was the jury who found him guilty. You didn't singlehandedly try and convict this man."

I grabbed a tissue and swiped at the tears trickling down my cheeks. "I know you're right. In theory, anyway."

She smiled. "How does it feel to talk about all this?"

I composed myself and considered her question. Despite being emotionally wrung out, I felt...lighter, somehow. As if a pack of bricks had been removed from my back. "Like I could sleep for twelve hours. But also relieved, if that makes sense."

She nodded. "The monster we harbor in our head is much more powerful than the one we push into the light of day. But be aware that the monster will try to worm its way back into the forefront of your mind. It will take insight and vigilance to keep it at bay."

"How do I do that?"

She sat back in her chair and crossed her legs. "First, cut back on the drinking. Alcohol is a depressant. I'll give you some healthier techniques for dealing with stress and anxiety."

She outlined a few coping strategies she wanted me to practice—cognitive behavioral stuff that sounded like techniques I'd used to train Woody. Despite feeling like the dog in this scenario, I agreed to try.

"And now we're at the end of our session. So what do you think? Want to come back for more?"

It was an easy decision. "I'd like that. As long as you promise not to tell my mother she was right."

She chuckled and checked her schedule, finding a weekly opening on Thursdays at nine. "One last thing," she said, as I put on my coat. "I want you to think about the link between the Jameson Jarrett situation and your desire to help Kimberly Lyon. Could it be that you are rushing in to save her as a sort of penance?"

My eyes narrowed, but before I could speak, she raised a hand. "Just think about it. And in the meantime...counselors aren't in the business of giving advice, but we all do it under the guise of—" her fingers made air quotes "—*suggesting*. My suggestion is this: disengage from the murder investigation. Let the police do their jobs, and focus your attention on healing from your own trauma."

I shrugged. "I promise I'll think about it. But to be honest, I don't see how I can sit back and watch Kimberly go to jail if she's not guilty."

She gave me a wry smile. "That's the thing about advice. You're free to take it or leave it. I just hope you'll consider it."

15

C onsider Dr. Lowell's suggestion I did—for the twenty seconds it took for me to descend the staircase from her office. My conclusion? I might not be imbued with volumes of insight, but one thing I did know: I could not be at peace if I stood by while another innocent person went to jail—and a guilty person went free.

When I reached the sidewalk, I glanced into the alcove on the off chance Brian lay in wait. Empty. Relieved, I inhaled a fudgy smell that tickled my nose and made my stomach growl. Where was Tonya?

I looked up and down the street but saw no sign of her. After a single, frustrated huff, I decided to draw on the brand new techniques from my counseling session. I could reframe Tonya's tardiness as an opportunity to get to know the village again. After all, the only place I'd visited since my return was Quicker Liquor.

A young woman pushed a stroller along the sidewalk, stopping occasionally to window shop. A man in a suit hurried toward the real estate office. A young couple strolled hand in hand, eyes only for each other. It was strange that life in the village seemed so normal when just two days ago a woman had been murdered.

That probably wasn't the kind of thinking Dr. Lowell would recommend. I took a few steps to my right, pausing in front of Tabitha's Treasures. The shop was shuttered for the season, a glittery poster informing passersby that they could find Tabitha "On a Beach—back in March." I'd worked at Tabitha's Treasures one summer during high school, and I immediately conjured a mental picture of my younger self in khakis and a white Oxford shirt, gritting my teeth as vacationers dragged their rugrats through rows of— well, I'd be kind and call it cheap crap—magnets and ornaments they bought as remembrances of their time in Rock Creek Village.

Smiling at the memory, I turned back in the other direction and scanned the row of shops leading to the end of the street. A narrow gap separated each shop from its neighbor, with a staircase leading to the second level. Office space topped each little store—real estate, insurance, law offices. It was an attractive, efficient arrangement. The town seemed to be caught in a time warp, hearkening back to a simpler, more innocent era.

As a journalist, though, I knew how deceiving looks could be. Here, as everywhere else, darkness hid beneath the cheerful façade. Human beings lived and worked here, after all. In my experience, most were driven by unattractive forces few wanted to admit: greed, lust, revenge, power.

Another dark thought that would surely be frowned upon by my new therapist.

Still no Tonya. I passed The Fudge Factory, and glanced in the window of the upscale clothing boutique I'd heard about: V&K's Fine Fashion. A Closed sign hung in the window. Now that one of the owners was dead and the other arrested for her murder, I wondered if the shop would ever reopen.

Then I noticed a blond man climbing the stairs to the office above the boutique, lugging a small suitcase behind him. I recognized him as Parker Lyon, and the office's sign read: *Rocky Insurance Company.*

So Parker's place of business was directly above his wife's—and his lover's—establishment. That had to have been awkward. Or perhaps convenient.

I bit my bottom lip as I wondered about the suitcase. This was an odd time to be traveling, with his wife in such dire straits. Then again, their relationship wasn't exactly a textbook example of how to have a happy marriage.

As I was lost in thought, a hand fell on my shoulder. Startled, I swiveled, my palm positioned for another nose punch. Instead of Brian, though, I saw Tonya, her face wreathed in an amused grin. "Calm down, grasshopper. Why so jumpy?"

"You shouldn't sneak up on a person that way. Especially when she's recently been accosted by an angry hulk and wrung out by a therapist."

Her brow creased. "Rough morning?"

"Walk in the park. I'll tell you about it later. Right now, I'm all atwitter over your big surprise. Which flavor of fudge does it involve?"

"No fudge, my sweet," she said, laughing. "But something I hope you'll find just as delectable. Follow me."

The journey took only a few steps. Nestled between the Fudge Factory and V&K's Fine Fashions was a storefront I'd passed without noticing, likely because it lacked a sign and sported a grimy plate glass window. Tonya brandished a key.

"What's this?" I asked. "Are you relocating *The Gazette* offices?"

Wearing a mysterious smile, she unlocked the door. A bell jingled, and she guided me inside. With a flip of a switch, overhead fixtures bathed the space in soft white light. Tonya swept a hand around the room, like a *Price is Right* model displaying a prize. "It's for you, dearheart. Your new photo gallery."

I scanned the space. "Photo gallery? What are you talking about?"

"Think about it," she said. "You seem to have soured on your journalism career. But with your talent and your passion for photography, I simply can't imagine you abandoning your camera. This is a perfect solution. I've seen your landscape and nature photography, most notably the ones hanging at your parents' lodge. People love them. Your mother told me tourists are constantly complimenting them and asking if they are for sale."

"Of course she would say that. She's my mother."

"Just listen for a minute," she said. "You could create art instead of documenting crime scenes. You could bring joy to people's lives and their homes. And financially, you could make a killing. No pun intended."

Even as I shook my head in disbelief, my feet started traipsing through the space. I had to admit, it was an intriguing idea. My own photo gallery? A feeling I couldn't identify percolated inside me. Excitement? Fear? "What did this place used to be?"

"An art gallery."

"Why did it close? Not enough business?"

"Quite the opposite," she said. "The artist who held the lease was recently offered an opportunity in L.A. She opened a gallery there and sells her art to the Hollywood elite. We did a feature on her last year." She beamed, as though personally responsible for the artist's success.

"So cool," I said. An art gallery. It explained the perfect layout. A polished gray concrete floor provided easy care under high traffic. The track lighting would emphasize displays on the smoky gray walls—perfect for black-and-white images. A half dozen free-standing pillars on wheels created options for temporary, movable exhibits. Little work would be required to turn this into a functional photography gallery.

Tonya glided to the rear of the studio, and I trotted along after her to a hallway containing four smaller rooms. I envisioned them as an office space, a small portrait studio, and a lab where I could teach photography classes. The fourth space could easily be transformed into a darkroom— old school, but for me, nothing beat witnessing an image coming to life in a tray of developing fluid. I visualized myself introducing the thrill of photography, both film and digital, to a generation of rookies.

Suddenly, I felt my heart pounding and my breath coming in spurts. This whole day had taken me way outside my comfort zone. First I'd bared my soul in counseling, and now I was actually considering my future. It was too much, too soon. I hurried back to the door, turning my back on the gallery. "It's a nice space," I mumbled, my voice tight. "But it's not for me."

Unruffled, Tonya skipped along behind me. "I had a feeling you'd say that. But you'll come around. We just have to hope no one else signs a lease before you do."

Tonya locked the gallery door and took my hand, leading me down the street. "Let's eat," she said. "My treat."

I pointed over my shoulder. "The Fudge Factory is that direction."

"No chocolate for lunch," she scolded.

"Quicker Liquor?"

"If you're a good girl and eat your meal, you can have dessert later. In whichever form you choose."

We strolled past a few more shops, finally reaching a cafe with a jaunty red and white striped awning. Snow Plow Chow. Sam's place.

I had a hunch I was being set up.

It had been Tonya, after all, who'd played matchmaker between Sam and me back in high school. Before I could object, the door opened and a couple stepped outside, followed by an aroma of such heavenly proportions that my rumbling stomach sounded like the angel Gabriel playing his trumpet. What could I do? My baser instincts almost always conquered my common sense. I followed my best friend inside.

16

A smattering of customers looked up as Tonya and I entered the cafe, unfamiliar faces that quickly turned back to their phones. A server I recognized as Dan the Bartender from the Snowflake Swirl moved toward us with an air of indifference—until he caught sight of Tonya. As she removed her coat, his apathetic expression morphed into a worshipful gaze.

I sighed. Some things never changed.

"Well, hello there, Tonya." His eyes traveled from her crown of curls down her red paisley tunic and black leggings to her knee-high leather boots. He had the decency to bring them back up to her face. "You're looking fetching today. Came to visit old Dan at work, huh?" He winked at her before glancing in my direction and grabbing two menus from the host stand. "Two of you today?"

She smiled at him. "Dan, you remember my friend Callie Cassidy, don't you? I believe you met Saturday night."

Recognition dawned on his face. "The photo lady, right? Chief Cassidy's daughter."

I nodded. I'd been a top-tier journalist for a quarter of a century, a pioneer of convergence media, a Felden Prize winning photographer. But now that I was back in Rock Creek Village, I was simply Chief Cassidy's daughter. "Good to see you, Dan," I said.

He snapped his fingers. "Hey, you found the boss lady

dead, right? Oh, man. That was one steaming pile of…well, you know." He cupped a meaty hand around his mouth, puffing sour breath into my face. "Was there lots a blood? Give old Dan some details."

I tried to stutter out a response. "Well, I can't—"

Tonya came to the rescue. "Dan, we're famished. Could you be a doll and tuck us into that cozy little booth?" She pointed toward a table near the fireplace.

He straightened and ran a hand across his scalp. "Course. Anything for you, babe." He waddled over to the red vinyl booth and laid menus on the table, extending a hand to take Tonya's coat.

He didn't reach for mine, so I draped it over my arm without any assistance at all.

When we got to the booth, Dan watched appreciatively as Tonya removed her gloves and hat, fluffed her hair, and slid into the seat. I mimicked her movements but drew no attention. When we were both settled with our coats tucked in beside us, Dan pulled an order pad and pencil from the pocket of his apron, touching his tongue to the tip of the pencil. "What can I get you beautiful ladies to drink?"

"Um, do you have hot chocolate?" I said.

His eyes flicked my way then straight back to Tonya. "Course. Whipped cream?"

Tonya and I looked at each other. "Make it two," Tonya said.

When Dan went off to get our drinks, laughter bubbled from our lips, and our easy companionship felt just like high school.

"That guy…" I said.

"He's not so bad." Tonya shrugged.

"Do I sense a budding romance?" She glared at me and picked up her menu while I assessed the surroundings. Sam had created an appealing space here, plush and homey. Along with tables and booths, several living room style seating arrangements clustered near a stone hearth, inviting small groups to enjoy coffee or cocoa and conversation around a crackling fire. Thick rugs dotted the rich, laminate wood flooring, creating an intimate atmosphere.

The only problem lay in the choice of wall decor: kitschy, cheap-looking paintings depicting Wild West scenes—grizzled old men with donkeys and covered wagons resting in the snow. I cringed.

"What's with the artwork?" I asked, gesturing to a lasso-wielding cowboy above our table.

Tonya snickered. "Guess Sam needs someone with a photographer's eye to help. You up for the task?"

I ignored her matchmaking. "He needs to replace this junk with local landscape scenes. It would take the ambience up a notch and provide diners with an interesting focal point."

She shot me a sly grin. "And I know just the photographer to help with that."

I kicked her under the table. Dan approached, balancing a tray with two glasses of water and two steaming mugs, white foam peeking above the rim. My mouth watered as he set them in front of us. Tonya's first.

"Ready to order?" he asked, pencil poised over pad.

I took a sip of the thick, creamy liquid, realizing this hot chocolate was so delicious it might make up for the fudge deprivation. I quickly wiped the foam from my lips. "I don't know what's good here," I said to Tonya. "You order for me."

"Well, everything's good. But for a first-timer, I'd always recommend ChipMunch." She stacked the menus and handed them to Dan. "Make that two."

Dan took a moment to write down the order. When he finished, Tonya asked, "Sam around?"

He shook his head. "Hightailed it outta here a few minutes ago. Elyse forgot her homework or some such. Usually he'd let her face the music, but he's feelin' sorry for her, what with her mom and all." He puffed out his chest. "Left old Dan in charge."

After our server headed toward the kitchen, Tonya leaned across the table, hands clasped. "Okay, Miss Marple. What progress have you made on your investigation? Off the record, of course."

I smirked. "You sound like Kimberly. Both of you seem to think I'm psychic or something—like all I have to do is consult my crystal ball and the killer's face will appear."

She chuckled. "Your reputation precedes you in this town. Villagers are wagering their hard-earned cash trying to guess when you'll get this solved."

"You're not serious?"

She smacked my hand. "Of course not, you silly goose. As for me, all my chips are still on Kimberly. Are there even any other suspicious characters worth considering?"

"Actually, I was hoping to get your help with that."

She leaned back and slung an arm across the vinyl seat. "I live to serve."

Just then, I spotted Dan at the front of the cafe, and an idea blossomed. I gestured to him, but he ignored me. Tonya gave me a look of confusion, but without asking for explanation, she came to my aid, waving a manicured hand. "Yoo hoo, Dan. Yoo hoo."

He responded to her summons immediately, treating her to a seductive smile. "Just couldn't get enough of old Dan, huh? Need a refill on the hot chocolate? Extra whipped cream. On me." He waggled his eyebrows. I subdued a gag.

Tonya smiled sweetly and turned to me, her dark eyes not sharing the smile. "I think we're fine on the hot chocolate. But Callie has a question."

"Sure thing," he said, eyes turning reluctantly to me.

"The other night at the Creekside—"

"You mean the night the house fell on the Wicked Witch?"

Oh my. "Um, yes. Do you remember who all was in and out of the place that day?"

He shifted his weight. "Course I can." He tapped his

index finger against his temple. "I got a, what do you call it, photographic memory for faces." He paused, his bushy eyebrows drawn together. "I'm not sure the cops would want me talkin' about it, though."

"Dan, be a lamb and tell us what you remember," Tonya said. "It'll be our little secret." She put a finger against her lips, and he quivered like jelly.

"What that detective don't know won't hurt him, right? There was me, course. And Darius the DJ, who they hired outta Boulder. Same with all the waiters. Got 'em from a temp service at the university, seven in all. I don't know all their names, but I could get 'em if you want."

"No, that won't be necessary," I said. "Just anyone local."

"Well, Snow Plow Chow was catering, so Sam was there. But you already know that. I saw you talking to him and his daughter."

"Did either of them go back to the office area before I arrived?"

"Didn't see 'em. Guess one of them coulda when I wasn't watching. Or when Sam sent me back here to the Chow to pick up some supplies. Anyone coulda gone in and out then."

So the Creekside had been left essentially unattended for periods of time. That certainly opened the window of opportunity. "Who else did you see? Maybe earlier in the day?"

He shifted his eyes to the ceiling. "Fran delivered the alcohol from Quicker Liquor. Then the two—" He glanced sidelong at Tonya. "—the lady couple came in. None too happy, either of 'em."

"Jessica Fannon and Summer Simmons?" Tonya asked.

Two names I didn't recognize. My lengthy absence from the village was clearly going to make this investigation more challenging. Luckily, I had a best friend who seemed to know everyone in a fifty-mile radius.

"Yeah, those two. Stormed in like someone lit a fire under 'em. Didn't stay too long. Left with their arms wrapped around each other."

He began to fidget, and I knew we were on the brink of losing his attention. A stroke to his ego might gain me another minute or two. "I can't believe you remember all these details," I gushed. "You weren't kidding when you said photographic memory." He looked pleased, so I continued. "Can you think of anyone else? What about Victoria's husband? Did he stop by?"

He wiped a finger across his upper lip and shook his head. "Nah, not him. But that puny guy Parker did, all decked out in a fancy coat. Headed straight back without even a how-you-doin' for old Dan." He looked from side to side and leaned in. "Him and the Wicked Witch were getting it on, I heard."

I twisted my face into an expression of astonishment to keep him talking. "Are you serious?" I asked in a hushed tone. "Wow."

A self-satisfied nod, followed by a whisper. "Couldn't a had time to, you know, do the dirty back there, though. That wife of his was hot on his heels. And she sure looked like she wanted to kill somebody."

17

I froze with my mug of hot chocolate halfway to my lips. I could see that Dan had enjoyed shocking me. From the corner of my eye, I could tell that Tonya's reaction mirrored my own.

"Yeah, but Kimberly couldn't have killed Victoria," he said. "Not then, anyway. She marched out a couple minutes later dragging the hubby behind her. Musta come back later when I was takin' my break."

The kitchen door banged open, and a man in a white apron stuck his head out. "Hey, Dan. You gonna pick up this order or what?"

"Yeah, yeah, I'm coming." He took off toward the kitchen.

"Well, that was a lot of information," Tonya said. "Not sure what to make of it, though."

I nodded. "Kimberly didn't mention that she and Parker had made an appearance at the event center earlier in the day. That would have been nice to know."

"Sounds like she was caught up in the heat of the moment, though. Would she really stop to rig the latch on that door in such an emotional state?"

"Ah, you're coming around to the dark side," I said. "Considering the possibility that Kimberly might be innocent." She waved me off, and I smirked. "The thing is, the latch might not even be related. From what Dan says, if the timing was right, anyone could have waltzed in and out right through the front door while he ran back to the cafe for supplies."

I was interrupted by the tantalizing aroma of seasoned beef and cheese. Dan shuffled across the room carrying two plates and plopped two orders of nachos in front of us. He struck what I assumed he intended as a sexy pose, hand on hip like a runway model. "Can I get you ladies anything else? And I do mean anything…"

Tonya, who'd always had a knack for handling enthusiastic admirers, poured on the charm. "Thank you, Dan. You're so sweet. We know where to find you." He smiled and sauntered off to the host stand.

I eyed my plate. So this was ChipMunch—nachos served on potato chips instead of the traditional tortilla chips. It was a unique concoction, and looked as delectable as it smelled. I lifted one of the chips, laden with a saucy beef mixture, chives, and sour cream, and popped it in my mouth. My eyes rolled back in my head, and when I returned to reality, Tonya's face was gleeful.

"That recipe is Sam's creation. It seems you approve."

"Oh, yes."

She took a bite, and we chewed together in silence for a few moments. Hot chocolate and nachos—the lunch of champions. I pictured the delightful yoga participants next door, but didn't feel the slightest bit guilty. That would come later, when I faced the scale.

A drop of thick liquid drooled from the corner of my mouth, and I reached across the table to grab a napkin from the dispenser. My hand brushed against a small vase filled with an array of tiny blue wildflowers. I did a double take and felt my gut clench as I recalled the image of a similar flower I'd seen.

Saturday. On the floor beside Victoria's dead body.

"Tonya. These flowers. Where did they come from?"

"What are you talking about? They've been there the whole time."

"No, I mean, where did Sam get them?"

"Forget-me-nots." She shrugged. "They're everywhere in alpine environments. Quite common. You haven't been away so long that you've forgotten forget-me-nots, have you?" She grinned at her little joke.

"It's winter, though. All the wildflowers should be dead."

"Not if they're grown in a greenhouse. Marlene Timor at the Village Florist keeps a supply of them. They're quite popular with tourists. Sam probably orders from her."

I nodded, trying to remember if I'd seen them elsewhere, perhaps as decorations on the ballroom coffee tables. Nothing popped into my mind. I'd need to look at my photos again when I got home.

Quite common, I repeated to myself. But still. Sam had access to the very flower I'd photographed at the murder scene. And there was that stain on his shirt. And his scornful expression when he'd mentioned Victoria's name…Had I made a mistake eliminating him from my list?

Absently, I took another meaty bite of ChipMunch. Tonya was staring at me. "What?" I said around a mouthful of chips. I dabbed at my chin with the napkin. "Am I a mess?"

"Oh, you're a mess, all right. Tell me you're not considering Sam as a suspect."

I managed a weak smile. "Of course not. That's ridiculous. Tell me about this Jessica and Summer couple Dan mentioned."

She pursed her lips and gave me a hard look but eventually started talking. "Jessica Fannon is the journalism teacher at the high school. Quite the firecracker. I just love her. Summer Simmons is her wife, owner of Yoga Delight. She'll almost be your neighbor when you open the photo gallery."

I ignored the last part of her statement and searched my mind. The name niggled at the edges of my memory. Then it clicked. Mom had told me about her instructor Summer when she'd been nagging me to go to class with her. As a sidebar, she'd mentioned Summer's recent marriage to Jessica.

"People are thrilled for them," Mom had told me. "Such wonderful young women—friendly, hard-working. But—like everywhere else, I suppose—we have a handful of bad apples in the village, the kind who squeak behind the scenes and try to get everyone in a tizzy."

Victoria had been one of the squeakers, I surmised.

"Dan said they seemed angry Saturday. Any idea what that was about?"

"No clue. But most people in town have had a bone to pick with Victoria at one point or another. Nothing new about that."

Tonya's phone buzzed with a text, and she leaned her head toward the screen as she pushed her plate away. She'd only eaten half of her meal. I, on the other hand, was scooping the last of the beef onto my final chip and shoving it in my mouth.

Once she'd finished reading, she motioned to Dan to bring the check. He tore it from his pad and laid it in her outstretched hand, lingering on her palm. Tonya squinted at the bill, then reached for her bag, a canvas and leather monstrosity I identified as Burberry. "Owning a small-town newspaper must pay better than I thought," I said, nodding toward the purse.

"It's a knock off, silly. Almost everything I own is fake." She brandished a pair of glasses. "These readers, for example. You might think they're the fancy version from Target, but I actually got them at Walmart. Quite a steal."

She handed over her credit card. Dan bustled away, returning with her receipt just in time to hold her coat as she slid into it. I struggled into my coat without assistance. Tonya graced Dan with a high-wattage smile, and we headed for the door.

The sky had darkened, as if someone had set the village's lights on dim. A thick layer of gray stratus clouds blanketed the mountains, concealing their peaks. To my eye, it looked as if they were just passing through, and wouldn't be dropping any of the snow Mt. O'Connell—and the Knotty Pine—so desperately needed. I said a little prayer to the snow gods as a frosty wind gusted down the sidewalk, rattling the Snow Plow Chow's awning and whipping tendrils of hair across my face like soft whips.

Tonya pulled a knitted beanie over her ears and air kissed in my direction. "Ta ta, sweetpea. Talk soon."

I grasped her upper arm, my fingers sinking into the padding of her parka. "One more question."

"Baby, it's cold outside," she said through chattering teeth. "Make it quick."

I looked around to make sure no one was eavesdropping and lowered my voice. "Off the top of your head, who do you think killed Victoria? You're not allowed to say Kimberly."

She tapped a gloved finger against her cheek, eyes turned to the sky. "Hmm. What about the lover? Who also just so happens to be the main suspect's husband? I'd say he's a top candidate."

"Parker Lyon? Everyone says he's so timid. And snobby. Would he really deign to get his hands dirty?"

"Still waters run deep, you know. And he has a reason to hold a grudge against both Victoria and Kimberly."

I shook my head. "Definitely not who I was expecting."

"Keep in mind that you made me exclude Kimberly. My money's still on her. And speaking of money, I have to go earn a living. Be good, lovebug. Don't go stumbling over any more bodies."

18

Without looking back, Tonya wriggled her fingers at me as she sashayed off. I stood for a moment, reveling in the depth of our friendship. I'd known some nice people in Texas and Washington, D.C., some of whom I'd even called friends. But as soon as they, or I, moved on, their faces faded like old Polaroid pictures. Not so with Tonya. Despite the physical and sometimes emotional distance, we'd fallen right back into the closeness of being best friends. Maybe the people who fluttered into our hearts when we were young nested there forever. Or maybe I'd just gotten lucky.

Across the street, a small herd of elk lazed in front of the Peak Inn. On the slope of the mountain behind them, a doe sauntered through the trees, occasionally dropping her head to graze on twigs. The wind swirled around me, its scent clean and fresh. I closed my eyes and inhaled the crisp air, realizing it wasn't just Tonya I'd missed. Or my parents. Without even knowing it, I'd been longing for Rock Creek Village.

And that was the paradox. One part of me felt safe here, cocooned and cushioned and protected. Another part felt like a huge failure. Coming home meant admitting defeat, telling the world I wasn't the big shot journalist everyone believed me to be.

Being here comforted my soul at the same time as it

punctured my ego.

From the lower village, the church bell chimed one o'clock. I turned in the direction of the resort, anticipating a little play time with my fur babies followed by a return to my suspect list.

Yoga Delight was currently devoid of contortionists or meditators, and the window of V&K's Fine Fashions was still shuttered. As I passed the empty gallery space, a glint of reflected light in the window drew me toward it like a magnet. I cupped my hands around my eyes and peered through the streaked glass.

A strange sensation filled me. After a moment, I identified it as anticipation. I'd told Tonya I wasn't interested, but she knew me better than that. I still felt a passion toward photography. And I was good at it—really good, if the reviews could be trusted. Could I redirect my passion toward something more upbeat and fulfilling than the world's dark side? Could I use my talents to make people happy?

I imagined the walls of the gallery covered in nature shots—snowscapes and wildlife and flower-filled meadows. A pinprick of emotion pulsed in me, straining to grow. Was this joy?

My cell phone buzzed in my coat pocket. I was so preoccupied with the gallery that I barely registered the words Unknown Caller on the screen. "Hello?"

A mangled noise emerged. At first, I wrote it off as a bad connection. Service could be spotty in the mountains, especially under cloud cover. I stepped toward the curb in hopes of better reception and pressed my finger in my other ear. "I'm sorry, I can't hear you—"

No response. I listened as hard as I could. Yes, I could hear someone breathing on the other end of the line. I rolled my eyes. Some crank caller had stumbled across my number. "All right, you've had your fun. But shouldn't you be in seventh grade math class? Don't bother calling again. I'm blocking your number."

As I went to disconnect, I heard an unusual metallic sound and placed the phone back to my ear. A voice spoke, mechanical and deep-throated, and I realized it was being filtered through a distortion device.

"You're in danger," the robotic voice said.

"Danger?" I repeated. "Why?"

"Stop," the voice commanded. Not much of a conversationalist. I couldn't tell if the person was male or female, much less guess an identity.

But whoever it was, I'd had enough. "No more games. Tell me who you are."

I wasn't surprised when I heard the beep indicating the caller had disconnected. My grip tightened on the phone as paranoia set in. An older gentleman sat on a bench in the park across the street, paying me no attention as he nibbled at a sandwich. A woman pushed a stroller down the sidewalk. Was it the same woman I'd seen earlier? Was she stalking me, using the stroller as cover?

But they both appeared harmless, and completely disinterested in me. I realized the person I was looking for was Brian Ratliff. Given our confrontation in the alcove, he seemed to be the likely choice.

But was he savvy enough to obtain and use a distortion device?

My thoughts jumped next to Preston's earlier call and his concern over Jameson Jarrett's release. Could the call have come from Jarrett?

I blew out a breath and watched the condensation it produced drift away on the wind. The call was curious, but it was probably just someone bent on intimidation. I wasn't scared for my safety. But I wouldn't be stupid. I'd watch my back.

I maintained a casual pace as I headed down the street, glancing in storefronts and smiling at passersby. No need for anyone who might be watching to think I was spooked.

Which, of course, I wasn't. When I got to the last store on the block, Quicker Liquor, I found Fran outside polishing the window. She looked over her shoulder and smiled when she spotted me. "Hey, Callie. Long time no see. How've you been?"

By long time, she meant three days. I'd last come in to replenish my stock on Friday. "I'm good," I said. "Been a little busier than usual."

"So I heard." Fran lowered her voice to a conspiratorial whisper. "Need something to take the edge off?"

I frowned, wondering whether she was trying to sell me wine, or something…stronger. "Umm…" I responded.

"I just got in a case of that boxed chardonnay you like. Or maybe you'd rather up your game with a nice chianti."

Remembering Dr. Lowell's suggestion to cut back, I nearly declined, but then I remembered two things. First, the wine box in my fridge was currently well below the half-full mark. Surely cutting back didn't mean being unprepared. Second, as a liquor store owner, Fran was the next best thing to a bartender. Nobody knew more about the underbelly of a town than bartenders and hairstylists. Maybe Fran could help refine my suspect list.

I followed her inside, refusing the chianti offer in favor of my old standby—cheap boxed wine. She sniffed, but produced the box. "Just one?"

I nodded, and she started ringing up my purchase. "So," I said. "You heard about Victoria Ratliff…"

She clucked her tongue. "Terrible business. And her best friend arrested. Things like that just don't happen here."

"So true." I paused, trying to figure out how to steer the conversation without sounding like I was grilling her for information. "Why do you think it happened?"

Her eyes lit up. "Well, I'm not one to spread gossip…"

Here came the "but."

"…but I would think having an affair with her husband would be reason enough."

I fought a wave of disappointment. Nothing new.

But Fran wasn't through. She leaned toward me conspiratorially. "And now Parker's been kicked out of the house."

Ohhh. I recalled seeing him with a suitcase earlier. "Really... How do you know that?"

"My friend Penelope called me. Parker checked into your parents' place about an hour ago. I bet we'll be reading all about it in *Sophie's Scoop* tomorrow morning. She gets all the good stories."

"You mean Sophie Demler? I doubt there'll be a column. Nobody seems to know where she's run off to."

Fran looked puzzled. "That's funny. I could have sworn I saw her just last night near the Creekside." She tapped her glasses. "Must be time for a new prescription."

Minutes later, I left Quicker Liquor with my box of wine and only two nuggets of information, neither of which seemed particularly useful. I felt stymied, but perhaps my mind just needed a break. I trotted across the street and took my usual shortcut through the copse of trees that marked the boundary line of the Knotty Pine property.

Under the canopy of pines, shards of light dappled the ground, and scattered pinecones peppered the path. Here in the perpetual shade, the temperature dropped even more. Small patches of snow, hidden from the sun, nestled like collars around the tree trunks. My footsteps crunched across fallen evergreen needles. The river, just out of sight, gurgled as background music. I stopped for a moment to inhale the pines' fragrance, so refreshing after years of breathing exhaust fumes in the city.

I wished I could capture the scent in a picture. My thoughts returned to the empty shop. The gallery. My gallery?

Could I make a life here, again? I quickly shook the question from my mind. Before I could concentrate on my future, I had a murder to investigate.

19

Before I emerged from the cover of the thicket toward the resort's riverview cabins, I noticed a man trudging down the sidewalk, toting a paper grocery bag in the crook of one arm. He passed my cabin and turned up the short walkway leading to the middle structure. I knew by the stylish blond hair and the tweed coat it was Parker Lyon.

Fran had just told me about Parker checking into the Knotty Pine, but it hadn't occurred to me that he'd be right next door to me. I wasn't interested in having a neighborly conversation with the man, so I retreated into the shadows and waited until he unlocked his door and closeted himself inside. Then I scurried down the sidewalk and through my own door, exhaling in relief.

But the exhale quickly became a whoosh. In my haste, I'd forgotten about Woody's traditional greeting. The ball of fur catapulted into my chest, wriggling and whimpering in excitement.

Carl sat on the bed and licked his paw. He may have raised an eyebrow in disgust.

I scratched my pup's ears and kissed his furry head before lowering him back to earth. After setting my purse and brand new wine box on the table, I lifted the cat into my arms and ran a finger down his spine in what I'd discovered was his favorite form of affection. He rewarded me with a contented purr. As I cuddled the creatures, I thought about Parker Lyon. Tonya had put him on top of her suspect list—just below Kimberly. Not a ringing endorsement of his character.

Also, he had motive out the wazoo.

Other than the fact that he was a cheater and a snob, I didn't know much about Parker Lyon. It was time I changed that.

"Let's go visit Mom," I said to the creatures. I had questions, and my mother was just the person to supply the answers.

Penelope called hello from behind the desk—nothing extraordinary there. But across the Great Room in the game room, an odd tableau greeted me. Mrs. Finney was bent over the pool table, gripping a cue stick and smacking balls into pockets one after the other. In a nearby chair, my mother sat with a ball of yarn in her lap, knitting needles clacking. I lifted my eyebrows at Penelope, and she shrugged. "Welcome to *The Twilight Zone*," she said.

I went to the game room and stood beside my mother. "Since when do you knit?"

She smiled serenely at me and waved a needle toward Mrs. Finney. "Hello, sweetheart. I believe the two of you have met."

I nodded. "Yes, we have. Mrs. Finney, isn't it?"

"Yes, dear, it's me." She leaned on the cue stick and smiled.

I turned back to Mom. "But for real. What's with the knitting?"

"Mrs. Finney is giving me lessons. I've been searching for a new hobby, and knitting is so relaxing. Much the same as meditation, which you would know if you'd join me for this afternoon's class. Mrs. Finney is going."

Mrs. Finney moved beside Mom and placed a hand on her shoulder. "I am looking forward to it. And in return for knitting instruction, your mother has been coaching me on the inversion table. Exhilarating." I had a mental image of the husky woman hanging upside down in my parents' study, and stifled a giggle.

Woody sniffed the skein of yarn in Mom's lap and rested his head on it as if it were a pillow. She stroked his ears as Carl wove between her feet and purred. "Maybe I'll knit these boys some sweaters," she mused. A lovely burgundy would set off their golden coats."

"All right, I'll go," I said suddenly.

Mom looked at me quizzically. "To meditation class," I said. "Sounds like fun."

Mrs. Finney clapped her hands. "Oh, how delightful."

My mother's expression was incredulous. "How spontaneous of you, darling. Quite unexpected. Run home and change, then. We'll be leaving in a half hour."

I hurried down the path, with Woody and Carl trotting along behind me. I'd let my mother think I'd acquiesced because of a counseling-inspired desire to seek serenity. In truth, though, the meditation class was a tactical move that would serve me in two ways. First, on the walk into town, I could casually pump my mother for information. Though she knew just about everything that went on in the village— even more than Fran—Mom was notoriously tight-lipped about what she perceived as gossip. But if I was able to phrase my questions in just the right way, perhaps she'd let some of her knowledge slip out. I only hoped Mrs. Finney's presence wouldn't make her reticent to share what she knew.

Second, since the class was led by Summer Simmons, I'd be in close proximity to one of the women Dan the Bartender had seen in the event center on Saturday. A little friendly interrogation might take Summer off my suspect list—or move her up a notch.

The wind had let up, but the afternoon was what we Coloradoans referred to as "brisk." In other words, the temperature hovered around freezing, and a chilly breeze prickled at any exposed skin. None of that seemed to affect Mrs. Finney, though. She danced through the parking lot and across the street singing some obscure tune and occasionally spinning in a clunky pirouette.

Mom and I grinned at each other, and she tucked her arm through mine. "This is such a pleasant surprise, sweetheart. I think you'll just love the class. And Thursday you can join me for yoga. We'll have such fun."

"Slow down, Mom. Let's just get through one class before you schedule my entire future."

Her laugh tinkled like wind chimes, and I couldn't help but smile. I squeezed her hand and decided to start my cautious probe. "I have a question for you…"

"Uh oh," she said. Ahead of us, Mrs. Finney did a little skip.

"Nothing to uh-oh over. Just wondering if you know where my high school yearbooks are. I'd like to flip through them. You know, for old time's sake."

"Oh, my," she said, frowning. "When we bought the resort last year, we got rid of a lot of things and put others in storage. We could hope they're in the latter category."

I waved. "No big deal. It was just a thought."

"Maybe Tonya would have hers. Or Sam." An impish grin crossed her face.

"Mom," I said, in a warning tone.

"I could have your father look through the storage unit. Though with all the boxes in there, I doubt we'd find your yearbooks before the spring thaw." She snapped her fingers. "Oh. I bet the school library would have a set."

"Good idea," I said. She'd provided me with the perfect segue into my next topic. "Speaking of high school, Tonya told me the journalism teacher there is married to our meditation instructor. Jessica Fannon, I think she said?"

Mom's face lit up. "That's right. I told you about them, too, didn't I? Lovely women."

"Well…" I let my voice trail off, hoping it would pique her curiosity.

She gave me a sidelong glance. "What?"

"Tonya and I were having lunch at the Snow Plow Chow—"

"Sam's place," she said, with a knowing nod.

"He wasn't even there, Mother." I drew out her name, knowing I sounded like a petulant teenager. "Anyway, this guy Dan who works there—who was also the bartender for the Snowflake Swirl—said Jessica and Summer came into the Creekside Saturday looking for Victoria. And that it didn't seem like a social call."

I could see the wheels spinning as Mom sifted through her mental database of knowledge. "Well, I can't know for sure, of course…" She hesitated. "I don't want to spread rumors, but I suppose it doesn't matter anymore now that…well, now that Victoria has passed. My friend, a lawyer at the Chamber of Commerce, told me Victoria had asked about instituting a morals clause for business owners. My friend told her that would likely be illegal, and Victoria didn't mention it again. But she got the impression it had to do with Yoga Delight."

"A morals clause," I said. "Talk about irony. What was Victoria's goal?"

Mom shrugged. "Nothing in particular, I expect. Victoria liked to have something on everyone, some bit of blackmail she could pull out when she needed a person to fall in line. You know how she was in high school. Age didn't soften her much."

An undercurrent of bitterness wove into my mother's voice. I squeezed her hand. "You didn't care for Victoria, I take it."

"Didn't like her as a teenager. Didn't like her as an adult." She let go of my arm and shook herself. "But these aren't feelings I care to nurture."

Mrs. Finney rejoined us in time to hear Mom's last line. "There, there, my dear. Everyone is entitled to a negative thought or two. We're only human, after all."

Mom gave the woman an affectionate smile. These two were developing a fast friendship. I studied the enigmatic Mrs. Finney. Who was this person, anyway? How had she found our little village? I decided it wouldn't hurt to do a little research into her background, though it would have to wait until the murder was solved.

As we approached Yoga Delight's entrance, Mom stopped in her tracks and put her hands on her hips. "Something just occurred to me. Are you truly here for meditation, or did you come with the idea of interrogating Summer Simmons?"

I could feel my cheeks warm. Hopefully, the color would simply look like exposure to the cold. "Dr. Lowell mentioned meditation at my appointment, Mom, and as much as you've hyped it, I thought I'd give it a whirl." Not exactly a lie…

She shook a finger at me. "Callahan Maureen Cassidy, I feel a great fondness for Summer Simmons, and I quite enjoy my time at her studio. I don't want you going in there and ruffling any feathers."

I grasped her finger and gave her what I hoped was a reassuring smile. "Of course not, Mom. You know me better than that."

20

Mom looked at me skeptically but ultimately chose to believe me. As we walked inside with Mrs. Finney, she insisted we grab a drink from the studio's juice bar. Her recommendation? An apple strawberry kale smoothie. The thought of it triggered my gag reflex, but when I asked if the place served Dr. Pepper, she squinted at me as if I were defective.

Mom handed me her coat. "You two go get settled. I'll get the drinks."

Mrs. Finney and I removed our winter wear and laid it in the heap near the door. She wore a blousy, purple knee-length caftan over pink leggings. When she removed her shoes, her pale feet poked out like dead fish. She wiggled her toes. "One is most likely to discover illumination when unconstrained by footwear."

"Naturally," I said. She stared at me until I slipped off my own sneakers.

Mom returned and handed each of us a glass of green swill she might have dredged from the bottom of a swamp. I wrinkled my nose. "That looks disgusting!"

"Oh, Callie, don't be such a baby. Take a risk once in a while." She took a drink and smacked her lips. Then she grabbed a cushion and settled cross-legged on the floor. Mrs. Finney followed suit.

I held the glass to my nose and inhaled a fruity aroma.

Appealing. But still. It was green. And healthy. I put my lips to the rim and took a tiny sip. My tongue didn't revolt, and my taste buds were attentive. A larger drink this time, and I decided I liked it.

Mom was right again. Go figure. The older I got, the smarter my mother became.

I took another gulp and glanced around. I was pleased no one seemed to be staring at me. The same had been true at Snow Plow Chow, I recalled. Perhaps I wasn't quite the subject of intense scrutiny I always imagined. I noticed Dr. Lowell positioning herself on a cushion across the room. She smiled at me, and I felt like a student who had earned a gold star.

I chugged the last mouthful of tasty green slime and set my empty glass on a tray near the window. I chose a cushion, settling in next to Mrs. Finney. "Come here often?" I wiggled my eyebrows, feeling mischievous and inexplicably cheerful.

She stared at me deadpan. "Bloody hell, Ms. Cassidy, are you hitting on me?"

Flustered, I stuttered, "N-no, it was just a joke…"

"My dear," she said. "I was—what do the young people say?—messing with you. Besides, I'm far too old for you. But to answer your question, I will continue to come here often. The door to the universe is a heavy one. Pushing it open requires great persistence."

Summer glided into the room, wearing tie-dyed yoga pants and a tank top. "Ladies and gentlemen, time to take our places."

I wriggled into the cushion, trying to get comfortable. The tightness in my chest betrayed my nervousness, and my brain created its usual repertoire of possible negative outcomes. What if I didn't enjoy it? Worse yet, what if I was no good at it? Would I flunk meditation? I saw Dr. Lowell watching me. Hoping to impress her with my Zen, I smiled serenely.

Summer fluttered into a sitting position and explained the

process for the benefit of us newbies. During the thirty-minute class, we would spend twenty minutes in total silence, becoming "aligned with the now" and practicing present mindfulness. A simple enough concept. I figured I could manage it.

"Today's theme is anxiety," she said, her voice soft and hypnotic. "Close your eyes. Accept your thoughts and feelings, positive and negative. They're all part of the human experience."

Though my eyes were closed, I felt them rolling beneath the lids. I'd always considered myself too cerebral for the yoga and meditation world. But I was here now. Might as well try.

"Watch your thoughts drift through your mind. Let them go, like balloons floating into a blue sky."

Her cadence was soothing, melodic. If I hadn't been sitting cross-legged and straight-backed, it might have lulled me to sleep.

"Focus on the rhythm of your breath. And now, silence. The only sound you'll hear will be a chime that rings every five minutes to recenter you from distraction."

Easy peasy, I thought. How hard could it be to sit here and breathe? I was going to get an A in meditation.

A couple of minutes passed. My mind started racing. I chased it.

What should I have for dinner this evening? I need to go over my suspect list again. Who is this Mrs. Finney? How are Sam and Elyse? And what's up with this Sanchez? Why does he dislike me? Why do I care? Is Woody asleep? Did Carl use his litterbox?

By the time I realized I had stopped focusing on my breathing, fifteen minutes must have passed. And I hadn't heard a single chime.

I cracked open one eyelid. The other meditators rested on their cushions, breathing evenly, hands on knees and peaceful expressions on their faces.

I squeezed my eyelids shut and tried to make it to Nirvana.

And so it went for the remainder of the session. I'd experience a few moments of what Summer called mindfulness, only to find myself right back in a state of mind-fullness. I was going to fail the class.

At last, what was apparently the final chime rang. Summer instructed us to open our eyes and guided us through a series of simple stretches. Everyone else looked placid and content, so I mimicked them. I shook out legs that had fallen asleep, struggled to my feet, and told Mom and Mrs. Finney to go ahead without me. Mom gave me the evil eye, but Mrs. Finney patted her arm reassuringly. "The universe expands as the universe is meant to," she said. I had no idea what that meant, but Mom nodded wistfully. The two of them donned their coats and left, trailing behind Dr. Lowell and the others in the class.

I limped over to the young instructor. "Thank you, Summer," I said, wondering if I should add a "namaste." I didn't know what it meant, but I thought the context might be right. "I've never attended a meditation class…"

"You're kidding," she said, her eyes twinkling.

Had my charade been that obvious? "If you have a minute, I wonder if I could ask you a few questions."

Curiosity played across her face. "Sure. Follow me."

We walked to the back of the studio, through a beaded curtain, and into a sixties hippie hallucination. The smell of sandalwood incense blanketed me. An honest-to-goodness lava lamp flowed on one end of a low teak table. The only seating consisted of four rainbow-striped bean bag chairs arranged in a circle.

Summer gestured toward the beanbags. "Please, take a seat." With no discernible effort, she folded her legs and appeared to teleport into the chair. I attempted the same graceful maneuver but thudded down on my left hip and wriggled around, trying to end up in a semi-upright position.

Summer rested the backs of her hands on her knees and

closed her eyes. Just as I decided she had descended into another round of meditation, her eyelids fluttered open. "So, Callie, what shall we talk about?"

I sank backward in the beans. "As I'm sure you've heard, I was at the scene of Victoria Ratliff's murder, and—"

"You've taken it upon yourself to play detective," she interrupted. "I suppose you know my wife and I had a rift with Victoria, and want our whereabouts and alibis."

I squirmed. The woman's Zen seemed to have evaporated. "That should cover it."

She sighed. "Why not? I have nothing to hide. Jess and I aren't exactly Snowflake Swirl types, so we went to the movies and spent the rest of the evening curled up at home. Snug as a bug, as the saying goes. A married couple covering for each other—not the strongest alibi, I realize. But it is what it is. As for motive, I'm a pacifist. I don't even step on spiders."

"Probably a good idea since you're not wearing shoes."

Summer hesitated then tilted her head back and laughed—a great belly laugh that served to cut the tension between us.

"You know," she said, "Jess has spoken of you over the years with great respect, bordering on hero worship. As a journalism teacher, she's in awe of your career."

"I take it you're not quite as enraptured of me."

"I adore your mother. And your father's pretty great, too. As for you, the jury's still out."

She softened the words with a smile, but there was no need. I found her bluntness refreshing. I really wanted to like her. "What was your opinion of Victoria?"

"You mean, did I hate her and wish her dead? Of course not. I hated the things she said and did, but I believe you can hate the action and love—or at least accept—the person. I don't hold grudges. They do more damage to the person carrying them than to the object of the hatred."

"And yet you went to the Creekside Saturday to confront her. Care to tell me what that was about?"

She lifted her shoulders. "In the grand scheme of things, it was nothing important. If it were up to me, I wouldn't have gone. But my wife has not quite achieved the peace, love, and understanding vibe. When she gets in a state, I sometimes tag along to provide balance. You know, infuse her with an external dose of calm."

I nodded. "Would you mind filling me in on your conversation with Victoria?"

She cocked her head and studied me. "Yes, I think I would mind. I'd rather keep it private for the time being."

Not what I'd hoped for, but I couldn't fault her. I had no authority to compel her to answer. "Last question, then. Who might have carried a grudge to the extreme, in your opinion? Who might have wanted Victoria dead?"

She tossed her braid. "Even if I had someone in mind, I wouldn't offer a name unless I was aware of specific facts. I try to avoid spreading negative energy."

A chime sounded from the studio, and Summer rose to her feet. "Another class beckons," she said, reaching out a hand to help me up. "I hope I have set your mind at ease. And I hope you find the peace you are searching for."

I followed her through the studio, retrieved my coat, and walked outside, inwardly processing our conversation. Though her demeanor hadn't indicated murderous vibes, I could never completely trust someone so limber and so irritatingly serene. Besides, she'd clammed up about her confrontation with Victoria. Could she be protecting her wife, who Tonya had described as a firecracker? I definitely needed to do a bit more exploration into the couple. For now, anyway, Summer's name stayed on the list.

21

At precisely five o'clock, I took the half-filled box of wine from the refrigerator, held a glass beneath the nozzle, and twisted, releasing a slow stream of golden liquid. After ingesting a kale smoothie and all that fake meditation, I'd earned a little decadence.

The sun's waning rays slipped through the half-closed blinds, depositing stripes of spun gold across the floor. I went to the fireplace, sent a psychic apology to Tonya, and crumpled a page of *The Gazette*. After shoving it between two scorched logs in the hearth, I pulled the trigger on the long-stemmed lighter, and touched the flame to the newspaper. Fire erupted from the paper and settled into the timber, sending a rush of sparks like lightning bugs up the chimney.

Woody lay on the floor, gnashing a rawhide chew toy. Carl nestled in the curved nook of his torso. Their copper-toned coats mingled together so that it was impossible to tell where one ended and the other began. That made me feel a little lonely.

I took a long sip of wine and reveled in that initial jolt just behind my jaw. The evening was my own, as so many of them had been over the past month. If things progressed according to my ritual of the past month, I'd eventually pop a frozen entree in the microwave, read a book, watch some mindless TV, and sip a glass—or two, or three—of wine.

But I vowed tonight would be different. Dr. Lowell had urged me o cut back on the wine, for one thing. Also, I had crime scene photos to study. Suspects to research. Motives, means, opportunities to outline.

I had stumbled onto a purpose.

Slouching in the wooden dining chair, I slid the legal pad in front of me. I rummaged through my purse and retrieved the suspect list I'd started last night. Kimberly Lyon, Brian Ratliff, Parker Lyon. Beneath them, a name I'd scratched through. Sam Petrie.

I crumpled up the paper and tossed it into the fire. Time to start a new list. Turning the pad sideways, I wrote the words Motive and Opportunity down the side. No need for Means, since the murder weapon—Victoria's letter opener—had been procured by the killer at the scene. Across the top of the page, I wrote the three names from the first list and added Summer Simmons and Jessica Fannon.

I tapped the pen against the pad and tried to think of anyone I might be missing. Dan had mentioned that Fran came by the center to deliver liquor, but I didn't think that warranted including her on the list. Next, I thought of Sophie Demler. Kimberly had mentioned her, and the woman was now suspiciously missing. Or was she? Fran thought she had seen her over the weekend, but she hadn't seemed too certain. Still, I jotted Sophie's name alongside the others.

Scanning my new list, I felt a flutter of anxiety. A name that wasn't there seemed to pulse from the page. A glaring omission. Sam Petrie.

I tossed the pen onto the pad and lifted my glass, swirling the wine before draining it.

My memory lit on the boy I'd known in high school. His sweet, tender smile. Twinkling blue eyes. His touch, always gentle, never violent or harmful. No capacity for murder.

Of course, that was then and this was now. I couldn't really know how the intervening years had shaped him. Like water pounding against rock, time and experience inevitably carved new contours and crevices into all of us.

I went back to the refrigerator. I knew I should throw Sam's name back into the mix, but that would require liquid courage. Refill in hand, I made my way back to the table, determined to do what I had to do. But before I could sit down, Carl screeched and Woody lifted his head from his bone. A second later, there was a rapping at the door.

I flipped on the porch light, nudged Woody away from the door, and pulled it open. At first, I thought my brief trip down memory lane had created a hallucination, but when I blinked, he was still there.

Sam had come calling, one hand clutching a red thermal food carrier, the other holding a cloth grocery bag.

I looked down at my fuzzy pink socks, my blue flannel pajama pants, and my long sleeved souvenir t-shirt from the Funeral Museum in Houston that read, "Any day above ground is a good one."

I felt my face flush as I remembered shucking off my bra when I got home. I crossed my arms over my chest. Sam looked at me, amused. "Can I come in?"

"Sorry," I said, moving back so he could get by. "I just…wasn't expecting you."

His face creased, and his eyes looked sad. "You forgot about our dinner date?"

"What? Wait—"

"Kidding," he said, the corner of his mouth curving upward. "You've been gone too long, Callie. You don't get my stupid jokes anymore." He lifted the containers. "I made you dinner. I was hoping to get lucky—" He realized what he'd said, and now it was his face that flushed. "I mean, I was hoping you hadn't already eaten."

I laughed, and he did too. Just like that, the whole crazy scene felt normal. I sniffed the air, fragrant with a familiar aroma. Despite the ChipMunch I'd devoured hours earlier, my mouth watered. "That smells like—"

"Lasagna," he said, the tiny lines around his mouth

creasing as he smiled. "Your favorite. At least, it used to be."

My immediate impulse was to grab the casserole dish from his hands and dive face first into its contents. "It still is."

"All right, then. May I?" He lifted the bag and gestured to the kitchen.

"Yes, you absolutely may."

After he deposited his treasures on the counter, Sam spent a few minutes on the floor scratching and petting the creatures. I sneaked into the bathroom and wrangled back into my bra. Since I was there anyway, I touched a little powder to my nose and a dab of perfume behind my ears. Not that I cared or anything…

When Woody and Carl had been sufficiently adored, Sam and I stood side by side in the tiny kitchen, hips nearly touching as we unwrapped the food. He filled two plates with oversized portions of garlicky noodles covered with meat sauce and ricotta, dripping with melted mozzarella. Crusty, buttery French bread and a crisp Caesar salad rounded out the offerings. I cleared the table, tossing the laptop onto the bed and tucking the legal pad upside down beneath it. I hadn't added Sam's name, but I felt guilty anyway.

He arranged silverware and steaming plates on the table. "I had a bottle of wine to go with the meal, but I forgot to pack it." He motioned to my wineglass. "Any more where that came from?"

"I'm afraid the only thing I have is cheap chardonnay from a box. On the plus side, I bought a new box today."

"Works for me, if you don't mind sharing."

I poured him a glass and topped mine off. Then I sat next to him at the tiny table and cut into my lasagna. When my lips closed around the first bite, I realized it was the second time today this man's food had made me moan.

While we ate in companionable silence, I stole glances at

him, trying to gauge his potential for violence. He grasped his knife and fork loosely, and his movements were graceful and easy. No intensity, no aggression in his posture. No way was this man a killer.

My eyes fell to his sleeve and a dark stain on the cuff, in almost exactly the same spot as the one I'd seen Saturday on a different shirt. I laid my utensils on the plate and reached across the table, lifting his arm and pointing to the offending portion of cloth. "What's this?"

He examined the stain and smiled wryly. "I get stains like this on just about every shirt I own. Elyse is always on me about it. I'm right-handed, and when I'm in the kitchen chopping, I have a bad habit of sliding my wrist along the cutting board after each slice." Picking up his butter knife, he demonstrated on his napkin, mimicking a downward motion and drag. "I end up pulling my sleeve through whatever liquid happens to be pooled there." He lifted his sleeve to his nose and sniffed. "Tomato, I think. Probably from this very lasagna."

Did that explain the similar stain on Saturday night's shirt? I sure hoped so.

We did the dishes together, with Sam washing and me drying. When Woody finally accepted that he wasn't getting any leftovers, he went to his food bowl and munched contentedly on his kibble. Carl pretended to ignore us all. The whole scene felt comfortable, congenial, and strangely domestic.

After the chores were complete, we moved to the living area. I sat on the bed, my back against the headboard. Woody stretched across my lap, and Carl perched on Woody's back. Sam took the armchair. He laced his hands behind his head and watched the flames crackle.

I cleared my throat. "Delicious as that meal was, and grateful as I am for a full stomach and good company, I think it's time for you to tell me why you're here."

The firelight played across his face, alternating light and shadow. He closed his eyes briefly and dropped his hands to his lap. "Rumor has it you've agreed to help Kimberly clear her name."

"Does that bother you?"

"Yes and no. It creates…a few conflicts. Something happened Saturday, before Victoria was killed. I got some news…I think you need to know."

I frowned. When Sam had explained the stain, I'd been filled with relief and congratulated myself for not adding him to my suspect list. I couldn't bear the thought that I was wrong and he was preparing to confess to murder.

The silence stretched on. Carl made a graceful leap to Sam's lap and settled atop his knees. The cat's tail swished as he stared into Sam's face, as if trying to transmit courage.

After a few seconds, Carl's magic worked, and Sam plunged into his story. "Saturday morning, as I was prepping for the Swirl, Kimberly showed up at the restaurant. It's never a good sign when Kimberly makes an appearance, and that morning, the expression on her face told me something was up. Something serious. She said she had information I should know, since it might become public knowledge in the next few days."

A long pause followed. Then Sam rose from the chair and started pacing, holding Carl to his chest.

"You'll feel better if you let it out," I said. "My new therapist says the monster in your head is stronger than the one on the table. Or something like that."

He nodded. "It's just…It's the hardest thing I've ever dealt with."

I said nothing, giving him time to find his courage.

"She said Elyse isn't my biological daughter."

His shoulders slumped. I immediately went to him and wrapped my arms around him, smooshing Carl between us. When we finally pulled apart, he dropped into the chair. I sat on the edge of the bed. "Oh, Sam. I don't know what to say."

"It gets worse. Her father...my baby's real father...It's Brian Ratliff. Victoria's husband."

I realized with a shock that this was Kimberly's secret, the one I'd been unable to pry out of her. No wonder she wanted to keep it to herself. It was a sordid situation—Kimberly getting pregnant with Brian's child, Victoria having an affair with Kimberly's husband.

Sam put a hand across his eyes. "I wish she'd never told me."

"Why did she? After all these years."

"She and Victoria got in a fight. Nothing new, but this one was apparently apocalyptic. Victoria rubbed her nose in the affair with Parker, and Kimberly lost it. She told Victoria she'd beaten her to the punch and had an affair with Brian years ago, and that Elyse was his child."

I shuddered but didn't speak. After a moment, Sam continued. "Victoria had just filed papers in a divorce case that was likely to get nasty. This was information she could use. It was all about to blow up." He took a deep breath. Woody whined softly, and Sam stroked his head. "But now Victoria is dead and Kimberly has been arrested. I'm not sure what to do."

"First things first: does Elyse know?"

Sam shook his head. "Kimberly said she couldn't tell her. They haven't been getting along—typical teenage girl and mom stuff, I think—but she said I needed to be the one to break the news. But how can I tell my baby I'm not her real father?"

I put my hand on his shoulder. "Sam, you are Elyse's real father. All these years you've dried her tears, listened to her laughter. Loved her. The biology doesn't matter. You're her dad."

He sighed. "Anyway, I guess this gives me motive. When I found out you were helping Kimberly, I knew I needed to tell you. I haven't gone to the police yet. I plan to, but I wanted to wait until I talk to Elyse."

I nodded. "No one will hear it from me. But the sooner

you tell Elyse, the better. In my experience, news like this doesn't stay quiet very long. It will look better for you if you tell the police before they find out on their own. And they will."

He looked at me, eyes pleading. "I didn't kill her, Callie. I hope you believe me."

"Of course I do, Sam. The thought never crossed my mind." I bit my bottom lip. *Just a tiny white lie*, I thought.

He turned his eyes to the fireplace. "Funny how life can be going along fine and suddenly everything crashes."

I could relate to that sentiment.

22

By unspoken mutual agreement, Sam and I turned away from heavy emotions and talked of trivial things: life in the village, the current tourism slow down, weather predictions. He told me funny stories about life as a cafe owner and chef, and I shared anecdotes from my journalism career.

When we'd polished off one last glass of wine, Sam said he needed to get going. I watched him zip his thick coat and pull his wool cap over his ears. We stood near the fire, inches apart. The aroma of dinner had dissipated, and now the scent of him was all around me. I closed my eyes and drew it in.

When I opened them, he was watching me. The bright blue of his eyes had darkened to a slate gray tone. Warmth spread through my chest. We were so close we could taste each other's breath. Fortunately, we'd both eaten the garlic bread. He tilted his head toward me.

We both jumped like guilty teenagers at the rap on the door. I put my hand to my chest. Sam drew his hand across his mouth. A single sharp bark issued from the dog. The cat was nowhere to be seen.

"Are you going to answer that?" Sam asked after a moment.

I patted my hair and pulled open the door. A gust of cold wind blew inside, causing me to shiver.

Or maybe it was the sight of Detective Sanchez standing on my porch.

Sanchez's eyes flicked from me to Sam and back to me. He raised his eyebrows briefly before returning to his I'm-a-stoic-detective-nothing-surprises-me expression. "May I come in, Ms. Cassidy? I was hoping to ask you a few questions."

I stiffened but moved aside. "Certainly, Detective." From the corner of my eye, I saw Sam's jaw twitch. Sanchez entered, and his eyes scanned the room.

Sam cleared his throat. "Well, I'll leave you to it, then." He looked at me, a plea in his eyes. I gave him a smile and a nod, hoping I was conveying the message he needed to hear. *Don't worry. Your secret is safe with me.*

What I said aloud was, "Sure. We'll talk soon."

Sam extended a hand to the detective, and they shook. "Nice to see you, Sanchez."

Then Sam departed, and I shut the door. Sanchez pulled off his leather gloves and stuffed them into the pockets of his coat. His hair gleamed black in the firelight. "Cute dog," he said, scratching Woody's head. "Where's the cat?"

"How did you know—?"

He swiped a finger across the footboard of the bed and held it up. "Cat hair. Also, I'm slightly allergic."

His gaze fell to the laptop and the legal pad beneath it. "Have a seat, Detective," I said quickly. "Can I get you a glass of water? I'd offer wine, but I assume you're on duty."

"Nothing to drink, thank you," he said. He settled in at the table and sniffed the air. "Italian food...lasagna?"

I smiled tightly and nodded. "Very good. But I'm sure you're not here to regale me with detective tricks. What can I do for you?"

He motioned toward the other chair. "Will you sit for a moment, Ms. Cassidy?"

"Callie," I said, taking a seat. "No need for the formality. We're friends here, right?"

"All right. Callie, then. I was next door talking to Parker

Lyon. He's filed a restraining order against Brian Ratliff."

"Huh," I said. "Did they get into some sort of confrontation?"

"I can't go into the details. What I can tell you is that Ratliff's aggressiveness seems to be part of a pattern. I'm here to see if you'd like to reconsider and file a restraining order as well."

I thought about it but didn't see the point. I'd already proven I could take care of myself. Rather than answering directly, though, I tried to pump Sanchez for information. "Is Brian a suspect in his wife's murder?"

He stared at me for a moment, and I figured he was deciding how best to deal with me. "I think we may have gotten off on the wrong foot, Ms. Cassidy—" I started to interrupt, but he put up a hand. "—Callie, that is. I'm sorry about that. I know I can come across as…territorial sometimes. But I still can't talk about an ongoing investigation."

I bristled. In my career, I'd been accustomed to being treated by detectives as part of the team. But I was in no mood to cajole or plead. Nor did I see any advantage to being adversarial. "I understand. To answer your question, I won't be filing for a restraining order, Detective Sanchez. If there's nothing else…"

I stood. After a beat, he did too. "Callie, I'd like to talk about your…efforts on Kimberly's behalf."

Ah, now we'd gotten to the real reason for his visit. "There's really nothing to talk about."

"Just hear me out. Please." It was the please that caused me to close my mouth. "Chief Laramie and I are conducting a thorough investigation. It's true this is my first homicide, but I've been well trained, and I work with a good mentor. I'm not just trying to quickly close the case. The truth is my highest priority."

"Well, the truth is that you might have arrested an innocent person," I said, though I wasn't totally prepared to stake my reputation on Kimberly's innocence.

He looked at the ceiling and took a breath. Counting to ten, perhaps, as people did when confronted with willful children. "Consider this. If Kimberly Lyon didn't commit this murder, someone out there has a vested interest in keeping the truth hidden. If you get in the way of that...well, let's just say I don't want to be investigating two homicides."

I thought about the anonymous call I'd received. But since there was no proof it had anything to do with Victoria's murder, I wasn't ready to share. "Your concerns have been noted, Detective. I assure you I will exercise suitable prudence. As I've been trained to do."

As soon as Sanchez started down the path, I closed the door, snatched up my phone, and dialed Kimberly's number. This was all her fault. And how could she have created such a mess for Sam—and for her own daughter?

After ten rings, I disconnected. It was probably fortunate she hadn't answered. Maybe I'd be more rational tomorrow.

I decided to expend my pent-up emotional energy on research. I sat at the table and booted up the laptop. Carl jumped up beside it, having reemerged from his hiding place. His ability to disappear and reappear on a whim fascinated me. Did he possess a special sense about people? Was he able to divine human traits that Woody and I couldn't? The cat had warmed up to Sam right away, but he'd hidden from Kimberly and hadn't even made an appearance for Sanchez.

Then the cat leapt to the floor and arched his back, hacking and heaving. A wet, tangled hairball flew from his mouth, landing on the floor with a wet plop.

Gross.

Perhaps I would be wise not to assign too much mysticism to the creature who had regurgitated that thing.

Once I'd cleaned up the mess, I took a seat at the computer. Carl reclaimed his spot on the table, looking pleased with himself. "Are you done?" I asked. "I can't have you leaving any disgusting globs on my keyboard." He yawned, then settled onto my lap, purring. The hairball incident was forgiven.

I turned to my suspect list, trying to decide where to begin. I no longer considered adding Sam's name. More than ever, I was convinced he hadn't killed Victoria, or framed his daughter's mother.

But once word of Kimberly's nasty secret leaked out—and I was surprised it hadn't already, in this sieve of a community—Sanchez couldn't help but consider Sam a person of interest. Maybe even the prime suspect. Though the end goal was the same—figuring out who killed Victoria—my priority had shifted from proving Kimberly's innocence to protecting Sam.

After the way I'd treated him twenty-five years ago, I owed him that much.

I decided to start with Brian Ratliff. Not only had I witnessed his tendency toward impulsive anger, but he had more than one reason to want his wife dead. After Kimberly's explosive confession to Victoria, I now knew he had reason to hate Kimberly as well.

A single Wikipedia click led me to Brian's claim to fame. Twenty years ago, he'd spent two years as a player with the Colorado Avalanche. His bio was short and not too sweet. College hockey at the University of Denver. Selected by Colorado in the second round of the draft. A year in the minors, followed by two with the Avalanche. He hadn't been a superstar, but he'd made it in the bigs for a while, more than most athletes could say. Then came a career-ending blown knee, and poof, his dreams were over.

Interesting, but relevant? Probably not. Despite their aggressiveness during games, the hockey players I'd known over the years displayed no particular propensity for off-ice violence.

The rest of the bio mentioned his wife, Victoria, and two children, Braden and Banner. No mention of a post-hockey career. I scrolled through the list of his yearly earnings. Not nearly enough to sustain the family's lifestyle these past twenty years. That told me all the money must be hers. And with a divorce looming, he'd be poised to lose a lot.

I pulled up his Facebook page, but the only postings were those in which his wife had tagged him—vacation photos, school activities, family events.

I recalled the alibi Brian had mentioned in the alcove—home with his boys watching a game—and pulled up his sons' Facebook pages. No recent activity there. When I tried Instagram, things got more interesting. There I found pictures of the twins reclining on a couch, surrounded by scantily clad teenage girls, each kid clutching what looked suspiciously like a joint. The time stamp showed they'd been posted Saturday evening, right about the time of the murder.

This could blow up Brian Ratliff's alibi.

Similar searches into Parker, Jessica, and Summer's social media yielded nothing of value. By this point, mental and emotional exhaustion made it difficult to concentrate, so I called it a night.

Despite the wine and my fatigue, sleep did not come easily. I squirmed in the bed, tossing off the quilt and then pulling it back across me. I rolled onto my side and watched the numbers on my bedside clock change. When I flopped onto my stomach, bouncing on the mattress, Woody, who was stretched out across the foot of the bed, yipped in irritation. Carl emitted a hiss. I tried to settle down. What had me so fidgety? I didn't want to admit it, but I knew.

It was Sam. Not only my worry for him, but also how quickly I was redeveloping feelings for him.

Or maybe I was unearthing feelings that had never completely disappeared.

I'd had relationships with other men since I'd left Rock Creek Village, two or three that had even lasted more than a few weeks, but nothing ever felt right. I'd blamed it on my independence, my career. But maybe I'd been subconsciously comparing all men to Sam and pulling away when they didn't measure up.

I rolled onto my back and draped an arm across my forehead, eliciting groans from the creatures. "Nobody is forcing you to sleep on the bed," I muttered. But they had a point. I pushed away thoughts of Sam and squinched my eyelids shut, willing sleep to come.

Eventually, it did.

23

My next conscious thought involved murder—specifically, strangling whoever was calling so early. I thrust my hand toward the nightstand, feeling around for my warbling phone. When I located it, I held it to my face and squinted at the screen.

"Ugh. What do you want, Tonya?"

"Good morning to you too, grumpy head. What are you doing?"

"Sleeping. Trying to, anyway."

"Honey lamb, it's almost ten."

"Long night." I pulled myself to a sitting position and rubbed my eyes.

"You can tell me all about it when I pick you up. Forty-five minutes."

"Wait, where are we going?"

"You'll see." Another tease. I wondered if we were headed back to the gallery.

I yawned, but it was mostly for show. "I'm still in bed."

"Better get a move on, then. Kiss kiss." Before I could object, the line went dead.

When Tonya said jump, people typically asked how high, and so it was with me. I climbed out of bed and started the coffee maker. While the morning magic brewed, I nudged the creatures off the bed, straightened the quilt, and plumped the pillows against the headboard. I was a product of my mother's raising, and she'd always told me if I did nothing else all day, I should make my bed.

I threw a coat over my pajamas, filled a mug with hot black liquid, and accompanied Woody outside for his morning constitutional.

As my dog darted off into the trees, I leaned on the porch railing. A gray blanket lay across the sky, monotone except for a few dark ripples, as if Mother Nature had also made her bed but neglected to smooth the cover. I thought this one might be a serious snow sky. A gust of wind circulated, and I pulled my hood over my head and held my mug up to my face so the steam could warm my cheeks. A crackling noise from behind startled me, and when I jumped, coffee sloshed onto my fuzzy socks.

Irritated, I turned on soggy toes, expecting to see an offending elk lumbering through the trees. Instead, stalking up the path toward my porch was my new neighbor, Parker Lyon, looking quite dapper for someone who had just been forced out of his home. His blond hair was tufted and gelled, and his coat was open to reveal an expensive black suit, salmon shirt, and designer tie. Someone had been living the good life. No doubt he was vexed at the prospect of losing it.

"Good morning," I said, tucking my wet foot beneath the dry one. "Parker Lyon, right?"

"Don't you good morning me." His thin, hawkish face screwed up in rage. I thought for a moment he might try to peck me with his beak. "Who do you think you are?"

I took a step back and lifted my coffee cup, assessing its viability as a weapon. If nothing else, the coffee was still hot. Flinging it in his face might stop him if he rushed me. "What on earth are you talking about?"

He crossed his arms and scowled. "You said I killed Victoria. Kimberly told me. Right before she kicked me out."

Ah. Now I got it. Parker Lyon blamed me for the breakup of his marriage.

"Did you?" I asked.

"Did I what?" The pitch of his voice rose an octave.

"Kill her. Did you kill Victoria?"

His face contorted again. If he'd been a cartoon character, smoke would have spewed from his ears.

Woody bounded around the cabin then, but when he spotted Parker, he skidded to a halt. After taking a moment to assess the stranger, he gave a low growl and moved in front of me. From inside, Carl clawed at the glass, hissing.

Parker stumbled backward and nearly fell off the porch. "Get your animals under control!" he demanded.

"May I remind you that you invited yourself onto my porch?"

Parker glared at me and scurried down the path, glancing over his shoulder to make sure he wasn't being chased.

It was all I could do to keep from laughing. I looked from my golden retriever to my tabby and wondered how I'd ever gotten on without them.

After a quick shower, I squeezed into jeans and a sweatshirt. Then I donned my winter wear and patted the creatures good-bye. Slinging my camera around my neck, I hurried to the parking lot, where Tonya's silver Chevy Tahoe idled.

"I said forty-five minutes," she scolded as I slid into the vehicle. "It's been forty-eight. What happened to your strict adherence to deadlines?"

I tossed my bag onto the floor. "Sorry. I was waylaid by an angry neighbor."

She put the car in gear. "Do tell."

As we drove, I summarized the encounter with Parker. Then I told her about Sam's visit, though I didn't mention the main subject of our conversation. Close as the three of us had once been, it was still his secret to share.

She shot me a sidelong glance. "Dinner with Sam, hmm? I'm very pleased."

I waved a gloved hand. "Don't get excited. Just two old friends having dinner. You and I have had several meals together since I've come back, and no one's gossiping about us being a couple."

She smiled. "Don't be so sure. Somewhere within the confines of one of these homes, someone is even now speculating on the nature of our relationship. That's just the way things go in Rock Creek Village."

When we passed the lake, now an ice pond, Tonya turned into the lower village onto a street lined with narrow, two-story, brick-and-wood-framed townhomes, their oversized windows looking worshipfully toward the distant mountain range. Each unit boasted a deep front porch and second-floor balcony. The homes were small but sweet, with postage stamp lawns and stone walkways. If I ever decided to live in the village permanently, this would be the type of place I'd want.

"This neighborhood is new," I said as she rolled down the street. "Cute homes."

"Not all that new. The development went up about ten years ago. You need to get out more." We slid to a stop in front of a place on the corner. Tonya turned off the engine and unbuckled her seatbelt.

"Whose house is this?"

"Sophie Demler's. Let's go." She got out of the car and strode purposefully up the sidewalk. I grabbed my bag and followed, the camera bouncing against my abdomen. Tonya pressed the doorbell and cupped her hands around her face, peering through the glass partition next to the door.

"Sophie's current disappearing act has lasted longer than usual," she said, her breath fogging the window. "I tried calling her mother. No answer there either. Thought I'd come check her house, see if anything seemed amiss."

"And you brought me because…?"

"You've always been my partner in crime."

She stepped off the porch and headed toward the back of the house, her spiky heels sinking into the soft brown grass. The woman had once again snubbed practicality for fashion. I nearly always took the opposite approach, and my unattractive yet practical winter boots pressed diamond patterns into the dormant grass.

When we rounded the back corner of the house, I gasped. Sophie's backyard was breathtaking. A stone fire pit rested atop the rock patio, flanked by two cushioned patio chairs. A small patch of lawn lay between the patio and the alley. Evergreen shrubs, lilac bushes, and a few young pine trees provided lush landscaping.

I tore my gaze from the idyllic scene and saw Tonya bending over a terra cotta urn on the patio. She hoisted it and moved it a few inches to the side. "Voilà," she said, lifting a dirt-covered key.

"You're going in? What if she's just upstairs sleeping? What if she subscribes to the stand-your-ground law and comes after you with a rifle?"

Tonya chuckled. "Where do you come up with these far-fetched scenarios?"

"I forgot to tell you," I said. "Fran thought she saw Sophie day before yesterday. Maybe she never left, and she's just staying out of sight for some reason."

She waved. "Honey, Fran sees a lot of things the rest of us don't see. Not too long ago, she tried to convince everyone Chris Hemsworth was in town filming a scene as Thor. And then there was the time when no one could persuade her she hadn't seen Elvis skiing down Mt. O'Connell. I love Fran, don't get me wrong, but I doubt she saw Sophie anywhere."

She inserted the key into the lock of the sliding glass door and turned. "Now come along, sunshine. I don't have all day."

Sliding the door open, she stepped into a large, open room. Despite my misgivings, I followed. "Doesn't this constitute breaking and entering?" I whispered. "Seriously."

"Sophie told me months ago where she'd hidden her spare key. She frequently darts out of town on a whim, and she wanted someone to have access. You know, water the plants and such." She put her finger to her cheek. "So here I am. Doing a good deed."

I looked around, not noticing a single plant. Still, Tonya's rationalization sounded like something I'd come up with, so I relented, perhaps a little too easily. From what I'd heard, Sophie accumulated nuggets of information the way a chipmunk hoarded nuts. Perhaps I'd stumble across something relevant to my investigation.

The lower floor of Sophie's home consisted of an open kitchen and eating area to the left and a spacious living room to the right. A neatly folded afghan lay across the back of a leather couch. A couple of books rested on a coffee table. It was a lovely, well-tended home.

My attention was drawn to an old-fashioned roll top desk nestled in a nook beside the living room. It was a journalist's dream—all those cubbies and drawers. Who knew what kind of secrets it held? I was practically salivating. "I think I'll just take a peek," I said to Tonya. "Maybe I'll find something that will tell us where Sophie is."

She gave me a skeptical look. "Is that really what you're looking for? I have my doubts." She sighed. "Go ahead. But make it fast. I'll run upstairs to see if Sophie took her suitcase."

As Tonya's heels tapped across the floor and up the steps, I sat in the oak desk chair, my adrenaline pumping. I started with the three drawers to the left of the knee hole. My expectations sank. All three were empty. What kind of sociopath didn't fill the drawers of such a magnificent desk?

Perhaps the treasures were buried within the belly of the beast. Scooting the chair in closer, I put my hands on the heavy cover and rolled it up into its pocket.

As Tonya said, *voilà*. Papers, books, pencils and pens, even a small fan cluttered the desktop. Perhaps here I'd find a clue to Sophie's whereabouts. But even more compelling was the idea I might find evidence of a murderer's identity.

I took a couple of establishing shots with my camera, in case I later needed a blueprint as to what had been found where. Then I studied the mess, trying to get a sense of Sophie's organizational strategy. Bills and other household papers made up the pile on the left. I flipped through them quickly, disinterested in how much Sophie paid for electricity.

Then I spotted a box of lavender notecards, just like the one I'd found tucked inside the cover of a yearbook in Victoria's office.

I chewed my lip as I considered the implication. Lots of people might own lavender notecards, right? But as a journalist, I'd always found coincidence suspicious. The notecard in Victoria's office probably came from this box. I gritted my teeth, frustrated again that I hadn't gotten a look at the inside of that card before Sanchez had interrupted me.

But I had a lot to look through and not much time, so I pushed the box aside and turned my attention to the two books resting near them. More yearbooks, I realized, just like I'd seen on Victoria's desk. There'd been four of them there, spanning our high school years. These two were from our freshman and sophomore years. I was intrigued.

I riffled through the freshman book, looking for anything that might be shoved between the pages. Nothing. In the sophomore book, I hit pay dirt. A snapshot fluttered onto the desktop. I studied the picture—the same group shot I'd seen on the wall of Victoria's office. The Vixens, dressed in their prom finery. Sophie posed at the left end of the group.

But unlike the photo hanging on Victoria's wall, only three of the five teenagers smiled out at me. Someone had cut Victoria and Kimberly's faces from the picture.

I leaned back in the chair and stared at the gaping holes. It looked as if the goal no longer revolved around establishing Sophie Demler's whereabouts. The new mission was to determine whether the woman was capable of murder.

24

I remembered Sophie from high school as a short, curly-haired girl, a bit on the chubby side. Not exactly prime pickings for Victoria's Vixens, at least physically, but her air of snideness and talent for gathering and dispensing gossip had earned her a position in the exclusive viper pit.

As I looked at the mutilated snapshot, I wondered if Sophie had turned on her former allies, just as Victoria and Kimberly had turned on each other. Kimberly had hinted that Sophie might possess a motive for killing Victoria and framing her. Perhaps she'd faked her disappearing act, sneaked into the event center, killed Victoria, and then skedaddled out of town for real. Far-fetched, perhaps, but feasible.

The click of Tonya's heels preceded the scent of her perfume. "No suitcases," she said. "Toiletries missing too—makeup, toothbrush. Looks like she left of her own accord, without telling anyone. As usual." She leaned over my shoulder. "Find anything?"

I showed her the photo. "Someone might be a little bitter."

"Oh my," Tonya said. "She really does hate them."

Laying the photo on the desk, I snapped a picture of the picture so I'd have a copy. "Obviously some bad blood there. What's the backstory?"

Tonya perched on the arm of the couch. "We talked about V&K's Fine Fashion, right?" I nodded. "Well, two years ago, before Victoria and Kimberly set up shop, that space was occupied by a store called Sophie's Stationery Source. Sophie wasn't necessarily doing a booming business, but she was getting by, making a little progress each year. Then the other two decided to open a boutique. And they honed in on Sophie's location."

I fingered the lavender notecards, likely a remnant of Sophie's now-defunct shop. "I think I see where this is going."

"Yup. Sophie loved her little shop and refused to give it up because of their whims. Besides, she'd sunk all of her savings into the place. But Victoria was president of the Chamber of Commerce. And, of course, the Chamber oversees inspections. City inspectors conveniently discovered a number of code violations, and when Sophie couldn't afford to pay for the required renovations, she was evicted."

"That's horrible," I said, my eyes resting on the group photo. "I haven't seen Sophie since high school, and it's not like we were friends even then. She ran around with the Vixens, so I wasn't predisposed to like her. But hearing that story, I feel a little sorry for her."

Tonya nodded. "It's why I hired her to work at *The Gazette*. She'd lost everything, to people she'd once considered friends. Of course, the Vixens had long since drifted apart. Two of them moved out of state. Only Victoria and Kimberly stayed tight. Until recently, of course."

"Hiring her was generous of you. Especially since, from what I've read, she doesn't have much talent."

"What can I say? I'm a regular Bill Gates." Her lips turned up, but her eyes weren't smiling. "To be honest, I don't like Sophie all that much myself. She's mean-spirited and dippy, as unreliable as a flight schedule. But her society reporting generates a lot of readership. Her stories have increased our subscription base, which we desperately need. You know how times are in the newspaper world."

Though I understood my friend's point, I had mixed feelings about her method of luring readers. *Sophie's Scoop* was nothing more than a glorified gossip column. I'd only read it once, and it caused me serious professional anguish. Calling Sophie a journalist was like saying Woody was a guard dog.

But this wasn't the time for a philosophical discussion or a critique of *The Gazette*. I pointed at the defaced photo. "In light of this, though, and Sophie's disappearance...Could she be a suspect herself?"

Tonya rubbed a finger across her lips, considering. "But why would she wait two years to get her revenge? I just can't see that."

"Revenge fantasies can fester for a while before they explode. If the time is right, feelings can turn into actions."

"I suppose you're right," she said, coming to stand beside me. "What else have you found? Anything that might show motive?"

"Not yet. Bills, receipts...a couple of yearbooks." I patted the books, and Tonya examined their spines.

"Freshman and sophomore years."

"Victoria had all four years' worth on the desk in her office. Coincidence?"

"I think not," Tonya said. She flipped through the volumes, and I turned my attention to a bright pink, reporter-sized notebook resting on the far corner of the desk. I picked it up but hesitated to open it, aware that I would be breaking an unwritten code among journalists— *Thou shalt not violate the sanctity of the reporter's notebook.*

Just as I was about to ignore my conscience and flip open the cover, my phone buzzed. I dug it out of my purse and looked at the screen. Unknown Caller.

I put my finger to my lips, cautioning Tonya to stay quiet. Then I pressed the Accept button and clicked on the speakerphone. Heavy breathing filtered from the phone, just like yesterday.

After the second breath, I'd had enough. "Whoever you are, you're pathetic."

The mechanical voice crackled through the line. "You're at risk."

"So you said last time. Now tell me who you are and explain this so-called risk or leave me alone."

The caller disconnected. Tonya stared at me with her hands on her hips. I shrugged. "Prank call," I said.

"I take it this isn't the first such call you've received?"

"Second time it's happened."

"What did the police have to say about it?" I averted my eyes. "You didn't tell them? What in the name of Bigfoot is wrong with you? You're being threatened. You have to report it."

"I'm sure it's no big deal…"

Her eyes blazed. "Callahan Cassidy. A woman was murdered two days ago just up the road. You're not some ditzy teenager who runs into a dark deserted basement to hide from a serial killer. You're an adult, a professional. Act like it."

The depth of her anger shocked me, and I realized how scared she was for me. I decided she was right. I was stupid to be so nonchalant about these calls.

I walked over and wrapped my arms around her. After a moment's hesitation, she responded to the hug. "I'll tell Dad about the calls when I get home," I said. "He'll tell me what I should do about them."

"After he takes you out to the woodshed. Deservedly so."

I released her and laughed. "The woodshed? Who says that anymore?"

She patted her hair. "All I know is that you'd better tell him. I'll be following up."

I made an X across my heart, and she rolled her eyes. "Any idea who it might be? I couldn't even tell if it was a man or a woman."

"I've thought about it since the first call. If I had to guess,

I'd say Brian Ratliff. After he…" I remembered I hadn't told her about him cornering me in the alcove yesterday. "Now, don't get mad—I just forgot to tell you…" I quickly highlighted the events, ending with, "But Detective Sanchez was there, so it's been reported. In a sense, anyway."

She sighed. "What am I going to do with you, Callahan Cassidy? You're a magnet for trouble." She thought for a moment. "But Brian Ratliff? I don't know. I can see him being pushy, aggressive even. But he doesn't seem sneaky enough for the anonymous caller thing. Or savvy enough to know about distortion devices."

She glanced at her watch. "We're going to have to play secret agent later. This visit has run longer than I anticipated, and I'm running late for a meeting. I'll just slide the key back under the urn, then we'll go out the front door and lock it behind us. That way, we won't have to walk through the muck again."

"But I'm not finished with Sophie's desk…"

"Yes, you are, *mon petit*. Gather your things."

I looked at the key in her hand, my mind churning with possibilities. She read my thoughts.

"Just because you know where the spare key is doesn't mean you can come back here later. That's completely unethical. You've always been committed to doing the right thing."

When she stepped outside, I looked back at the desk, wondering if she was right about my devotion to ethics. Sophie's pink notebook shone like a beacon on the desktop. I decided my ethics were a little more…pragmatic than Tonya might have guessed. I took a quick peek over my shoulder and saw her bent over the planter. I tucked the vandalized picture inside the cover of the pink notebook and slid the whole package into my purse.

Back in the Tahoe, the heat blasted around our feet. The first tiny flakes from the oncoming snowstorm drifted onto the windshield. Instead of driving, Tonya sat with her hands on the steering wheel, and I could tell something was bothering her.

I put a hand on her knee. "What's wrong?"

She shook her head. "Nothing. It's just…that picture of the Vixens stirred up some bad memories. They wreaked a lot of havoc back in the day."

I nodded. "Before I found Victoria's body, I was remembering that poor girl she humiliated at graduation."

"Melissa Masterson. Perfectly nice person. Moved out of town as soon as she graduated. She didn't deserve all that bullying."

"None of them did." The trace of an image flickered around the edges of my memory—a girl sobbing, the Vixens circling around her. But it drifted away before I could capture it.

Tonya tapped the wheel. "Most of The Vixens were decent enough at one time. Kimberly, for example. I can't help but think she—and most of the others—wouldn't have turned so vicious if Victoria hadn't energized their baser instincts."

She finally put the car into gear and glanced at me. "Ah, well. These melancholy ruminations are best left to another time. Preferably a snowy evening at your parents' lodge with a mug of mulled wine."

As she pulled onto the street and prepared to make a U-turn, I made a decision. "Wait," I said. "Instead of taking me home, can you drop me off at the high school?"

Her eyebrows furrowed. "Why?"

"I'm ready to figure this out once and for all. To do that, I need to eliminate as many suspects as possible. Jessica Fannon would be a good start." I looked across the console. "You're friendly with her, aren't you? Will you call and wrangle me an invitation?"

"You're like a dog with a bone, sweet potato," Tonya said. But she pressed the Bluetooth button on her dashboard and made the call.

25

I n the two hours since Tonya and I had left the lodge, the temperature had plummeted. Fingers of blustery wind reached beneath my hood and tousled my hair. I pulled my coat tighter around my neck and looked at my old stomping grounds—Rock Creek Village High School. Memories tumbled from the place like ghosts, filling me with a strange sense of both perpetual youth and weary age. I was at once seventeen and seventy.

As I started toward the school's glass entry doors, my phone rang. A spurt of anxiety whooshed inside me. Was it my anonymous caller, wanting to remind me again that I was at risk? A glance at the screen told me it was almost as bad. Kimberly Lyon.

She'd ignored my call last night, so in a petulant move worthy of my teenage self, I hit the Decline button. The phone buzzed again almost immediately, this time with a text.

I need a progress report.

I stifled my irritation, reminding myself that her life was, after all, on the line. *Still gathering info.*

It's been two days! Frown emoji.

Irritation blossomed into indignation, and I pounded out my response. *I don't work for you. If I'm moving too slow, get someone else.*

Three dots flashed, flashed again, and again. *I don't want anyone else. Sorry. Can you come to dinner tonight? Talk then?*

At last, a little humility. But I'd promised my mother I'd eat dinner at their place tonight. I'd rather stick my tongue to the frozen light pole than bail on a commitment to my mother.

Can't tonight. Busy.

Three dots flashed. *Breakfast tomorrow?*

That works. Where?

You'll have to come here, she responded. *Stupid ankle monitor. Eight?*

Ah, yes. I'd forgotten about her home imprisonment. *OK.*

Don't have anything here to eat. Be a dear and bring breakfast with you. Something low cal.

I shook my head and walked inside.

A middle-aged woman with black shoulder-length hair sat at a computer, pecking away at the keyboard. She lifted a finger to acknowledge my presence. While she completed her task, I removed my gloves and parka. I glanced in the mirror and saw static electricity crackling in my hair. I looked like a dying dandelion. I licked my palm and smoothed my hand across my head.

After a few more keystrokes, the woman rose from her chair and approached the waist-high counter that separated the elite school personnel from the riff raff.

Her face wreathed into a grin. "If it isn't Callie Cassidy, Rock Creek Village's claim to fame." She thrust her hand forward, and I took it. "I heard you were coming. I'm Selena Sanchez, secretary, receptionist, and jack of all trades."

"Pleased to meet you, Ms. Sanchez. Any relation to Raul?"

She beamed. "My son," she said. "Detective Raul Sanchez. You've heard of him."

I suspected calling him by his title never got old. "We've met," I said, forgoing the details. "He seems to be...dedicated to his job."

"He's the best, if I do say so. But you didn't come here to listen to me brag on my baby. Jessica Fannon called. I'm supposed to send you back post haste. Your presence is highly anticipated."

I followed Selena's directions to the school's journalism department classroom. The door was open, and I stepped inside without being spotted. A spritelike woman, probably late-twenties and barely cresting five feet, energetically addressed a group of twenty students. Her red hair fell above her ears in a pixie cut. Freckles peppered her skin, and green eyes peered from her pale skin. She was one of those cute young things who made me feel clunky and ancient. Her students gazed at her with reverence.

My camera hung around my neck, and I quietly shot a couple of pictures of Jessica with her class. At the last snap of the shutter, a girl looked over her shoulder and pointed in my direction. "She's here."

Jessica smiled and beckoned. "Come in. Students, meet Callahan Cassidy, winner of the Felden Prize for Excellence in Journalism."

The kids applauded, as did Jessica. I felt myself blush. "Enough! You're inflating my ego. Heaven knows I don't need that."

They giggled as if I had just told the funniest joke ever. At Jessica's direction, they took their seats, watching me with the same level of awe they had bestowed upon her. A heady experience, to be sure.

"Ms. Cassidy, we only have fifteen minutes until the bell. Please share some sage advice with my future journalists."

Advice? Me? Other than *Abandon all hope, ye who enter here*, what did I have to offer? I set aside my cynicism and chattered about networking, willingness to start at the bottom, practicing fundamentals, and the other clichéd but worthy guidance I had received along the way. The students nodded and took notes as if I were providing answers to a riddle that would unlock a treasure.

When the bell rang, they lined up to thank me. Several asked me to come back. Could I critique their work? Could they interview me for a story? I assured them I was excited to help them on their journey.

I enjoyed the experience more than I would have imagined.

When the room had emptied, Jessica led me to the teacher nook at the back of the room. "You made their day," she said. "Mine too. I can't thank you enough for coming."

I felt a stab of guilt about the true reason for my appearance. "It's a pleasure," I said. "Your students are delightful, and they clearly think the world of you. But I'm afraid I have an ulterior motive…"

She waved and gave me a congenial smile. "I know. I saw Kimberly's post on Facebook yesterday. And Summer said you already cross examined her mercilessly."

My cheeks flushed again. "Oh, I didn't mean to—"

Jessica laughed, a titter that crinkled her eyes. "I'm just kidding. She found you intriguing. I think she likes you, though she's not ready to admit it just yet."

She removed a few items from a small box refrigerator behind her desk. "Okay if I eat while we talk? I only get a half hour for lunch."

I assured her it was fine and watched as she unwrapped a peanut butter and jelly sandwich on white bread, a bag of barbecue chips, and a carton of chocolate milk. She took a bite out of the sandwich. "Don't tell Summer about all this," she said around a mouthful of food. "She's a health nut. At home, I'm forced to ingest organic stuff and veggies. Lunch is my hidden rebellion. Wait till you see the size of my brownie. Sorry, but I'm not sharing."

I grinned. Tonya was right about this whirling dervish. She'd drawn me in like a magnet. My gut reaction said she hadn't killed Victoria. She was too forthright, too in-your-face to attack surreptitiously. But recent experience had taught me my gut instinct couldn't always be trusted.

"I already talked to the cops," she said, crunching on a chip. "But I'm happy to answer any questions you have. From what I've heard, though, you found Kimberly Lyon standing over the body, so it seems pretty cut and dried to me." She cringed. "Sorry. Pardon the pun."

I shrugged. "It might be as simple as it appears. I just want to erase any doubt in my own mind. For me, investigation always involves a process of elimination. I start at the periphery and work my way toward the core. In this case, I want to rule out the people least likely to have committed the crime."

"Well, I'm grateful to be in your *least likely* category." She crumpled her chip bag into a ball and tossed it into the trash can. "Ask away. I'm ready to be ruled out."

I shifted in my seat. Summer had already provided me with their alibi, so I didn't feel the need to hear that again. What I really wanted to know was what had caused Jessica's rage in the first place.

"Why did you go to the Creekside Saturday? What had you so riled up?"

She ran a hand through her hair, and her face tightened. "Long story. I'll have to go back in time a few days so you'll have context."

I nodded, gesturing for her to continue.

"Victoria showed up here Wednesday during my conference period and requested—demanded—that my staff write an article about her twins. I'm standing there thinking, we could write an article, all right, about their lives as slugs and dopers. But she wanted some glorifying puff piece about the boys' contributions to the school."

"What did you tell her?"

"What could I say? Of course the answer was a gargantuan 'no way.' But Summer's got me working on this inner peace stuff, so I tried to stay calm. I told her I'd mention it to the staff, but content decisions ultimately belonged to the students. Blah, blah, blah."

I nodded, impressed. "How did she respond?"

"The witch told me I should be the authority figure in the classroom, that it was my responsibility to tell students what to do. Otherwise, I had no business as a leader of teenagers. This from the woman whose sons deal their own Ritalin."

She swallowed the last bite of sandwich. "Then she smiled sweetly and began listing the names of school board members, her *dear friends*." Jessica lifted her fingers into air quotes. "She mentioned the endowments she and her two-timing husband had given the school. And she leaned over and whispered that a certain group of parents wasn't supportive of teachers with alternate lifestyles." Jessica's face reddened, and her green eyes blazed. "Can you believe that? She then informed me she had the clout to swing the pendulum whichever way she chose."

It was a terrible story—one of blackmail and intimidation—but I wasn't surprised. This was exactly the Victoria I remembered from high school, one who would stop at nothing to get her way. One who delighted in tormenting others.

"This happened on Wednesday?" I asked. "Why'd you wait until Saturday to challenge her?"

Jessica pulled out the brownie, and my eyes widened. The thing was bigger than my hand. "I didn't worry about it much," she said. "Victoria has delivered cloaked threats in the past, and nothing ever comes of them. But then Summer got home from her Saturday yoga class and said Victoria had stopped by to enlist her help in persuading me. She reminded Summer that she was Chamber of Commerce president and insinuated she could influence the success— or failure—of Summer's business. I was livid. It's one thing if she's just threatening me. Another thing entirely to try to browbeat the woman I love."

Wow. If this behavior was typical, it was no wonder Victoria was dead.

"Wow," I said. "She hasn't changed a bit," I said.

Jessica lifted her shoulders. "She's always been a bully, and she just keeps poking until she finds a person's soft spot. Most bullies don't quit. People tell you if you ignore them, they'll go away, but that hasn't been my experience. Unless you put a stop to it, they continue until they break you. I'd guess murder was someone's way of putting an end to Victoria's bullying. Permanently."

I nodded. "Okay. Let's change gears for a minute. What do you think of Kimberly? Is she a bully too?"

Jessica wrinkled her nose. "She wouldn't get my vote for Woman of the Year, but she's not nearly as bad as Victoria. And her daughter has turned out well, though that's probably a result of the father's influence."

A little smile crossed my face. It figured Sam had a reputation as a great dad. "Let's suppose for a minute that Kimberly didn't kill Victoria. Who do you think did?"

She pondered, rubbing her freckled chin. "Tons of people hated her. But enough to kill? And sneaky enough to frame Kimberly? Has to be someone with a grudge against both of them. The first person who pops into my head is Kimberly's husband. No tangible reason—just a sense I get around him. He's too mild mannered. Seems phony. Probably concealing a smoldering pit of rage."

I thought about Parker marching onto my porch, the indignation in his eyes. Jessica's assertion wasn't outside the realm of possibility. I had once interviewed a forensic psychologist whose favorite tagline was, "We all have a murderer within us. Some of us just keep him in a tighter cage than others."

I wondered if Parker had unlocked the cage.

26

J essica's lunch break ended, and now I stood in the hall of my old school during passing period, amidst a swirling maelstrom of teenagers. The noise level equaled a rock concert. Amazing that just over three hundred students could generate such a field of energy. I plucked one from the stream to ask directions to the library, and he rewarded me with an irritated look and a finger pointing to my left.

Though the school resembled the one I attended a quarter of a century ago, it was more of a distant cousin than an aging twin. Much had changed, and I had only a hazy sense of familiarity. Hallways had been rearranged, additions made, windows replaced, paint and hardware upgraded.

As I navigated the direction indicated by the moody adolescent, a commotion attracted my attention. Across the hall, two boys had cornered a girl, whose hands covered her face as her shoulders shook. Laughter or sobs? I paused to watch the scene play out. When the girl dropped her hands, her expression reflected desperation.

I recognized all three faces: Sam's daughter and Victoria's twins.

Without a plan, I marched toward the trio and faced the boys, shielding Elyse. I widened my stance and placed my fists on my hips, trying to project my inner Wonder Woman.

"What the hell is going on here?" I asked.

Whether because of my aggressiveness or because they'd just heard an adult use a minor curse word in a school setting, the boys looked nonplussed for a moment. Then the one closest to me smirked. "Mind your own business, lady. We were just offering our con... con..."

"Condolences," his brother prodded.

"Yeah. Because her *real* mom is going to prison. Now she only has her *fake* daddy." He peered gleefully at Elyse. I realized the boys had just revealed to Elyse the secret Sam had told me yesterday. The twins' father had probably told them. I wondered if he'd also mentioned that Elyse was their half-sister.

I was stunned at their callousness, coming as it did on the heels of their own mother's death. I leaned forward an inch, conscious of the desire to protect Elyse while still allowing the boys to save face in front of a growing group of onlookers. I kept my voice low. "Listen, little boys. I'm not intimidated by punks like you."

In unison, the twins' eyes widened. I waited to see which response they would choose: fight or flight. Before they could react either way, a bald figure wearing a suit rounded the corner and strode toward us, glaring at the twins and glancing at my visitor badge. "Is there a problem?"

I raised an eyebrow at the brothers. "No problem. These young men were just helping me find the library."

Tweedledee and Tweedledum nodded, with identical expressions of compliance that barely concealed their humiliation. Authority Figure cocked his head. "That's very chivalrous of you, boys. As a reward, I'll escort you to your next class." He turned to the students gathered across the hall. "The rest of you get moving. Bell rings in two minutes."

When the crowd dispersed and the boys slithered away behind the bald guy, I took a calming breath and pivoted toward Elyse. I had a quick daydream of the girl throwing her arms around my neck, grateful I was there for her when she found out the hard way Sam wasn't her biological father.

Another Wonder Woman fantasy destroyed.

Pain clouded her eyes, and her lips tightened into a thin line. When I reached out to put a sympathetic hand on her shoulder, she jerked back as though I might electrocute her. "Stay away from me! Leave my father alone, too!" She stomped off, leaving me with my arm extended and my mouth agape.

I brushed my fingers through my hair in a futile attempt to regain some dignity. My mind reeled as I wondered how to handle this. Should I tell Sam? If I did, Elyse might view it as further interference and hate me even more. But if I didn't, Sam might see it as a betrayal. I was in a no-win position.

When I am undecided, I often decide to not decide, and so it was right now. I spied the library down the hall and made up my mind to follow through on my visit. The right answer would hopefully materialize while my mind was otherwise occupied.

As I walked into the library, the sweet, musky smell of books wrapped me in a cocoon of contentment and comfort. *My name is Callie, and I am a book junkie.*

The library was a pleasant space that, like the rest of the school, had been renovated since my high school years. Back in my day, the library had presented as austere and harsh, metal folding chairs surrounding wooden tables. Now, oak bookshelves lined the pale-yellow walls, and plush chairs were arranged in groups, inviting readers to escape into fictional wonderlands.

Across the room, I saw a polished wooden checkout desk. The woman behind it offered me a warm smile. I blinked twice and realized I was looking at Mrs. Barney. Her hair was streaked with gray, and her figure was softer and fuller than the twenty-something woman I remembered, but she was the same librarian who had catered to my thirst for reading.

I trotted across the room, returning her smile. "Mrs. Barney! What a wonderful blast from the past! You may not recognize me—"

"Callie Cassidy! How could I forget such an avid reader— and such a lovely person. I've followed your career…" Her smile faded, and she cast her eyes downward. "I have been so sorry for your troubles."

"That's kind," I said, eager to change the subject. "But I'd rather talk about you. What's new with my favorite librarian?"

She lit up as she talked about her college-aged daughters, her husband the firefighter, her work with teenagers. It sounded as if she had a good life.

"But enough of my rambling," she said. "What brings you to my den of knowledge?"

"Nostalgia," I said. "Now that I'm back in the village, I find myself yearning to walk down memory lane. Simpler times and all. But my mom has my yearbooks packed away in some inaccessible corner of a storage unit. I was hoping to look through the library's copies."

"Certainly, but someone has beaten you to them. Funny thing is, no one has requested those books in two decades, and now two people in one day. But I imagine she'll share."

Mrs. Barney pointed toward the back of the room, and I turned to see which former classmate was flipping through the pages of our mutual history. When I recognized the woman at the table, my eyes widened. Not a classmate, but the perpetually present Mrs. Finney, clad in a purple polyester pantsuit and a matching fedora, complete with a blue and violet peacock feather. She appeared amused as she waggled her fingers at me. I excused myself and started toward her.

"Mrs. Finney." I said.

"Yes, dear, it's me."

"You're looking at my high school yearbooks."

"Indeed I am."

I waited for her to elaborate, but she merely offered a knowing smile.

"What are you researching?" I prompted.

"The best way to understand a new place is to examine its history, my dear. And," she added in a wistful tone, "the roles we choose in adolescence forge the paths of our lives."

"Right," I said. Then I sat next to her and leaned over to look at the yearbook laying open in front of her. It was my senior year, the portrait section, and a picture of smiling eighteen-year-old Callie Cassidy stared from the page.

"That's me," I said.

"Indeed it is. I stumbled upon your delightful portrait just before you entered the library."

I sighed, trying to reconcile the girl in the photograph with the woman I had become. Part of me still felt eighteen, twenty, thirty. But another part of me felt ancient and remote, as if those versions of myself were as fictional as the books lining the walls. Where had those younger versions of me slipped off to? Could I get them back?

Would I want to even if I could?

From the corner of my eye, I noticed Mrs. Finney watching me. "Hard to believe I was ever so young," I said.

She nodded. "Yet the wisdom of our youth is perpetual."

She pushed the open yearbook in front of me and lifted herself from the chair. "I believe I'm finished here, dear," she said. "Your turn. Remember, oftentimes one can only solve problems by facing backwards."

I tilted my head. She had touched on the subconscious reason I'd wanted a peek at these books—the feeling that this murder might have more to do with Victoria's high school self than her adult self. Had Mrs. Finney concluded the same thing? Was she spouting gobbledygook or sending me a message? "Is there something you want to tell me, Mrs. Finney?"

She waved. "Don't mind me, dearie. I'm just a silly old woman."

She smiled sweetly and strutted off. The word "shrewd"

floated into my head. This was the second time in as many days that I'd felt the desire to research her background. But it would still have to wait. For now, my past beckoned.

Starting with my freshman yearbook, I spent the next hour browsing through the four volumes, flipping past pictures of Sam, Tonya, and other classmates I hadn't thought of in years. I hoped an image or word might transform the persistent itch in my mind into a premise. But when I returned to my own portrait in the senior yearbook, I sighed in disappointment. I'd discovered nothing.

I looked at the old me one last time, smiling at her ambitious, hopeful expression. Then I closed the book and stacked it atop of the other three, resting my hands on the pile. I couldn't escape the sense that there was something I should see in those pages, something to lead me in the right direction. But the more I reached for it, the further away it drifted. Best to let it go. For now.

I hoisted the stack of books and carried them to the check-out desk. Mrs. Barney moved toward me. "Did you find what you were looking for?"

"Not yet. I wondered if I might take these home for a couple of days and keep looking."

She glanced over her shoulder as if she were preparing to commit a crime and needed to inspect the area for potential witnesses. "These are reference materials, so I'm not supposed to let them out of the library. But it's my own rule, so for you, I'll make an exception. Just promise you'll return them in pristine condition."

After I pinkie swore, she handed me a canvas bag in which to conceal the contraband. I exited the library and then the school, lugging the books back toward the village. As I had expected, while I was concentrating on something else my subconscious had decided what to do about Elyse. As much as I dreaded telling Sam what I'd seen, I knew it had to be done.

27

The snowfall had relented, but gray clouds had settled like smoke rings over the mountaintops. A brisk wind whistled through the branches of the pine trees and stung my exposed cheeks and nose. A storm definitely loomed, though the timing was difficult to predict. Storms that appeared imminent could stall over the mountains for two days before heading into the valley.

I jaywalked across the street and climbed the hill into the upper village. Ten minutes at a powerwalking pace brought me to Snow Plow Chow. As I opened the door, the bell jingled in cheery greeting and the heat lured me inside. Sam, who stood behind the cash register, brightened when he spotted me.

How I hated to destroy that smile.

He looked concerned when I said we needed to talk, and he spoke a few words to Dan before placing a hand on the small of my back and guiding me into the kitchen. A single cook loitered near the steel prep table, his thumbs tapping at the screen of his phone. When he glanced up and saw his boss, he swung his arm behind his back. Sam smiled at him. "Relax, Rodger. I don't care if you're on your phone, as long as we're slow. But listen, could you give us the room for a few minutes?"

The man looked from Sam to me and back, a knowing smile creeping across his face. "Sure, boss," he said. "I'll just go out back and grab a smoke."

The cook pulled on a coat and stepped through the back door. Sam leaned a hip against the table and crossed his arms. "What's up, Callie? You're wearing your serious face."

I squirmed as I summarized the scene at the high school. "I feel sure they told Elyse that... well, you know..."

Sam's face turned a deep shade of crimson. He turned to the prep table and pounded a clenched fist into the stainless steel. "This is Kimberly's fault. I could...I could kill her."

I jerked my head toward the kitchen door and saw Dan peering at us through the window. "Sam," I whispered. "You need to calm down."

The blood drained from his face as he replayed what he'd said. He rubbed the back of his neck in a familiar gesture.

"I didn't mean that." The breath hitched in his chest.

"Of course you didn't. But you need to be careful what you say right now." When I looked back to the door, Dan had disappeared.

Sam slumped against the wall. "I'm blaming Kimberly, but it's my fault too. I should have told Elyse as soon as I found out. Secrets always come back to bite you in the butt."

"Maybe. But as Tonya would say, it's water under the bridge. The question is, how are you going to handle it now?"

He shoved his hands in his pockets. "I don't know what to do. Being a parent is hard under the best of circumstances, and this... Should I pick her up at school right now? Should I wait for her at home? Should I tell her I know what happened, or wait for her to talk to me? Can I google this?"

I put my hands on his shoulders. "You know your daughter, Sam. Trust your gut. What feels right to you?"

He thought for a moment. "I'm going to get her. This shouldn't wait a minute longer."

I nodded. "I think that's a good plan."

He wrapped his arms around me and squeezed. Then he pulled back, his face inches from mine. "Thank you for defending my daughter. I'm…I'm glad you've come home."

"I don't get the idea Elyse feels the same way."

"She will. Someday. For now, I am grateful enough for both of us." He released his grip. "Are you hungry? I know I can't repay you, but I can make sure you're fed. Order whatever you want—on the house. Forever on the house."

He moved to the back door and swung it open, summoning Rodger back inside and explaining that he was leaving, likely for the rest of the day. Then he grabbed his coat from a hook on the side wall and led me back into the dining room. Pulling Dan aside, he spoke in a low voice and pointed at me. With one last nervous smile in my direction, he strode through the front door, a blast of cold air replacing his warmth.

Dan approached me. "Boss says to give you whatever you want. No charge."

I thanked him but declined. "Listen," I said, "whatever you heard—"

In quick succession, he held a hand across his eyes, then covered his ears, then his mouth. "I didn't hear nothin'. Saw nothin'. Won't say nothin'. Sam's a good man."

I smiled and patted his arm. The wall clock read two-fifteen. I could use some Woody and Carl time to clear my head. After that, I'd get back to work. Maybe I'd find answers in the pages of a pink notebook and some yearbooks.

The yoga studio was once again in full delight mode. I peeked through the window and saw Summer, her long braid bouncing across her lithe back as she led a dozen women through painful-looking stretches.

Amidst the group of yogis, I noticed Mrs. Finney, her body twisted into an impossible pose. For a large woman, she was surprisingly flexible. Her head hovered near the floor, and her upside-down face peered through the triangle of her legs. She smiled as she spotted me and raised her right hand to waggle her fingers at me.

I tore myself away from the incongruous sight and kept walking. At the Fudge Factory, I saw Dr. Lowell inside, scanning the content of the cases. I nearly joined her, but I wasn't in the mood to discuss my feelings, so I kept walking. I paused at the empty gallery, noticing movement behind the glass. Two people traipsed about inside as if they owned the place. My immediate response—angry, jealous, territorial—surprised me. In spite of what I'd said to Tonya, I felt attached to the place. I fought the urge to march inside and vanquish the intruders.

But I was saved from myself by the weather. A squall ushered in the front edge of the storm we'd been waiting for, and snow began to fall in a thick blanket. I stepped from beneath the awning and opened my mouth to let wet flakes land on my tongue. A few things in life immediately transported you back in time to the age of seven. Hostess cupcakes. Footie pajamas. Snow on your tongue.

I spotted Sanchez a few doors down, exiting Quicker Liquor with a paper bag clutched in his fingers. When opportunity presents itself, a good journalist doesn't pass it up. I hurried toward him, raising my hand in what I hoped was a friendly gesture.

He looked like the proverbial deer in the headlights.

"Afternoon, Detective," I said. "Just wanted to see if you've made any progress with the investigation."

He narrowed his eyes. "I thought we'd come to an understanding. I do the detecting. You do...whatever it is you do that doesn't involve this case."

I pursed my lips. "The only understanding I've come to is that justice must be served."

Sanchez sighed and shook his head. "I don't know why you assume I'm not capable of doing my job. Your father was a cop. A good one. And he helped train me. I'm not interested in convicting an innocent woman. There's plenty of evidence implicating your friend, including the fact that you yourself found her in the room holding the murder weapon."

"First of all, she's not my friend. If she's guilty, I want to see her pay for her crime as much as you do. Second, I've never tried to imply you don't know how to do your job. It's just that, as a private citizen, I have access to people in a way you don't."

"Leave it alone," he said. "I don't want to see you in any danger."

I hesitated, trying to decide whether to walk away. I decided to give it one last try. "At least let me tell you what I've found out. Maybe you'll find some of it useful."

He shook his head again but pointed to his car at the curb. "Five minutes," he said.

We got in the car, and he turned on the engine so the heater would run. I took a moment to get settled, mostly so I could organize my thoughts. I didn't want to waste my one chance at an audience with the king.

He leaned across his seat and stored his paper bag in the back. "All right, tell me what you have."

I started with Summer and Jessica, the motive I'd uncovered, and their response to my questions. "I haven't tried to verify their alibi, but I believe them. They're at the bottom of my suspect list."

His eyebrows shot to his hairline. "Suspect list? You have a suspect list? I don't remember seeing your badge."

The bag of yearbooks dug into my thigh, and I shifted in my seat. "Poor choice of words. It's more of... an inventory. People who might have wanted Victoria dead and who might want to frame Kimberly."

He rubbed his eyes. "I looked into Jessica and Summer, even though their motive wasn't all that compelling. Several people saw them at the movies and the grocery store. Alibi confirmed. Who else is on your little list?"

I forced myself to ignore his condescending tone. After all, Dad had pegged him as an intelligent and skilled detective. And to be fair, the guy was hearing me out.

"Well, there's Victoria's husband. He said he was home

watching hockey with his sons, but I found an Instagram post that indicated they were at a party that afternoon. He's high on my list."

"I'd be disappointed if he wasn't. Every armchair detective suspects the husband, as do the professionals. And you're right, he lied about his alibi. He does have one, though. Just not the one he said. Turns out he's been engaging in a little extracurricular activity of his own. After some prodding, he confessed that he'd been... otherwise occupied... at his lady friend's apartment in Denver. We still have to verify, but it sounds legit. Also, you have to wonder why he'd go to the trouble of framing Kimberly."

Yikes. I couldn't provide the reason without revealing Sam's secret, and I wasn't prepared to do that. I considered telling him about Sophie, but I didn't want to turn over the pink notebook before I'd leafed through it.

I shrugged. "I'd look into Parker Lyon, Kimberly's husband."

Sanchez nodded, seeming unsurprised. "Anything specific about him? Besides his affair with the deceased?"

I told him about our morning clash, and a spark of anger flashed across his face. "Did he threaten you?"

"No. He was just being a jerk. Trying to intimidate me. But I'm not easily intimidated."

The corner of his mouth twitched. "I noticed that yesterday, when Ratliff had you in the alcove." The smile faded then, replaced by a stern expression. "You're not invincible, though. I'm telling you again, you need to stay out of this, for your own safety. Let me do my job. I'm not incompetent."

I lowered my eyes. "I never meant to imply that you were. My father speaks well of you, and from what I've seen, you're smart and capable. It's just been...a rough time for me lately. I don't know, maybe I thought I could redeem myself for past mistakes. I didn't mean to step on your toes."

I started to open the door, embarrassed at having

divulged my emotional baggage and not sure what had compelled me to do so. Sanchez put a hand on my arm, and when I looked at him, I saw a flicker of compassion in his eyes. Maybe there was a heart in that broad chest after all.

"It's not that I'm unappreciative of your efforts. But there could be a murderer in our village. I feel an overwhelming duty to keep the people here safe. Including you."

I nodded, blinking back tears. Then I slung my bag of books over my shoulder and smiled at him. "Thank you, Detective Sanchez. Guess I'd better get back home before I'm buried in a blizzard."

"Want a lift?" he said, his tone verging on friendly.

"No, thanks. I rather enjoy walking in a snowstorm."

I got out and shut the door behind me. He lifted a hand, and I waved back. I wondered if we just might have become allies.

28

When I got home, I found a note tacked to the cabin door: "Don't forget about dinner tonight. 6 o'clock sharp. I'm making your favorite." I salivated, though I had no idea what delicious meal Mom had in store for me. With the exception of tuna casserole, every meal she cooked was my favorite. One perk of living right down the path from my parents was the frequency of home-cooked meals.

As I turned my key in the lock, I reminded myself to brace for canine assault. True to form, Woody propelled himself through the air, paws landing on my collarbones, tongue slurping my chin. Carl sat calmly on the bed, watching the display of affection with apparent disdain.

I knew I should train Woody not to leap on me, but the truth was, I loved his enthusiasm at the sight of me. Anyone needing a self-esteem boost should adopt a Golden Retriever, I thought. Then, for a healthy dose of humility, a cat.

Once I'd disentangled myself, I sat beside Carl and trailed a finger down his spine. He rewarded me with an arched back and a soft purr. I'd never considered myself a cat person, and as a stray, Carl probably hadn't been a person cat. But we were forging an amicable relationship.

And Woody was loving it. He jumped onto the bed and squeezed between us. Both the animals snuggled against my legs. Life was good.

But after a few minutes of mutual lovefest, I needed to get back to work. Nudging the creatures aside, I fanned the yearbooks across the bed. Carl's ears perked up, and he stretched across the bed to sniff the books. My brain churned. Something still tickled my memory, a clue I suspected could be found between the covers of those yearbooks. If I could just latch on to it...

But possibilities wouldn't come. Between the search of Sophie's house, my trip to the high school, the scene with Elyse and the twins, my meeting with Sam, and my heart-to-heart with Sanchez, I was mentally and emotionally drained. I needed some physical exertion to break the logjam.

When Woody saw me grab my ice cleats and realized a hike lay in his immediate future, his tail pumped in excitement. With my camera resting around my neck, I waved goodbye to the indifferent cat and led the pup outside.

It was snowing steadily, and I shot a few pictures of Mt. O'Connell cloaked in white. By this weekend, I predicted skiers would be skimming down the slope. Good news for Dad—and all the local business owners.

We crossed the wooden bridge and started up the path. Woody darted ahead and doubled back, his rear end shaking in joy and his nose dusted with white powder. I turned to face the village nestled below us and snapped a few wide angle shots. Then I switched to the zoom lens for some close-up work. Emerald green pine needles thrusting through a blanket of snow. Branches extending from a fallen tree like the legs of a centipede wriggling on its back. It felt good to take photos filled with the peace of nature rather than my usual fare of death and destruction.

Woody plunked down in front of me, his tail creating a snow angel. I shot his portrait, and together we trudged up the familiar path.

When we returned from the hike, Carl was reclining on the bed atop my sophomore yearbook. He stared at me as if trying to send me a message. Unfortunately, I wasn't a cat whisperer. He reminded me of the enigmatic Mrs. Finney. Maybe I should get the two of them together for a seance.

I opened my laptop and uploaded the pictures from the hike, trying to view them as a stranger would. They were good, really good, and I thought the photographer who shot them might even be able to make a living selling them. I thought of Preston's invitation to return to *The Sentinel* and its fast-paced, on-the-edge lifestyle. Then I thought of the gallery, imagining my landscape shots covering its walls. I sensed myself moving closer toward a life-changing decision, a chasm that would forever separate my past life from my future one. The idea filled me with a heady mixture of excitement and fear.

I skimmed through the nature photos one last time, feeling more content than I had in a long time. A few minutes later, humming in the shower, I felt the flutter of a smile on my lips. After I'd toweled off and dressed in my best pair of jeans, I dried my hair and even used a curling iron on it. I dabbed on a bit of perfume, then dug through a box of toiletries I hadn't looked at since I'd moved. When I found a tube of lipstick, I smoothed it across my lips. My parents weren't going to know what hit them.

My mother did not tolerate latecomers. At precisely five to six, I shrugged on my coat, grabbed my bag, and set off for the short walk to my parents' place. I cradled Carl in the crook of my elbow, and Woody trotted along beside us. Dusk had fallen. The storm had subsided, and a soft wind moaned through the branches of the evergreens. The three of us stopped for a moment of reverence, quiet and appreciative.

A sudden cracking sound broke the calmness. I jumped,

Woody growled, and Carl hissed. I squinted into the gloom, searching for the origin of the noise. A shadow moved through the trees. My pulse accelerated, and the mechanical voice of the anonymous caller replayed in my mind. "You're at risk." Then I heard Sanchez's words: "You're putting yourself in danger." But I shook off the nervousness and forced out a quavering laugh. I'd simply forgotten about the sounds and sights of mountain life. "No worries," I said to the creatures. "Just a deer. An elk, maybe. Or a bighorn sheep."

Suddenly, Carl wriggled from my grasp, landing on all fours on the path. Then he darted away, into the trees and out of sight. I called after him and took a few steps off the path, to no avail. Even in the light of day, I'd never be able to catch him. Woody stayed beside me, whimpering, and I crouched down next to him. "He'll be back, big guy. Carl possesses the spirit of a wanderer. He's just not accustomed to answering to family. But he'll come home." I hoped I wasn't feeding the dog a placating lie, but it was all the comfort I had to offer. I rose and gave his collar a gentle tug, guiding him to the lodge.

When I started up the stairs to my parents' home, the aroma of ham and au gratin potatoes lifted my spirits, but not Woody's. He plodded along behind me, downtrodden. My mother took one look at him and frowned. Dad stepped in from the kitchen, carrying a handful of silverware, and I told them about Carl's vanishing act.

"Oh, dear," Mom said. "Well, he's a creature of the night, you know, used to his independence. Perhaps he just needed some time to himself. I predict he'll be back on your doorstep by morning."

Woody seemed unconvinced, but I did my best to role model optimism. "I'm sure she's right, big guy. He loves us—you, at least. He'll be back."

Dad finished setting the table, and Mom carried platters of meat and potatoes from the kitchen, along with buttery homemade biscuits and crisp green beans. The perfect comfort food for a winter day. I dug in with enthusiasm, but Woody positioned himself near the stairs with his head resting on his paws, refusing even a nibble.

Across the table, my mother studied me. "You look lovely tonight, darling."

"You smell good, too," my father added.

"What's the occasion?" Mom asked.

"Why does there need to be an occasion to look—and smell—good?"

Mom lifted an eyebrow, and I decided to fill them in on Tonya's idea about the gallery.

"I've been doing some thinking..." I began.

"Uh oh," Dad said, laying his fork on his plate. Mom watched me without speaking.

"Tonya took me on a tour of an empty storefront on Evergreen Way yesterday. Used to be an art studio, from what she said. She thinks the space would be perfect for a photo gallery—"

Mom squealed. Dad grinned. "I know the realtor, Willie Wright," he said. "I'll be glad to contact him tomorrow."

"And I'll start creating flyers with my new graphic design program," Mom said. "You'll love them! I even took an adult education class."

I held up my hands. "Slow down, you guys. Let me breathe for a minute." I inhaled, my adrenaline pumping under the blanket of their exuberance. "I'm good with you contacting the realtor, Dad. I want to be there when you meet with him, though. I am a grown up, after all." He grinned, and I turned to Mom. "As for the flyers, I appreciate the offer, but that needs to wait. I'm just in the thinking stages. I'm not even sure my work is suitable for framing."

Mom guffawed. Dad snorted. Despite myself, I smiled. "You sound like farm animals. Seriously, though. I know a big part of my career revolved around photography, but not this type. I'm not sure I have that kind of artistic talent."

"Sweetheart, have you looked lately at the landscape

photos you took years ago? The ones we have displayed in the lobby?" Mom asked. "I can tell you our visitors have. We hear compliments about those beautiful shots every day. Even requests to purchase them."

"You could definitely sell them," Dad said. "No doubt about it."

I felt a surge of confidence. Still, my parents agreed to take it easy. I'd always been a kid who turned south when anyone tried to force her north, so my parents knew better than anyone to let me find my own way toward this decision.

During dessert—the most delicious chocolate and strawberry cake ever created by motherkind—I got a text from Tonya. *Did you tell your dad about the calls?*

Ugh. I was riding high on talk of my photography and definitely didn't want to broach the topic of anonymous threats right now. *Soon,* I responded.

She sent an angry-faced emoji, followed by *I'm calling him myself at noon tomorrow.*

I didn't bother to respond. Instead, I made small talk with my parents as we cleared the table and did the dishes. Finally, Woody's patience had eroded. He nudged my thigh persistently.

"Poor baby," Mom said. "He thinks Carl will be outside waiting for you."

"I hope he's right," I said.

After hugs and cheek kisses, Woody and I headed down the stairs. I waved to Jamal at the desk and stepped through the sliding doors into the dark, moonless night.

Woody's eyes searched for his fur brother in the shadows. Tree limbs rustled. I could see the frosty puff of my breath. As we neared the cabin, I noticed my porch light was out. I'd need to mention that to Dad in the morning.

Three feet from the door, Woody stopped in his tracks. His tail stiffened, and the hair rose on his neck. I craned my neck and listened, but heard nothing.

With a screech, Carl leapt from the darkness and onto the porch. Relief washed through me, followed immediately by apprehension as I heard a low growl from Woody's throat. He took a tentative step toward the cabin.

And that's when I noticed it.

The door to my cabin was ajar.

29

I pushed Woody behind me and crept toward the cabin door, listening for sounds of a trespasser within. Only silence—and darkness—seeped through the opening.

I tried to remember leaving the cabin earlier. Had I neglected to pull the door all the way closed? Was this a matter of simple negligence?

I thought about the crackling sound we'd heard on our way to dinner—before Carl's abrupt sprint into the forest. At the time, I'd written it off as a deer foraging for an evening snack. Perhaps the noise had been something more nefarious. After all, I had rubbed a few people the wrong way over the past few days. The anonymous call replayed in my mind, the mechanical threat.

I told myself I was getting worked up over nothing. What would I do if I were back in D.C.? I'd put on my big girl panties and handle things.

Taking a deep breath, I snaked my arm through the opening and felt around for the light switch. Brightness surged inside the cabin.

Still no sound. No movement.

Then Carl scurried through my legs and into the cabin. I yell-whispered, "Carl, get back here!" But one thing I was quickly learning about cats, or at least the one who lived with me: They were not especially obedient. Then again, neither was my dog. Maybe I should consider the common denominator.

It was time to bite the bullet. Figuratively speaking, I hoped. The hinges squeaked as I pushed open the door and strode into the cabin, hoping I exhibited courageousness I didn't actually feel.

Carl crouched on the table like a demon cat, eyes glowing red and ears flat against his head. Otherwise, the room appeared empty.

But not undisturbed. My eyes scanned the floor, where the contents of my dresser drawers had been dumped. Clothing lay in clumps, and papers were strewn across the floor.

This wasn't the product of an errant gust of wind. Someone had been inside my cabin. Might still be inside, I realized with a start.

I nudged the door closed with my foot and grabbed the fireplace poker. Then I edged into the bathroom. Wrenching back the shower curtain, I thrust the poker forward to impale any lurking prowler. A spider the size of a pinhead scuttled toward the drain.

Turning back to the main room, I dropped to my knees and bent my face to the floor. No intruders skulked beneath the bed. As I crouched there on all fours, Woody ambled over and licked my cheek as if to rebuke me for overreacting. "Whatever, you big chicken," I told him. "I saw you quaking back there, just waiting for me to take the lead. Great protector you are." He wagged and smiled, tongue lolling. Carl joined us, his body swaying gracefully as he pressed against Woody's hip. "And what about you, cat? Did you see someone out there earlier? Were you trying to chase off a prowler?" Carl just stared at me.

I replaced the poker and rested my hands on my hips to assess the damage. It appeared to be a surface mess, nothing more. My computer was intact, and my camera lay on the table where I had left it. The television rested in its usual spot atop the armoire. As far as I could tell, all my belongings were accounted for.

Then the cat hopped onto the bed, scrambling across the quilt.

I realized the yearbooks I'd borrowed from the library were missing. And in their place was a white piece of paper, with three words scrawled in thick black marker. YOU'RE AT RISK.

Beside the note lay a tiny blue flower.

Twenty minutes later, Woody and Carl relaxed by the fireplace, as if nothing out of the ordinary had happened. Dad, Mom, Detective Sanchez, and I stood shoulder to shoulder in a semicircle around the bed, as if preparing for an exorcism. Sanchez wore latex gloves, and he held up the threatening note. "Once again, did any of you touch this?"

"Asked and answered," I said. "I already told you we didn't."

I was feeling particularly defensive because I was already in the doghouse with my parents. The content of the note— *You're at risk*—had forced my hand, and I'd told them about the anonymous calls. My father had given me a stern look and lapsed into that disappointed silence that used to get under my skin as a kid. My mother had gasped and wrung her hands as if I'd been shot at. And here was Sanchez holding the note up again, rubbing salt in the wound.

But he took my tone in stride. "Not even when you first found it?"

"I guarantee you I did not, have not, and will not touch that note, Detective Sanchez." I glanced at Carl. "You're likely to find cat prints on it, though."

He nodded, and his eye swept around the cabin. "Call me Raul," he murmured offhandedly.

Those words shocked me even more than the note and the theft. Mr. Professional, Mr. All Business was allowing me to call him by his first name? I wondered if I had imagined it. "Okay. Raul." I tensed, waiting for the inevitable reprimand.

No such response. Instead, he glanced at me with what almost appeared to be kindness. "Take me through it again. Every detail you can remember, even if it seems insignificant."

I reported the series of occurrences as they flashed through my mind—the sound in the woods, Woody's behavior, Carl's sudden departure and later reappearance, the open door, my search of the cabin. When I mentioned that the little blue flower was the same kind I'd seen beside Victoria's body, he leaned toward the bed and scrutinized it.

I ended with my call to Mom and Dad, who had hurried over. Dad hadn't even slipped into his coat. Through my story, Raul watched me intently, and now he appeared... dare I say it?... impressed.

"Well, you shouldn't have gone in alone," he said. My mom nodded vigorously. I opened my mouth to protest, but he held up a hand. "Who do you think might be responsible?"

I said the first name that popped into my mind. "Parker Lyon." The three of them looked at me, eyebrows raised. "It just seems like his style. So passive-aggressive. Plus, he's living next door. Easy access."

A scowl lined my father's face. "He's not there now. I checked while we waited for Sanchez to arrive."

"Doesn't mean he didn't do it," I said. "If I were him, I wouldn't stick around either."

"Anyone else?"

I paused, thinking through my suspect list. Then I thought of Preston's call, Jameson's note of forgiveness. I told them about my former boss's concern. "I doubt it amounts to anything," I said. "Just thought you should know."

Raul scribbled in his notebook. "Seems unlikely. But I'll look into it."

"Let's not look past the elephant in the room," Dad said. "What about Kimberly? Maybe she murdered Victoria after all, and feels like you're getting too close to the truth."

"Could be," Raul said. "If it wasn't for her ankle monitor. Still, I'll double-check her whereabouts."

We stood in silence for a moment, considering the possibilities. "I just don't understand the yearbook aspect," Mom said finally. "I mean, why would someone break in to steal a set of books?"

"There's got to be more to it," Dad said. "Something we're just not seeing. There's no way the intruder broke in for that purpose alone."

"I don't know," I said thoughtfully. "Maybe it *was* just the yearbooks he's after. I've had this nagging feeling that there's something in them, but I can't quite grasp what exactly. It's been tugging at my subconscious. That's why I wanted them in the first place. I hoped if I kept looking through them, the answer might come to me. Maybe someone wanted to keep me from finding it."

"Seems like a long shot," Raul said. "See if you can get your hands on another set, though. Nothing to lose."

Mom offered to search the storage unit for my copies. Dad gave her a skeptical look, and we decided I should call Tonya to see if she had easier access to hers. Then Raul closed his notebook and tucked it into his coat pocket. "I think I have all I need for tonight. I'll go over this with Frank first thing in the morning." He turned to me. "In the meantime, I assume you'll be staying with your parents?"

I frowned. "Why would I?"

He crossed his arms and gave me a "duh" look. "For your safety, obviously. The note says it all. You're at risk. Somebody wants you running scared, at least."

"Exactly why I shouldn't capitulate," I said. "I'm not one to give in to threats. Besides, I don't believe anyone truly means me harm."

"I see," he said. "So Victoria's murderer is at heart a nice person who doesn't intend to hurt Callie Cassidy." He closed his eyes and took in a breath. When he exhaled, he focused on my parents. "I strongly recommend that Callie move out of this cabin for the time being, but of course I can't enforce that. I'll leave the three of you to figure it out."

He handed me a card with his cell phone number scrawled on the back and left. Dad folded his arms, and Mom pursed her lips. I knew then that arguing was pointless. But I argued anyway, and we finally negotiated a compromise. Woody, Carl, and I would bunk in my parents' guest room until Dad could have a security alarm installed in my cabin. Though I hated to knuckle under to a threat, I had to admit I took comfort in the idea of being nestled a few doors from my father—and his gun. Secretly, I wondered if even an alarm would make me feel secure here again.

No, only one thing would make me feel completely safe—catching the killer. I wished I could tell the intruder that the break-in had produced the opposite effect of what he'd intended. Because now I was even more determined to solve this crime.

30

A plump cream-colored duvet rested across my legs as I leaned against the queen-sized bed's padded headboard. Positioned as I was, right down the hall from my parents' bedroom, I felt a little like a teenager again. I giggled softly as I imagined trying to sneak out of the house without being caught.

In truth, though, there was nowhere I'd rather be. The room was warm and comfortable. The creatures were rolled into furry balls at my feet. A mug of mulled wine simmered on the nightstand.

A girl could get used to this kind of luxury.

I pulled my computer onto my lap to use as a makeshift desk and placed my legal pad on top. It was past eleven, but the break-in and subsequent relocation had rendered me wide awake—and more determined than ever to unmask the murderer.

First, I scanned the names I'd written across the yellow paper—Kimberly, Brian, Jessica, Summer, and Parker.

By virtue of being huddled over the body holding the murder weapon, Kimberly was still a top suspect. But given the ankle monitor currently strapped onto her leg, I didn't see how she could have broken into my cabin and stolen the yearbooks without the police knowing she'd left her house. Plus, why would she want to warn me off when I had signed on to help her?

As for Brian, he checked all the boxes for a person of interest. He was aggressive, with an obvious potential for violence. In light of Victoria's affair and their looming divorce, he possessed a clear motive for wanting her dead. And as far as framing Kimberly, odds were he'd found out Elyse was his biological daughter. He might either be incensed that the news had been kept from him or, more likely, furious that Kimberly had told his wife. And in spite of Tonya's assessment that Brian wasn't devious enough, I felt certain he had the skills necessary to procure and maneuver a distortion device and to make the anonymous calls. The only glitch was the alibi Sanchez—Raul—had discovered. Apparently, Brian had been in Denver with a lover at the time of the murder. Until that was a hundred percent confirmed, though, Brian stayed high on my list.

Jessica and Summer were a package deal, in my opinion. If one of them had been involved, so had the other. Dan had seen the two of them storm into the event center together, and from what Raul had told me, they were together the rest of the day. Besides, after having talked with each of them, I didn't believe they were murderers. Jessica was a spitfire, sure, and that might make her dangerous if we were looking at a crime of passion. But I couldn't see her plotting to kill one woman and frame the other. Besides, Summer was a pacifist, and I figured she kept Jessica grounded. I wouldn't go so far as to cross them off the list, but I wouldn't expend much energy looking into them, either.

And that brought me to Parker. Currently, he topped the list—mine, at least. As Kimberly's husband and Victoria's lover, he had means, motive, and opportunity. Dan had seen him at the Creekside the afternoon of the murder, and he could easily have rigged the door latch. Both Tonya and Jessica had mentioned his name when I'd asked about potential suspects. Living next door gave him easy access to my cabin, and he seemed just the type to make furtive phone calls. I replayed my conversation with Raul and couldn't remember him mentioning Parker's alibi. I decided the man warranted further investigation.

Then, much as I didn't want to, I turned my attention to a name that was absent from the list: Sam. With his catering gig, opportunity was a given, though eluding Elyse long enough to commit a murder might have presented a challenge. Motive was easy, too—Victoria knew Sam wasn't Elyse's biological father, and there was no doubt she would eventually reveal it to the world. But blood ties or not, Sam loved his daughter above all else. I couldn't see him framing the girl's mother. No, unless another clue surfaced that pointed in his direction, I simply refused to add his name. It might not be my most unbiased decision, but as I'd often been reminded, I wasn't a detective. I could suspect—or not suspect—whomever I chose.

After a moment's consideration, I uncapped my pen and added one more name: Sophie Demler. Reaching across the bed, I grabbed my bag and rummaged inside until I found the purloined pink notebook. I opened the cover and pulled out the group shot, with two faces sliced from the photo. Definitely the result of a fit of rage. I laid it aside and began exploring the notebook's pages. Most of the content seemed innocuous—upcoming social events, village squabbles, ideas for what looked like a novel.

But then things started to get interesting. I turned to a page on which Sophie had scribbled a series of initials and dates. *EP 03/13 KW&SP 08/12 KW & BD??* It didn't take a professional detective to decipher the code. Elyse Petrie, born March 2013. Kimberly and Sam hadn't gotten together until August 2012. Kimberly Wainwright and Brian Dunleavy had engaged in a fling prior to that.

Sophie had uncovered Kimberly's secret.

I thought of the lavender notecard in Victoria's office— a match for the boxed set at Sophie's house—and wondered if she'd revealed her discovery to Victoria.

If so, Sanchez, now in possession of the items on Victoria's desk, was likely already privy to Sam's secret. A wave of apprehension swept through me.

I turned to the next page and found an even more mysterious entry. *BW SIS?* Someone's initials? I riffled through names in my brain but couldn't come up with a match. I'd run them by Tonya tomorrow. She knew everyone in town. Perhaps she could figure it out.

That was the last page of the notebook, but one surprise still awaited. A piece of copy paper had been shoved into a pocket on the back cover. When I unfolded it, a tiny blue flower fluttered onto the comforter. My heart began to race.

I flattened the paper across my laptop to find a hand-drawn picture of a tombstone. The lettering on the monument read, RIP SOPHIE'S SCOOP. Beneath the drawing were three familiar words: YOU'RE AT RISK!

The threat, so reminiscent of the calls I'd received and the note left in my cabin, could have provided the impetus for Sophie to so suddenly leave town. Sanchez needed to know about this.

I picked up my phone to call him, but I hesitated. It was nearly midnight. Was this discovery urgent enough to disturb the detective's slumber? The note had to have been delivered to Sophie several days ago. In the interim, she had gotten herself to a safe place. At least, that's what her packed bag and missing toiletries suggested.

One way or the other, there was little Sanchez could do about it tonight. The call could wait until morning. Better yet, I'd stop by the police station after my breakfast meeting with Kimberly and hand over the entire notebook.

I wondered if Tonya had heard from Sophie since our visit to her house, but I didn't want to text or call her this late either. I was at loose ends, wanting to do something productive, but constrained by the late hour. Then it occurred to me that Sophie probably had a social media presence. Like the Las Vegas strip, the internet was perpetually open for business.

I booted up the laptop and opened Facebook, but as soon as I pulled up her page, I realized I'd struck out. There had been no activity since Friday afternoon, when she'd posted a photo of the Snowflake Swirl preparations. Since she'd been missing in action when Mom had tried to contact her Saturday morning, I had to assume she'd received the threat and skedaddled out of town Friday night.

After stewing over Sophie's timeline another ten minutes, I felt my eyes getting heavy and my brain turning sluggish. I put the laptop and notebook on the nightstand and switched off the bedside lamp. Then I snuggled beneath the covers and let my mind empty itself of murder and intrigue.

It would all be waiting for me in the morning.

31

Kimberly's house was situated in an upscale neighborhood west of the lower village. A car was parked at her curb, so I stopped in front of the house next door. Through the windshield, I conducted a quick assessment of the Lyon home. Beige stucco covered a two-story façade accented with stone and rustic wood. It was tasteful and suitable for a small mountain village, but it certainly didn't rise to mansion status. It was the stunning view of the Rockies that likely valued the house in the seven-figure range. I'd heard Kimberly inherited a sizable sum from her absentee father when he died. She'd either sunk it into this house or had a mortgage that would make me shudder.

Two doors down, I noticed a man shoveling his front walk. He was bundled up and wore a ski cap low on his forehead, but when I squinted and leaned toward my windshield, I saw that it was Brian Ratliff. So the Lyons and the Ratliffs were neighbors. No doubt that made for some interesting—and awkward—interactions at the mailbox.

I got out of the car and scuttled up the sidewalk, hoping Brian wouldn't catch sight of me. I was in no mood for another confrontation. My hand was still smarting from the last punch.

As I reached the front door and lifted my hand to knock on the solid oak, it swung open, and I found myself face to face with Dr. Lowell. "Oh," she said. Her expression of surprise mirrored my own.

She stepped outside and closed the door. "How nice to see you, Callie. Is Kimberly expecting you?"

I held up a bag of bagels I'd pilfered from my parents' lodge. "We have a breakfast meeting."

"Ah. I guess that means you've decided to pursue your investigation. How is it going?"

I glanced over my shoulder. Brian was gone, and I felt my shoulders relax. "It's…interesting. Did you hear someone broke into my cabin last night?"

Her eyebrows rose. "No. I went to bed early last night and came straight here this morning for…"

Her voice trailed off, and I assumed she didn't want to tell me she was seeing Kimberly professionally. "A house call?" I asked.

"A visit," she said. "But tell me more about this break-in."

The door opened behind her, and Kimberly stuck her head out. "Callahan? Come in. I'm starving." She looked at the bag in my hand. "That's not bagels, is it? I asked you to bring healthy food. All those carbs…" She wrinkled her nose.

"I'm not your personal shopper, Kimberly. Take it or leave it."

Dr. Lowell tried to hide a smile. "Well," she said, "I'll leave you two to it."

"See you tomorrow," I said. "I'll fill you in then."

Frowning, Dr. Lowell shot a glance at Kimberly. I realized she was concerned about my confidentiality. I waved. "It's okay. I don't mind Kimberly knowing I'm a client."

"All right, then," she said. "Tomorrow. But if you need to talk before then, feel free to give me a call."

She stepped off the porch, and Kimberly grabbed my arm and pulled me inside, taking the bag from my hand. "I'm starving," she said, hurrying down the hall.

"Thank you for coming, Callie," I said in a falsetto voice. "Can I take your coat? How about some coffee?"

She threw a glare over her shoulder and marched into the kitchen. When I walked in behind her and looked around, my mouth dropped open. I almost had to pinch myself to make sure I hadn't crossed over.

There was no other way to put it. The kitchen was white. Not cream, not eggshell, not ivory—bright and blindingly white.

To be fair, soft gray highlights rippled through the marble floors, and the appliances were stainless steel. But those were the only splashes of color. White quartz countertops. White pendants hanging above the bar. White leather seating surrounding a white-and-glass table topped with white placemats. White lacquered cabinets.

This kitchen might be as close as Kimberly would ever get to heaven.

"Wow," I said. "I may need to get my sunglasses."

Kimberly didn't even crack a smile. I studied her more closely.

It wasn't a pretty sight. Her hair hung limp and tangled around her shoulders. Her face was pale, and shadows beneath her eyes gave her a ghoulish mien. I didn't think I'd ever seen her without makeup.

"You look awful," I said.

She took two small plates from a cabinet and set them on the countertop. "Thanks," she said. "I look like I feel."

I shrugged out of my coat and draped it across the back of a white barstool. Despite myself, I felt a little sorry for her. "Here, let me do that," I said, opening the bag and doling out bagels. "They're blueberry. That's healthy, right?"

She slouched into a seat at the table. "I made coffee," she said, her voice as flat as her hair. "Help yourself."

I poured myself a cup of dark brew and carried it to the table. When I'd settled myself into a chair, I leaned across and grasped one of her hands. "Kimberly. What's going on?"

Tears filled her eyes, and she dropped her head onto her arms. Her shoulders shook with sobs. I patted her back and waited. After a minute or two, she lifted her head and swiped the back of her hand beneath her running nose. I scanned the kitchen and retrieved a tissue from a white lacquered box, handing it over. "Talk to me," I said.

She dabbed at her eyes and blew her nose. "Everything is falling apart," she said. "Parker and I are done. My boutique is history. And everyone thinks I killed Victoria."

After one last crying jag, she finally seemed cried out. "But the worst part is, my own daughter hates me."

"She doesn't hate you," I said, but the words sounded hollow.

Her voice rose to a screechy pitch. "She does! She came here last night to grab a bunch of clothes and said she wasn't ever coming back."

I didn't know what to say. In reality, I figured their relationship, if not severed, would be grievously damaged for a long time to come. Nothing I could say would soften that blow. So I steered the conversation in a different direction. "I've been doing some digging. Want to hear what I've got?"

She snuffled and took a bite of her bagel. "Please. Tell me you've found something that will get this thing off me." She pulled up her pant leg to reveal the ankle monitor.

First, I mentioned Parker's name. She shook her head adamantly. "You're wasting your time on him," she said. "He may have cheated on me, and our marriage may be over, but I will never believe he murdered Victoria and framed me."

I started to interject, but she held up a hand. "I won't listen to anything regarding Parker. Move on."

A wave of annoyance nearly convinced me to pack up my bagels and leave, but I looked at her again. She was so forlorn. I'd probably be hard pressed to believe my husband could betray me like that either. I'd let her slide.

"All right," I said. "In my opinion, Brian Ratliff is a top

contender. His wife was having an affair and proceeding with a divorce, so there's definitely motive for murder. And as far as framing you…"

I hesitated. Her face colored, and she looked out the window. "Sam told you, didn't he?"

I nodded. Kimberly took a deep breath. "I was hoping it wouldn't have to come out," she said. "For Elyse's sake."

"I understand. But she knows now, so let's not have any more secrets."

"Okay," she said, her voice barely above a whisper. "It was such a long time ago. I was so ashamed. All I wanted was to bury the whole issue. I'd even halfway convinced myself Sam really was her father. Then when I found out Victoria and Parker were…well, I lost it, and the secret just spilled out. When I realized what I'd told her, it was too late. The damage was done."

She got up and went to the coffee maker, taking her time to refill her mug. She tried to lock eyes with me and couldn't do it. Instead, she stared out the window again, her lip trembling.

I felt a tiny bit of empathy. She'd made a horrible mistake, some wretched choices. But then, hadn't almost everyone?

"Listen, Kimberly, the introspection and guilt are going to have to wait," I said. "Our immediate concern should be figuring out who killed Victoria. Let's get back to Brian. He probably blames you for destroying his marriage, so I doubt he'd have any compunction about setting you up for his wife's murder. In my mind, that puts him high on the suspect list."

She thought about it for a moment and finally nodded. "It makes sense, in a sick way. But didn't Detective Sanchez say Brian had an alibi?"

"It's sketchy," I said. "We'll see how that plays out. In the meantime, he's the one I'm focused on. Him and…I know you don't want to hear it, but I'm going to look hard at Parker too."

"Do what you have to." She sighed. "So, Brian and

Parker. That's all we've got?"

I shoveled half a bagel in my mouth, chewed furiously, and washed it down with coffee. "I've eliminated a couple of people," I said, wiping crumbs from my chin. "And I'd like to have a word with Sophie Demler, but no one seems to know where she is." I snapped my fingers. "That reminds me. Do the initials BW mean anything to you? Or SIS?"

She frowned. "No. Should they?"

"Just a puzzle I'd like to solve. Probably nothing to do with the murder." I rose and put on my coat. "Anyway, that's today's update. I want you to spend some time thinking about any suspects we might have missed. Especially anyone who might have held a long-term grudge against you and Victoria. I just have a feeling everything is linked to the past somehow."

Her expression was skeptical. "Doesn't seem like someone would hold on to a grudge this long."

"You did," I responded, and she flinched.

She walked me to the door and leaned in like she was going to hug me. I pretended to be fiddling with my gloves. "By the way, Kimberly, that ankle monitor doesn't mean you can't take care of yourself. Throw a plastic bag over it and get in the shower. You'll feel better. We all will."

That elicited an actual laugh. But as she closed the door, I saw her sniff her armpit.

32

I drove my red Honda Civic through the neighborhood and down the street to the police station, again finding a spot in front of the door. I grabbed my bag, said a little prayer that Sanchez wouldn't rake me over the coals for stealing Sophie's notebook, and headed inside.

The same woman I'd seen Sunday sat behind the reception desk, Betsy Purcell according to her nameplate. She looked past me hopefully. "Is Chief Cassidy with you?"

"Not today. Just me." I smiled. "What a lovely sweater."

She beamed. I knew from experience that the person truly in charge in any bureaucracy was the admin, so I always did whatever I could to make nice.

"Thank you," she said, fingering the cuff and lowering her voice conspiratorially. "I paid more than I should have, but I couldn't resist."

"Money well spent," I said. "The color sets off your eyes."

Her cheeks pinked up, and she gave me another broad smile. "You're so sweet. Must take after your father. What can I help you with, Ms. Cassidy?"

"I was hoping to see Detective Sanchez. It's a matter of some importance."

I saw the flash of curiosity and figured she and Fran from Quicker Liquor were fast friends. "I'm afraid he's not here at the moment. If you have something for him or want to leave a detailed message, I'll be happy to pass it along."

"Thank you, Ms. Purcell, but I really need to speak with him personally. Do you know where he is? Or when he'll be back?"

She chuckled softly. "He's not one to give details on his whereabouts. Very secretive." Her eyes sparkled as she whispered her next words. "Takes himself awfully seriously. But if you tell him I said so, I'll deny every word."

I smiled. "All right. I'll try back later." I started toward the door but turned back. "What about Chief Laramie? Is he around?"

"No, the Chief attends a tri-county meeting every Wednesday morning. He'll be in this afternoon." Her brow furrowed. "Is this an emergency, Ms. Cassidy? I can page Detective Sanchez if you need me to."

I shook my head. "No, it can wait, thanks. I appreciate your help."

I hadn't been inside long enough for the interior of the car to get cold, but I turned up the heater anyway, letting the warmth blast across my feet as I considered my next move. The presence of Sophie's notebook weighed on me, but at least I could say I'd tried to turn it over to Raul. It wasn't my fault he was gallivanting around somewhere, unavailable to receive the evidence.

I decided to make a pit stop at *The Gazette* before heading back to the lodge. I wanted to ask for her help with the acronym I'd found in Sophie's notebook. It would mean divulging my…theft, but so be it. Someone needed to hear my confession. It might as well be Tonya, who was responsible for leading me into the temptation of Sophie's desk in the first place.

The newspaper office was located in a strip mall a couple of minutes outside the lower village, between a dry cleaner and a furniture refinishing place. During the short drive, I rehearsed how I'd tell Tonya that I'd taken Sophie's notebook. I didn't want to face her wrath, but she needed to know about the threat to her employee.

The office was small and sparse, consisting of an open space holding three desks, two of which were currently unoccupied. Behind them was a tiny office with a glass door. A young man with a pencil clutched between his teeth tapped away at a keyboard. "Help you?" he said without looking up.

"I'm here to see Tonya," I said. No response. I raised my voice. "Tonya Stephens. The editor. Your boss."

His eyes flicked up and back to the keyboard. Then he did a double take, and the pencil dropped from his mouth and clattered to the floor. "Wait, are you—?"

"Callie Cassidy," I said. "Would you let her know I'm here?"

He gazed at me with an unreadable expression, either starstruck or slightly stoned. Before I could decide which, the office door opened and Tonya stepped out, resplendent in tailored black slacks and a mauve satin blouse. "Look what the cat dragged in," she said. "I wasn't aware your car still functioned, sweet potato." She turned to the young man, who was still staring at me. "What's the problem, Phil? You've never met a Felden Prize winner before? Close your mouth, my friend."

I smiled at him. "Hi, Phil. Good to meet you."

"Yes, it's good. We meet." He blushed. "I mean to say, it's a pleasure to meet you, Ms. Cassidy."

"Please, call me Callie." I gestured to his computer. "I'll let you get back to your story. Don't want you missing a deadline on my account. I've heard your boss is a vicious taskmaster."

Tonya laughed and waved me into her office. Phil's eyes followed as I walked inside and shut the door behind me.

"You seem to have an admirer," she said, gesturing toward Phil.

"Since when did you start hiring twelve-year-olds?"

She grinned. "We're getting old, sweetpea. Everyone looks twelve to us. Phil is actually twenty-two, just graduated from college. Getting his feet wet here in our little town before catapulting into a bigger posting. Probably sees you as a means to an end."

"Thanks a lot," I said, settling into the lone guest chair. I looked around. It didn't take long. The office was the size of a broom closet.

Tonya sat behind her desk and followed my gaze. "It's not as magnificent as *The Sentinel*, but it's mine," she said, leaning back in her leather chair. "I admit, I'm shocked to see you here. Not as shocked as Phil, apparently, but still. What brings you to my humble place of business?"

"Can't a girl just drop by to see her best friend at work?"

"Good one," she said. "But let's get real. What's wrong?"

I inhaled and puffed my cheeks as I blew out the breath. Might as well rip off the bandage. "I took something from Sophie's house yesterday. Her reporter's notebook."

She sat up straight and lifted her eyebrows. Silence stretched between us. I wriggled under her sharp gaze. "Aren't you going to say anything?"

"What are you expecting? Absolution?"

"I don't know...I guess...I..."

She leaned back again and crossed her legs, a sly smile creasing her face. "Callie, you are not the mastermind you think you are. I saw you slip the notebook into your bag. I wondered if you'd ever tell me."

"You knew?"

"Of course. I'm a journalist, just like you. Nothing gets by me."

I narrowed my eyes. "You just wanted to see me squirm."

"One of the little pleasures that makes life worth living. Anyway, I assume you found something in the notebook worth sharing?"

I pulled the pink book from my bag, opened it to the pages near the end, and pointed. She scanned the initials and dates. "So Sophie found out Brian is Elyse's biological father," she mused.

"You knew about that too?"

"Sam told me last night. He said he'd already talked to you about it and wanted me to know before the news spread all over town. But it seems Sophie was already aware of this little nugget of information." She flipped to the page with *BW SIS* scribbled on it. "What's this?"

I shrugged. "I was hoping you could decipher it."

She shook her head. "Not a clue."

I took the folded paper from the pocket in the back of the notebook and spread it in front of her. Her eyes went round when she saw the tombstone and the words *You're at Risk.*

"It seems you and Sophie have something in common," she said. "These are the same words your anonymous caller used."

I nodded. "I went by the police station to turn this over to Sanchez, but he wasn't in. I'll try again later. In the meantime, I thought you should know. Maybe you need to intensify your search into Sophie's whereabouts."

"I'll get on it right away." She pointed a finger at me. "As for you, girl, you need to take this seriously. It's lucky I got you this little gift."

She reached inside her desk drawer and pulled out her purse, digging inside before brandishing a small pink tube with a keyring attachment. At first, I thought she was handing me a fancy feminine hygiene product, but further examination revealed a flip top and a trigger. "Pepper spray?" I asked.

"I'd like to keep you around for a while."

I smiled. "I'm not going anywhere." Just the same, I shoved the canister in the pocket of my coat.

"I have something else for you." She reached behind her chair, hoisted a bag, and set it on her desk. I peeked inside and saw four yearbooks. "Don't let these get stolen. I couldn't bear to lose the ego-boosting words my classmates penned in those pages."

"Such as, 'Have a great summer'?" I said, opening the cover of our freshman yearbook.

"They get better as the years pass. More mature and sincere. There's even one in the senior volume that refers to me as a BFF. Oh, wait. The person who plumbed those emotional depths was you."

A surge of affection washed through me. I got up and pulled Tonya into a hug. "Do you know how much I adore you?"

She patted my cheek. "Words for a yearbook, my sweet. All this sentiment makes it hard to kick you out, but I have to get back to work. Especially now that I have to search for a missing employee."

"Call me if you find anything."

"Same to you," she said. "And Callie, seriously. Don't be complacent. Watch your back."

33

P hil ran around his desk, insisting on carrying the bag of yearbooks to my car. Over my shoulder, I saw Tonya smirk. Phil and I made small talk, and as he tucked the bag into the passenger seat, he asked if I would be amenable to an interview. "You'd make a great feature story," he said. "You know, hometown success and all…"

Though I'd told Tonya weeks ago I wasn't interested in being the subject of scrutiny, this kid's puppy dog eyes melted my resistance. I told him I'd think about it. Between him and the young journalists at the high school, I was starting to forget the horrible lapse in my journalistic judgment that had brought me back here in the first place, tail between my legs. I wasn't sure I was ready to revisit all that for the sake of this young man's ambitions, but perhaps it would be healing.

One way or the other, though, there would be no interview until Victoria's murder was solved. As I drove back to the lodge, I reflected on the events of the past few days. Finding Victoria's body. Agreeing to help Kimberly. Getting two anonymous phone calls. Pilfering Sophie's notebook. Then there was last night's break in. Events seemed to be escalating. When I walked through the doors into the lodge, my plan was to take a quick hike and then hole up in the guest room and continue investigating. But my father had other ideas.

Mom sat behind the registration desk, chatting with Mrs. Finney. "Don't take off your coat," she said to me. She pointed to Dad, who was stoking the fire in the Great Room. "Your father has been waiting for you."

He spotted me and strode across the room, grabbing his coat from the rack beside the door. "No time like the present," he said.

"Where are we going?"

"The gallery, of course. I talked to Willie Wright this morning. He's on standby in his office. Just let me give him a quick call."

Dad kept the tone light as we walked into the village, and I sensed he was trying to calm my nerves. The security company would be installing an alarm that very afternoon, he said, so I was free to move back into the cabin. He asked if I would be available to supervise the installment, since he needed to drive into Denver for supplies.

"Sure," I said. "Nothing else on my dance card."

As we reached the empty shop, my pulse rate accelerated. *No need for anxiety,* I told myself. *We're just looking.* A smooth-looking thirty-something man in a black suit approached us and shook hands with Dad before turning to me. "You must be Callie," he said, introducing himself as William "Call Me Willie" Wright. "Let me show you around."

The three of us walked through the open space. As Willie talked, I envisioned walls covered with landscapes such as those I'd shot yesterday. In my fantasy, customers moved from one framed, spotlighted photo to the next, murmuring appreciation and pulling out checkbooks.

Dad touched my shoulder, retrieving me from the daydream. "What do you think?" he asked.

I tried to play it cool. "It has possibilities."

He grinned, knowing me well enough to read the enthusiasm hidden beneath the nonchalance. The realtor must have sensed it too. He said, "Let's go to my office and talk details."

Call Me Willie's office was housed directly above the gallery space. It was a welcoming place, designed to make clients feel comfortable about handing over their life savings. Willie took our coats and offered coffee, which we declined, then led us to a pair of wing chairs. He stepped behind an oak desk large enough to make him seem trustworthy and sank into an expensive leather chair.

We discussed the lease price, and Willie said the company that owned the place might be flexible since the shop had been vacant for several months. Even if that didn't happen, the asking price seemed reasonable enough. He tried to persuade me to commit right away, but pressure was always a counterproductive approach with me, and I told him I'd let him know. Dad and I got back into our coats, shook hands all around, and promised to talk soon.

At the bottom of the stairs, Dad draped an arm around my shoulder. "What do you think, Sundance?"

"I don't know, Dad. It's a big decision. I need time to think about it."

Always careful with his words, he was silent for a beat. "It's good to be a thinker and a planner," he said at last. "But sometimes it's a relief to just be a doer. To take the plunge and let yourself have something you want without overanalyzing and sucking the joy out of it."

I opened my mouth to protest, but he squeezed my shoulder. "My two cents. Take it or leave it. Let's head back. I need to head to Denver so I can get home before dark."

As we turned toward the lodge, footsteps sounded behind us. I swiveled to see Sam jogging toward us from the Snow Plow Chow.

"Hey, Butch," he said. The men shook hands, and Sam looked at me. "Got a minute?"

"You go ahead," I said to Dad. "I'll be along in a bit."

He nodded. "See you this evening. I think your mother is expecting you for dinner again."

I watched for a moment as he walked away, tall and strong, the daddy who had always taken care of me.

"He's a good man," Sam said, and I nodded. "Listen, Callie, I heard about what happened last night. I've been worried. I was going to call you, but when I saw you and your dad out here, I decided to check in person."

His voice sounded tired, and I looked more closely at him. He wore jeans and a red plaid shirt, hair swept back and blue eyes bright. He'd run outside without a coat. His only bow to the weather was a knitted red scarf wrapped around his neck. He was handsome as ever, except for the puffy bags under his eyes. He, too, had been through the wringer the past day or so. I should have reached out to him last night, but with all the chaos, I'd let it slide.

"That's sweet of you, but I'm the one who should be checking on you. How did things go with Elyse?"

"Not as bad as I expected. From what she told me, she'd suspected the truth before the Ratliff boys even said anything. She's furious with her mother for all the years of lying. But she said I'm her dad, and that's all there is to it. I think we'll be fine."

"Oh, Sam, I'm so glad," I said. "I knew she'd feel that way, but it's got to be a relief to have the secret out in the open. I...um...talked to Kimberly this morning. She was quite upset. I guess she and Elyse had an epic blowout."

He frowned. "I heard. But Elyse asked me to stay out of it, and I told her I would. I'm supportive of their relationship—Elyse needs her mom in her life—but I'm not going to push her. The healing will have to take place on her timeline."

A ruthless gale whipped Sam's hair like a bird's nest. He wrapped his arms around himself and shivered. "Listen," I said, "it's way too cold for you to be out here in your shirt sleeves. Get back inside. I don't want to be responsible for you getting pneumonia."

He grinned. "I'm not going anywhere until you tell me how you're holding up. The break-in—you must have been terrified."

"I'm fine. Really. It's no big deal. I stayed with my parents last night, and Dad is having a security alarm installed in the cabin this afternoon. No worries."

"Good." A lock of hair rested on his forehead. I resisted the urge to reach up and brush it back. Sam gestured toward the cafe. "Want to come in for some hot chocolate?"

I smiled. "Tempting as that is, I need to get back and rescue the creatures from my mother." I touched the end of his scarf. "She's taken up knitting. I'm afraid she may be fitting them for sweaters."

That familiar sexy grin spread across his face. "Rain check, then. But make it soon." He leaned toward me and brushed his lips against my cheek. Then I felt his breath in my ear. "Take care of yourself, Callie. And let other people take care of you too."

He pulled away and locked eyes with me, then walked back toward the cafe. I stood for a moment, rooted to the spot, hormones sweeping through me. Was I really reexperiencing these same old feelings twenty-five years later?

I drew a deep breath and pushed those thoughts away. I had too much to do, too much to think about, to chase romance.

I took one last glance through the gallery window before I started home. My heart pounded. It was overwhelming to be considering this giant career change. I wasn't worried about the money. My frugal nature had allowed me to stockpile a decent percentage of my earnings. Also, my grandmother had bequeathed her only grandchild, me, a sizable nest egg when she passed several years ago. She had left her only child, my father, an even bigger chunk, enabling him to buy the resort. Did I dare to follow in his footsteps and pursue a dream I never even knew I'd had?

Despite Preston's encouragement, I'd decided I

wouldn't—couldn't—return to my career. My last assignment had irretrievably damaged my passion for journalism. Could I find a new passion here in Rock Creek Village?

As I strolled down Evergreen Way, my mind reeled with indecision. It was an unusual state for me. My tendency was to weigh options once and immediately choose a path, never looking back. In retrospect, that method hadn't always served me well. And now it had brought me to the crux of my indecisiveness.

I was scared.

Scared to make the wrong choice. Scared to add yet another regret to my resume. Scared to embark on a new journey.

But ultimately, I was even more scared to do nothing, to continue the way I had the past month, or even the past year.

My mother was right. It was time to forgive myself and move forward.

When I arrived at the lodge to retrieve my things, Mom was still behind the registration desk, now with the phone pressed to her ear. Just as well. I wanted time to myself to call the realtor and revel in the prospect of my new life.

I went upstairs and greeted the creatures. Then I gathered the few things I'd brought over last night, and after a wave to Mom on the way out, the three of us headed back to the cabin. Woody and Carl chased circles around each other and gallivanted through the trees. I soaked in my surroundings. To the north, mountains jutted upward from the horizon to the sky. Above me, dark clouds marched toward the valley, presaging an impending storm. My parents' lodge, with its gabled roof, wide eaves, and intricately carved balconies, beckoned to visitors. Behind it, Mt. O'Connell glimmered proudly.

And below me, Evergreen Way and its picturesque shops,

one of which would soon become the cornerstone of my new life.

Along with exhilaration, I felt a deep sense of peace. That's how I knew I was making the right decision. No more fear.

I dug my key from my pocket and opened the door. The creatures rushed in ahead of me. I settled the litterbox in the corner, positioned the camera on the table, and shuffled through my purse for my phone. Time to make the big phone call.

I dialed the realtor's number. Call Me Willie said he was thrilled to hear from me and had been expecting my call. Just let him contact the owner, settle on a price, and draw up the paperwork. Could I meet at ten tomorrow morning?

The only thing on my agenda was my nine o'clock appointment with Dr. Lowell, whose office was a few steps away, so we made it a date.

In less than twenty-four hours, my new life would begin.

I sprawled into the armchair, a little dizzy. Carl had tired of playtime and swatted Woody's nose, so the dog turned to the next best thing: me. We spent a few minutes engaged in a fierce tug-of-war competition, which Woody won.

"You, my friend, are a lucky guy," I told him. "When I die, I want to come back as a dog owned by someone like me."

Then I hugged him, feeling like a pretty lucky creature myself.

34

I figured it would be nice to begin this new chapter of my life without an unsolved murder hanging over my head, but I didn't have a clear plan of attack. I turned on the computer and skimmed through Victoria's Facebook page again—for what, I wasn't sure. First, I scanned the comments. Not much new. More condolences, and a few more observations regarding the dead woman's character. Again, nothing hotheaded enough to suggest murderous intent.

I shuffled through Victoria's photos again, landing on the New Year's Eve shot of Parker ogling Victoria's cleavage. I knew she had chosen to display this particular photo as a way to humiliate and hurt her former best friend. I gazed at the expression on Victoria's face—arrogant and hateful. Gleeful at the prospect of causing pain. It was a countenance I'd seen many times during our high school days. Again, a tickle crawled at the outskirts of my brain. The look on Victoria's face triggered some old memory, one that ached to be released.

But for now, it was out of reach. Sighing, I went to the kitchen and made myself a cup of hot chocolate. Woody roused himself from his nap and whined at the door, wanting a bathroom outing I was sure he didn't really need. Still, a breath of fresh air might invigorate my brain cells. I tossed my coat over my shoulders and carried my mug to the front porch.

The dog scurried off into the trees, and I brushed a thin layer of snow off the rocking chair before sitting down. I watched the snow falling and rocked, willing my mind to make whatever connection I was missing.

I hadn't gotten far in my quest when Woody bounded back onto the porch and stood stiffly beside me, a low rumble coming from his throat. I shook myself from my thoughts to find Parker Lyon standing on the sidewalk, watching me. My hand went to my pocket and wrapped around the canister of pepper spray I'd stashed there.

"I come in peace," Parker said, lifting his hands as if in surrender.

Woody growled again, and Parker took a step back. "Sit," I said to Woody. For once in his doggie life, he complied.

"What are you doing here?" I glanced down the sidewalk to see if anyone was within shouting distance in case I needed rescuing, but there was no one in sight. I'd have to rely on the ferocious guard dog beside me and the pepper spray in my pocket.

I figured it would be enough.

Parker wore a gray wool coat over black slacks and dress shoes. He hadn't put on a hat, and his fashionably cut blond hair was damp with snow. He clasped his manicured fingers in front of him, wearing a repentant expression on a face that had seen more than its share of skin care products. Here was a man who took meticulous care of his appearance, even in the wake of his wife's arrest and his girlfriend's death. It was still nearly impossible to envision him as a threat, but that's likely what Victoria thought, too, before he thrust a letter opener into her chest. If, indeed, he did.

"I want to apologize for how I spoke to you yesterday. Perhaps explain my behavior." He looked up at the falling snow and pulled his coat tighter around him. "Could we possibly step inside?"

"Are you kidding? You think I'm letting you in my home?" I flashed to last night's break-in. "But then again, I guess you've already been in my home. By the way, I want those yearbooks back. They belong to the high school library."

Confusion crossed his face, and he pursed his lips as if trying to decide just how nutty I was. When he spoke, he enunciated slowly, the way people do with someone who doesn't speak their language. "I don't understand what you're saying. But I admit I acted atrociously. It was uncharacteristic of me, ungentlemanly. It won't happen again."

The opportunity was too good to pass up. If I could placate him, maybe I could extract some information. I softened my expression and tone. "I know my digging into all this has made you angry."

The words spilled from him now like a child trying to get a parent's approval. "No, no, not anymore. Well, at first yes, because Kimberly said you'd accused me of murder. But now I realize it's only right that you investigate. It even works in my favor. You can erase everyone's doubts about me. I want you to find the real killer and tell the world. And most importantly, that it wasn't me." Tears welled, brightening his blue eyes. He was either completely genuine or a skilled actor.

"Well, then. How about answering a few questions?"

"That's why I'm here. Ask me whatever you want. Give me a chance to defend myself."

A bitter wind swept a flurry of snowflakes across the porch, and I shivered with the chill. I made my decision and ushered Parker inside, gesturing toward the armchair. He edged past Woody and Carl, eyeing them warily, and sat on the edge of the chair without removing his coat.

I tossed my own coat over the dining chair, but not before I tucked the pepper spray into my palm. I lifted my laptop from the table and turned the screen to face Parker. "I was just looking at this photo on Victoria's Facebook page. You don't exactly present the portrait of Kimberly's loving husband here. Care to explain?"

His face reddened when he saw the photo, and he averted his eyes. "I'll tell you the whole sordid story. You'll think I'm a terrible cad, but I'm certain you will no longer suspect me of murdering Victoria."

Cad? I suppressed an urge to roll my eyes. Aside from former Ivy League frat boys in darkened cigar clubs, who used that word? Was Parker trying to impress with the image of an upper-class aristocrat?

He continued, unaware of my inner sarcasm. "Kimberly and I married twelve years ago…" He must have noticed my look of impatience because he held up a hand. "I know. Keep it brief. I don't intend to detail each of those years. That would be boorish."

Someone had studied for his SAT once upon a time.

A sudden forceful pounding interrupted his saga. "I'm expecting the security company," I told him, scrambling the three steps to the door.

But it wasn't security. At least, not in the form I'd been anticipating.

"Mrs. Finney," I said. Today she resembled a huge, stuffed teddy bear in her lavender faux fur coat and matching knit cap topped with a pom. Her face was tinted pink, except for the skin around her eyes. "What happened to your face? It looks like you're wearing a mask."

"Yes, dear, it's me. Just a little sunburned around my goggles. Forgot my bloody sunscreen when I went snowshoeing." The pleasant words did not match her firm tone and scowl as she twisted her head to peer around me before pushing her way inside. "Are you in danger, dear?"

"No, I'm fine." I closed the door. "Why do you ask?"

She glared at Parker through squinted eyes, and he squirmed under her scrutiny. Her arm shot forth, and a stubby purple-gloved finger pointed at him. "I was out for a stroll and saw this man outside your cabin. What do you have to say for yourself, Parker Lyon?"

"I… uh… well…"

"Mrs. Finney," I interjected, "Parker is here to persuade

me he didn't kill Victoria. I want to hear him out. It's all very civilized."

She dropped her arm to her side and relaxed. But just a bit. Then she turned her taut gaze to me. "Nevertheless, I'm not leaving here until he does."

My mouth gaped. When had this strange woman become my protector? It was slightly annoying, but also sort of sweet. I glanced at Parker and shrugged. Mrs. Finney wriggled out of her coat, removed her gloves, and yanked off her hat, tossing the winter wear across the foot of the bed. She pulled a chair from the table without taking her eyes off Parker. Her gaze was so fiery I thought she might unleash some pyrokinetic skills.

Then she smoothed her hair and settled primly onto the chair, back straight, ankles crossed, hands folded in her lap—the perfect British gentlewoman. "One mustn't play hide and seek in the garden of good and evil, young man."

Confusion lined Parker's well-tended face. "What? Who *are* you?"

"I am a force to be reckoned with. Now, get on with your story and keep it short. You've wasted enough of my Callie's time."

My Callie? More intimacy. Despite myself, I was growing rather fond of it. Meanwhile, Woody pranced over to Mrs. Finney, who stroked him with appropriate adoration. Since I had been relegated to second chair in this orchestra, I rotated a finger at Parker, signaling him to continue.

His story was predictable. When the company he worked for, the unfortunately monikered Rocky Insurance, relocated him to open a Rock Creek Village branch, he fell in love with Kimberly "at first sight." They'd married, and though Elyse never completely warmed to him, the union worked well. At least for the first ten years.

Then, Parker said, Kimberly developed an increasing obsession with Victoria. It was a rivalry born from a friendship based on a mutual feeling of superiority and disdain toward others—contingent on Kimberly's submissiveness. Kimberly's first rebellion—pre-Parker—had resulted in Elyse. Having the secret child of her friend's husband had allowed her to maintain the status quo for years.

But as Victoria's power in the village expanded, Kimberly grew restless, desperate for Victoria to know that she had covertly one-upped her. "It was a horrible time for me," Parker said. "All Kimberly could think about was herself."

Seemed to me they were a match made in hell.

Parker and Kimberly's marriage deteriorated, a casualty of the women's covert war. "Victoria was a constant presence in our lives that last year," he said. "There were three of us in the marriage. Figuratively speaking."

Until it became literal. One day Victoria showed up in Parker's office and seduced him, the two of them flailing about on the couch right above the boutique where Kimberly worked. He'd known it was a mistake right away, he said, but the damage was done. "She had me by the… you know. If I didn't capitulate to her demands, her whims, she threatened to tell Kimberly."

"Pathetic," Mrs. Finney murmured. Carl's furry head bounced up and down, as if he were agreeing with her assessment. Parker dropped his eyes to his lap.

"How long had the affair been going on?" I asked.

"Just a few months. We mostly…met…in her office. She'd prop open the back door. Expected me to sneak in through the staff entrance." He sniffed.

That explained the paper jammed into the door latch. It hadn't been left there by the murderer after all. But that didn't mean the killer hadn't made use of it.

"I tried to end the affair. I swear I did," he said. "But Kimberly found out before I could."

The smoldering volcano inside had erupted then. Kimberly could no longer keep her secret—Elyse's secret—to herself. She told Victoria everything.

Parker said he'd begged Kimberly to forgive him, even dropping to his knees. "She told me she wanted to try. But first, she said the two of us had to go to Victoria's office. She wanted to watch me tell Victoria it was over."

"And did you?"

"Yes. It was the most uncomfortable moment of my life. Victoria laughed at us, said good riddance. She said she'd already proven she could take whatever Kimberly had, whenever she wanted. Kimberly was so mad she was shaking. When we left, I tried to calm her down, but Victoria's taunting made that impossible. Kimberly told me she needed to make some decisions, and I should pack my things and get out of the house."

"And then…?" I prodded.

"I did as she said. I went to my office. After an hour or so, I tried to call Kimberly, but she didn't answer. I texted her but still got no response. I slept on the couch that night, hoping she'd be more reasonable the next morning." He gazed at the ceiling. "But that night, Victoria was killed. And there's speculation that I did it. I had to rent that awful cabin next door. It's been horrible for me."

"Not to mention for your wife, who was actually arrested for the murder," I said, my voice cold.

"Well obviously, her too. But I'm certain she'll be exonerated. Nothing ever touches her. Besides, she has you on her side."

I had grown tired of this self-absorbed, pitiful little man, and Mrs. Finney apparently had too. She rose from her chair. "I think we've heard enough." She looked at me with a question in her eyes, and I nodded. "Best be on your way now, Parker Lyon. Your moment in the limelight has ended."

He looked addled as he stood and faced me. "But you believe me, don't you? Will you tell everyone I didn't do it? My reputation…"

"We don't give a Fig Newton about your reputation," Mrs. Finney said. "As for whether we believe you, that remains to be seen. Now begone with you." She waved her hand like a wizard.

Parker lumbered across the room, seeming to have aged twenty years. I held the door open and he left, disappearing into the billowing snow.

35

W hen I turned back from the door, Mrs. Finney was wrestling into her gloves and coat. "Must get back to my room," she said, her tone as light as if she had been paying me a social call. "My Agatha Christie novel isn't going to read itself, you know."

"Before you go," I said, "what did you think of Parker's story?"

"Well, my dear, I don't trust Parker Lyon any more than I'd trust a disgraced politician. Nevertheless…" She tapped a finger against her chin. "I'm simply not convinced he's your killer."

I heaved a sigh. "Everything is so convoluted. I just don't know where to go next with this investigation."

She patted my arm. "Trust your instincts, my dear. I suggest going back to the beginning. The answers often lie where the end began."

The creatures and I watched through the window as Mrs. Finney, in her sensible purple galoshes, strode toward the lodge. Her fortune cookie message echoed what I had been thinking myself: "The answers lie where the end began." As for trusting my instincts, my gut told me that Victoria's murder was entwined with Kimberly, but not by her hand. And that this crime hadn't been set in motion by the marriage to Parker, or Elyse's parentage, or the threats to Jessica and Summer.

It was conceived long before that.

So often, the act of murder seemed impulsive and unplanned, but in reality, even a crime of passion was usually the culmination of a series of events, emotions, thoughts. What events had transpired to steer inexorably toward Victoria's murder? What collision of wills, what feelings of rage, pride, hopelessness, or fear led inevitably to her death? I felt certain the answer lay behind us, buried in a past I would have to exhume to expose the truth.

Two things nagged at my subconscious. One: I couldn't explain those stupid wildflowers. Two: Some image in those yearbooks provided a key that could unlock this entire case. Whatever it was, my brain refused to grasp it. I needed to open my mind, focus on the details, and stop relying on assumption in my vision. It was time to view this puzzle as if it were a photograph.

My high school photography teacher had once taught a lesson on perspective. She said when you look at a live scene with the naked eye—a friend walking toward you in a coffee shop, for example—your vision focuses on the friend, automatically filtering out distractions. Your conscious mind doesn't acknowledge the cashier in the background, the people at a nearby table, the coffee spill on the floor. You can turn your attention to those objects, but then your friend becomes peripheral. That's how the eye prioritizes; it doesn't allow you to see everything with the same level of intensity at once.

Not true of the camera lens. You can set a camera to achieve selective focus, but in an ordinary photo, in an ordinary setting, the lens captures everything with the same level of relevance. Every detail is equally acute. Without our own personal perceptions and biases, the spill on the floor in a photo is as meaningful as the smiling friend.

That's what I needed from my brain and my eyes right now: to focus on the details.

I burrowed into my armchair and opened the freshman yearbook, vowing to stay put until I either solved this or the security guy arrived. Woody curled in front of the fire, and Carl sat on the bed, watching me fiercely. "Freaky cat," I said. "Go read a book or take a nap or something. Just quit staring at me. It's too much pressure."

I flipped through the pages, studying each photo with as much objectivity as I could muster. I scanned backgrounds and foregrounds, details I might not notice at first glance. Some shots elicited a smile, others a grimace, but nothing set off warning bells.

Sixty seniors smiled up from the pages, girls in off-shoulder black drapes and boys wearing fake tuxedoes. As freshmen, we had considered the older kids so mature, but now they looked like babies to me. A few of them I remembered well, while others were a vague blip within my gray matter. The same was true of the junior and sophomore portraits. As I moved closer to my own class, my recollection grew broader and more vivid, but nothing reached out and grabbed me.

My pulse quickened when I reached the freshman section. My peers. What my subconscious wanted me to spot lay buried somewhere in here. I felt it acutely. I examined each portrait, matching it with the name to the side, trying to give that person substance in my memory, to create a three-dimensional image.

When I got to the one labeled *Callahan Cassidy*, I did a double take. Had I really ever looked so young? I kept moving through the portraits. Sophie Demler smiled awkwardly, trying to hide her silver braces. There was Victoria Dunleavy, haughty and proud, alive, the promise of a bright future in her eyes. I smiled at the sight of Sam Petrie, remembering him as a boy, sweet and funny. And there was Tonya, bold and alluring, a vision even during awkward adolescence.

On the last page of the portrait section, Kimberly

Wainwright appeared, with her thickly lined lips and trendy white eyeshadow. No hint of murder in those eyes.

I noticed a cheerful dark-haired girl in the next picture. A soft nagging erupted—the niggle of a distant memory.

Bethany Weller.

The hard drive in my brain spun, trying to locate data on this girl but unable to pinpoint any. She was familiar, but I had no clear memory of her. Had I seen her grown-up version around the village recently? Had I failed to recognize the teenager within the adult?

The blood pounded in my temples. Somehow, this girl was important. I recalled a technique involving mental time travel I had learned in a college psychology class. Though it sounded far-fetched, it had worked for me in the past. What did I have to lose?

I settled into the chair, leaning back and closing my eyes, envisioning Rock Creek High School as it had looked my freshman year. Faded beige tile floors appeared beneath my feet, and cream-colored walls surrounded me. I imagined my younger self walking those halls, searching for the mysterious Bethany Weller.

Before I could catch a glimpse of her, a knock at the door sucked me back into the present.

The security person had arrived. Dressed in a blue button-up uniform top with her name embroidered above the left pocket, Gretta was a chatterer, one who apparently adhered to the notion that good customer service entailed constant vocalization. She started by crouching and cooing baby talk to Woody ("Who's a good boy? Dere's a good boy. Dere's a snuggle wuggum"). Carl darted under the bed and hid from the drivel, but the dog disappointed me by adoring Gretta. After a few minutes, the woman finally rounded up her equipment and offered me a detailed analysis of the installation process, sounding more like a NASA engineer than a security alarm installer.

As she settled into her work, I plopped back into my chair, hoping to return to the mystery of Bethany Weller.

Alas, it was not to be. Gretta proved an able multi-tasker, tinkering with wires while regaling me with a detailed autobiography, interrupted by occasional remarks relating to the impending storm. Woody stared up at her with reverence. Three times I called him, even resorting to his full name—Woodward Cassidy—a technique which usually resulted in him slinking toward me with a guilty face. Today, he responded with a cursory glance before returning his big brown eyes to the worshipful gaze of his new idol.

For two hours, my contribution to Gretta's monologue was limited to "Mm hmm," "Really?" and "Oh wow." I remembered one of my mother's favorite quips: "It's a terrible death to be talked to death." Finally, a miracle occurred. Gretta said, "That'll do it. I'll show you how to work this gizmo, then I'm outta here."

Ten minutes of instruction rendered me thoroughly confused. Gretta handed me a manual, though I doubted it would help. After helping me program my PIN, Gretta squatted one last time, and Woody placed a big paw on her shoulder as if knighting her. She laughed and rumpled the fur on his head, making more unintelligible noises that enchanted him. "I'm sure I'll see you again in the next few days," she said.

"What? Why?" I asked. "I mean, great," I added quickly.

"Didn't your dad tell you? He decided to install these contraptions in every cabin. Said he wants his guests safe. Started with yours because… well, the break-in…"

Was nothing hidden from public knowledge in this grotto? And if everyone here knew everything, how did Victoria's murderer manage to remain concealed?

36

After Gretta departed, I turned my mind back to Bethany Weller. Something about the girl—something I'd seen in the past couple of days—still tickled at my memory, just out of reach. I burrowed into the chair for another attempt at self-hypnosis, but I found myself moody and distracted, unable to concentrate on slipping back in time.

I opened the next yearbook and searched for Bethany's sophomore portrait, finding it located once again next to Kimberly Wainwright. No smile from Bethany this time. Just a distant, faraway expression that made her look older than her years. Her hair was frizzy, and a patch of pimples spread across the bridge of her nose. I flipped back to the freshman picture and held them side by side. The difference was alarming. Was it simply the onset of puberty? An isolated rough day? Or had something happened to cheerful fourteen-year-old Bethany that sparked a metamorphosis into sullen fifteen-year-old Bethany?

I grabbed the junior yearbook from the bed and thumbed through the pages to the portraits. Kimberly was present and accounted for, but no Bethany. And she was nowhere to be found in our senior yearbook either.

Bethany Weller had disappeared from Rock Creek High School after our sophomore year.

I leaned back and closed my eyes, forcing my mind back

to the school hallway. Images swam to life around me as if I were watching a photograph being born in a tray of developer fluid. Visions of vaguely familiar classmates appeared, swarming through the passageway as they rushed to their next class.

Suddenly, I found myself in the gym, walking into the girls' locker room. I hesitated, feeling anxiety well inside both me and the vision of myself. At the back of the locker room, I saw several girls clustered around another girl I couldn't yet visualize. There was Victoria, and next to her, Kimberly. I still couldn't make out the unseen girl in the center of the group, but I knew instinctively who it must be. Bethany Weller.

As I edged toward the group, I heard them cackling like hyenas surrounding a wounded antelope. I peeked through their arms and saw her. Bethany cowered near a bench, arms wrapped around her torso to cover herself. Clad only in white cotton panties and a bra, she shivered. Victoria reached forward and pinched a roll of fat at Bethany's waist, and the other girls screeched their delight. I saw Sophie in the group, fidgeting uncomfortably but forcing a laugh. Kimberly hesitated, but under Victoria's daring gaze, she also grabbed a fold of skin and tugged. Bethany squealed, and tears leaked from her eyes.

Part of me began to levitate then. I floated above the scene, observing my teen self push through the group and position myself in front of Bethany. My arms were splayed in a protective gesture reminiscent of the Wonder Woman pose I'd used in my misguided attempt to protect Elyse yesterday. My face felt hot, and my voice was fierce as I spewed vulgarities I didn't remember knowing at that age. I intimidated even myself.

Though Victoria startled, she quickly regained her composure and narrowed her eyes at me before addressing her posse.

"Come on, ladies. Let's give these two lovebirds their privacy."

Hooting and linking arms, the girls skittered out the door. Victoria took a moment to glare at me before following in their wake. Kimberly risked a fleeting glance over her shoulder, and I thought I saw sympathy there.

When Bethany and I were alone, I helped her collect her scattered clothing from the floor.

"Just ignore them." I'm sure at the time I believed it was a kind thing to say, but in retrospect, the words sounded bland and empty.

Still, she looked up at me with gratitude. "Thank you for trying to help. No one else ever does." She turned her eyes away, and her voice shook. "But you shouldn't have. They'll just come after you."

I waved dismissively, full of youthful bravado. "I can handle them. How long has this been going on?"

"Forever," she whispered.

"You need to tell a teacher, or the principal…"

"I've tried. It only makes things worse." She finished buttoning her shirt and stared at the floor. "Don't worry about me. I'll be fine."

I saw myself vacillate and remembered that moment of indecision. Sympathy coursed through me, but also—what was that emotion lurking beneath it? I hated to admit it, but it was repulsion. I'd been disgusted by Bethany's weakness and fear. Her fragility had threatened to awaken the vulnerability buried in myself—an emotion I even now tried to ignore.

Bethany and I walked out of the locker room together, but I didn't remember ever talking to her again. And after that school year, she was gone.

I shook myself out of my hypnosis. Woody's head was in my lap, his brown eyes watching me. Carl sat on the arm of the chair wearing the expression of a teacher who wondered if his student was ever going to get it.

Seized by an overwhelming desire to find out what had happened to Bethany, I picked up my phone to call Tonya. Maybe the girl was somewhere far away, living a happy life filled with family and friends. But before I could dial, the device vibrated in my hand.

It was a text from Kimberly. I flashed to the image of her pinching Bethany's waist and felt a shudder of disgust.

Can you come over? Need to talk to you.

Just text whatever you want to say, I responded.

Please. It's vital. I think I figured something out.

Before I could answer, she sent another text. *I'm baking hot hors d'oeuvres, and I have a nice bottle of wine.*

I paused. Was it the information I wanted, or the sure-to-be-expensive wine she dangled in front of me like the proverbial carrot? Or did I want one last look at her, one last chance to inspect her eyes for the truth, before I fired myself as her private detective? I got up and walked to the window, peering through the blinds at the low, dark clouds. No precipitation, but the signs in the sky were ominous.

That storm was definitely coming.

Information. Confrontation. Wine. The hot hors d'oeuvres I could live without, but the rest of it was persuasive.

Despite the looming storm, I agreed to go. Maybe Kimberly could explain Bethany Weller's disappearance. If not, at least I'd make her answer for her long-ago locker room behavior.

It took a minute for me to remember how to set the security alarm. When I finally entered my secret number, the display warned me I had forty-five seconds to exit, ramping up my anxiety. I hurried Woody and Carl outside. Before I closed the door, I spotted the pepper spray Tonya had given me and skittered across the room to retrieve it. Sophie's notebook also caught my attention, and I tucked it inside my purse. The creatures and I left the cabin with a mere thirty seconds to spare. I wasn't sure I could handle this pressure every time I left home.

A fire roared in the lodge's huge fireplace. Mom sat in an

armchair, knitting needles clicking, while Mrs. Finney stood near the window, watching the clouds move in. Dad sat behind the desk, a pencil in his hand. "Hey, Sundance," he said, without looking up. "What's a five-letter word for someone who strips in a club?"

I frowned. What kind of puzzle was he doing? "No idea, Dad."

Behind me, Woody stopped on the entrance rug and shook the snow from his coat in a wave. He traipsed over to Mom and rested his head on her lap. She cooed and stroked his damp fur. Carl licked his paws and sauntered across the wooden floor to wind himself between Mrs. Finney's ankles.

"Can I leave Woody and Carl with you guys?" I asked. "I need to run a few errands before dinner."

My parents answered at the same time.

"In this weather?" My mother sounded horrified at yet another of my misguided decisions.

"Are you taking your car?" My father jumped to his feet and reached for his coat. "Let me scrape the snow off the windshield. And I'll warm the engine too."

"Daddy, I can do it. Don't trouble yourself."

"No trouble, Sundance. Give me five minutes." He hurried through the door.

"Let him go," Mom said. "It makes him feel good to take care of you. And in answer to your question, those sweet boys are always welcome here."

Mrs. Finney turned from the window to inspect me, lifting an eyebrow above her raccoon eyes. "May I ask what errands you have that are so urgent as to brave the impending storm?"

Mom stopped knitting and looked up at me. "Yes, sweetheart, where are you going? Not too far, I hope."

This must be how the Protestants felt during the Inquisition, I thought. I resisted the urge to cower under the dual gaze. "Here and there. I'll be back by dinnertime."

Mom seemed satisfied and returned to her project, but

Mrs. Finney continued to stare me down. I squirmed. "I'll go see how Dad is coming along with the car. You ladies have fun. Back soon." I hurried toward the door, glancing over my shoulder to see Mrs. Finney still surveying me, as if anticipating my imminent doom.

37

My little Honda chugged along in high spirits, much merrier than my own. Mrs. Finney's portentous demeanor had enveloped me, and the world felt gloomy and ominous. Steel gray clouds hung like tumors over the village. The stoplight at the intersection blinked red, an evil eye warning me to return home. Not yet five o'clock, but dusk had settled on empty streets and sidewalks.

A sudden sense of futility swept through me. I pictured Bethany Weller again, defeated and trembling. Then I envisioned Victoria's lifeless body. In the background of both pictures: Kimberly. Why had I stuck my nose into this? Did I really think I knew better than a trained detective—even if he was still a rookie? Was this just a feeble attempt to restore my dignity after the debacle of my last *Sentinel* assignment?

Then I thought of my session with Dr. Lowell—the hopefulness I'd felt as she talked to me about self-acceptance and self-forgiveness. I was sure she would advise me right now to shake off my dark thoughts—though I doubted she'd approve of where I was headed. But I felt in my gut that seeing Kimberly was important.

Maybe the new information she claimed to have would provide a turning point in the investigation. Or, at the very least, she might be able to fill in the gaps regarding Bethany

Weller. For whatever reason, I had woven Bethany into this, and I needed to figure out why.

Once I reached Kimberly's street, I rolled forward in the swelling darkness and parked in front of her house. As I unbuckled my seat belt, I heard pinging sounds on the roof of the car. I glanced through the windshield to see tiny pellets of ice bouncing off the glass.

Sleet.

Snow I could handle, but sleet just plain irritated me. Driving on ice-slicked roads always made me feel like an uncoordinated skater in a slapstick version of the Ice Capades. I considered turning around and making my way home before the sleet completely coated the streets.

But curiosity and compulsion superseded the desire for warmth and safety, so I tugged my hood over my head, grabbed my purse, and heaved myself from the car. Tiny icicles pelted my exposed cheeks as I scrambled to the front porch. I lifted my hand to knock on the door's smoked glass inlay. Then I gasped and stumbled backwards.

The door was ajar. It was déjà vu all over again.

I should have returned to my car right then. I should have called the police, or at the very least, my father. I should have internalized all the lectures I had so recently endured about taking unnecessary risks.

But I was never very good at "should." I nudged the door open and peered inside.

Darkness shrouded the entryway, with only a dim light piercing the shadows from deep inside the house. The light at the end of the tunnel, or an oncoming train? Behind me, the pattering of sleet and the howl of the wind created a physical force that launched me into the house. As I had done yesterday at my cabin, I reached a hand around the door jamb and found the light switch, flooding the foyer with beams from the overhead fixture.

I fumbled inside my pocket, transmitting a silent thank you to Tonya as I wrapped my fingers around my pepper spray. Holding it in front of me like a crucifix, I stepped over the threshold and twisted from side to side, mimicking the cop shows I watched. I wanted to shout, "Clear!" but instead I screeched, "Kimberly?" My voice emerged too high-pitched and squeaky to sound authoritative.

No answer. No noise at all, other than the pattering of sleet as it intensified.

I left the door open to facilitate the possibility of a quick escape and tiptoed through the entryway, trying to move stealthily. Though I had just announced my presence, this was how they did it in horror movies, so it had to be right.

Of course, in those movies, the monster inevitably snatched up and devoured the clueless damsel.

But still.

I made my way toward the brighter section of the house, trying to convince myself that *going to the light* was a good idea and not an otherworldly symbol foreshadowing my doom. "Kimberly?" I squeaked again, my finger on the trigger of my little pink canister. If she came traipsing around the corner, she would get a well-deserved face full of pepper spray.

At the end of the hall, I found the family room and kitchen devoid of human presence. A baking sheet dotted with frozen mini quiches and tiny egg rolls rested on the countertop next to the oven, its digital display indicating four hundred degrees. Two crystal wine glasses sparkled atop the bar, one empty and one containing gold-tinted liquid—evidence that Kimberly was around here somewhere, or had been recently.

I dropped my arm and cradled the pepper spray next to my thigh, my anxiety dissolving into annoyance. This was so Kimberly. No concern for anyone else. Probably ran to the store for a last-minute item. Probably hadn't even thought to text or call to let me know. Probably simply hadn't latched the door.

But still. Would she leave the oven on? The wine on the counter?

And what about the ankle monitor? Wouldn't it report

her to the police if she left the premises?

I slid fingers across my upper lip, wiping away beads of perspiration. The kitchen was hot. I set my pepper spray on the counter and shrugged out of my coat, draping it across a barstool. Then I took out my phone and dialed Kimberly's number.

A warbling noise sounded from across the room. On the kitchen table, a cell phone lit up as the ringtone played. Kimberly's phone. That couldn't be a good sign.

I disconnected and picked up her phone, swiping a finger across the screen. Password protected, of course. Then I heard a muted noise coming through the kitchen window, like water running across rocks, gurgling above the tinking of falling sleet. I didn't remember a stream near here, but it had been a long time since I'd been in the lower village. I edged toward the back door, listening intently. The sound was closer now. It had to be rushing water.

As I glanced back into the kitchen, my eyes fell on a smudge of blue on the white quartz near the wineglasses.

A tiny blue flower, just like the ones I'd found beside Victoria, in Sophie's notebook, and on my own bed.

Now I was on high alert. Kimberly could be in serious danger. I snatched up my pepper spray and put my hand on the doorknob, hesitating only a fraction of a second before turning it. The gurgling noise swelled even louder outside.

Through the murky ambient light, a bulky shadow loomed to my right. The mystery sound was coming from that direction. After patting the wall in an unsuccessful search for a light switch, I grabbed my phone and used the flashlight app to locate the wall plate, pressing the small lever upward. Garish flood lights spread across the back porch, illuminating a covered wooden deck and an immense above-ground hot tub.

Bubbling and steaming, the tub resembled a huge cauldron, potent and dangerous. I crept closer, irrationally fearful that a hand might emerge from the depths and grab my wrist.

When I peered over the lip of the hot tub, I staggered backward. My cell phone clattered to the wooden deck, and my hand rose to my mouth to shield the shriek that threatened to erupt.

Kimberly hadn't run off to the store after all.

38

Heart racing, I dropped to my knees and patted the deck in search of my fallen phone so I could summon help. The rough wood boards scraped my fingers. I peered over my shoulder, half expecting to find a menacing stranger swooping toward me. Just as panic started to set in, my right hand closed around the phone. I pushed myself upright and shoved my other hand into my pocket, digging for the pepper spray. I clutched it to my chest, my finger poised above the trigger.

Then I inched forward for another peek inside the hot tub.

Kimberly floated face up in water, eyes closed, body bobbing in the jetted sprays. Blond hair floated around her head like a paradoxical halo. She was clothed in black slacks and a gray silk blouse that clung to the contours of her body. A diamond choker lay around her neck, sparkling in the pulsing sprays. The ankle monitor flashed around her leg.

Her lips moved, and her chest rose and fell. My eyes went wide, and I gasped. Kimberly was still alive. But water bubbled across her mouth and her nose. I had to get her out of there before she drowned.

Steam swirled around me, and the gurgling of the jets thundered in my ears. I shoved my phone and the pepper spray into my coat pockets and climbed the hot tub's two wooden steps. Thrusting my hands into the hot water, I grabbed her right shoulder, twisting her until I could wedge my hands into her armpits. Water splashed down the front of my shirt and jeans as I yanked the unconscious woman over the edge. Her torso clunked down the steps. Panting, I carefully laid her on the deck. Her wet body had been heavier than I expected.

I shivered convulsively as the frigid air attacked my wet body. And Kimberly was even more soaked than I was. I needed to get us both into the warm house before hypothermia set in.

Grunting with the effort, I dragged her across the deck. When I reached the house, I released her and reached out to open the door.

The knob didn't budge.

For a horrifying moment, I imagined myself trapped in the back yard with a seriously injured woman and a savage killer lurking in the shadows. My parents often accused me of harboring a vivid imagination, but two bodies in less than a week? I was entitled.

Further examination disclosed that my palm was slick with chlorinated water. I wiped it across the rear of my jeans, still mercifully dry, and tried again. This time the knob turned, and the door swung open. I hauled Kimberly across the threshold and slammed the door, locking it behind me. Then I remembered leaving the front door open and realized any old neighborhood killer could waltz right inside.

I pushed that thought out of my head and pulled my cell phone from my wet pocket. I pressed 9-1-1, putting the phone on speaker as I knelt on the floor beside the drenched woman. It wasn't until I lifted the diamond choker to check her pulse that I noticed red welts on her neck. Ligature marks? Contusions left by fingers clenched around her airway? I filed the information and gently probed the skin until I located her carotid artery. Her pulse was weak but steady. When the dispatcher answered, I conveyed the information. I couldn't remember Kimberly's address, but she assured me she could look it up. Before she could request that I stay on the line, I disconnected and ran across the kitchen to retrieve my purse, jostling through the contents until I found Raul's card.

Hands shaking, I dialed the cell phone number he'd scribbled on the back of the card. After a single ring, his voice boomed in my ear. "Sanchez."

"Raul, it's Callie Cassidy. I'm at Kimberly Lyon's house, and, um, she's been seriously injured. I just hung up with 9-1-1, but I thought I should call you too."

"Injured? Elaborate."

"Well, she texted me to come over, and I did, and when I got here, I found her floating in the hot tub. She was—is—unconscious, with marks on her neck. She's breathing, though, and she has a pulse."

"Slow down. Where are you right now?"

"I told you, I'm at Kimberly's."

A pause. "Specifically, I mean."

"Oh. In the kitchen."

"Lock all the doors and stay put. I'm on my way." He disconnected.

I darted down the hall. After I closed and bolted the front door, I detoured to the thermostat and jacked up the heat. In the family room, I grabbed a wool blanket that lay folded over the back of the couch. I knew better than to try to get Kimberly's wet clothes off, but I could at least try to warm her up.

When I crouched over her, I had another bout of déjà vu, remembering the tableau of Kimberly hunched above Victoria's body. It occurred to me that someone walking unexpectedly through the door might think I had strangled this woman. First impressions could indeed be deceiving. Perhaps Kimberly had been telling the truth about being lured to the scene of Victoria's murder—and set up.

I considered that as I tucked the blanket around Kimberly. On my knees, I scrambled around to her head. Wet, worm-like tendrils of hair clung to her face. I smoothed them back. Then I got to my feet and hurried to the kitchen to grab a dish towel, wiping the moisture from her cheeks and forehead. Leaning in, I studied her neck. Three marks on each side, slightly less obvious on her right. Red and oblong. The shape of fingers.

I gently lifted one of her eyelids. Small blotches of red on the white of her eye. Though it could be the product of the hot tub's chlorine, combined with the bruises on her neck, I figured it must be petechiae—a sure sign of strangulation.

"Hang in there," I whispered to her. "Help is on the way."

Goosebumps prickled on my wet skin. I went back to the kitchen, stripped off my wet shirt, and pulled on my coat, zipping it tight around me. Sirens wailed in the distance, drawing closer, perhaps a couple of minutes out. Kimberly didn't require CPR or any other medical attention I could give her, so I took a moment to explore before emergency responders would arrive and make my search impossible.

As I'd established in Victoria's office, I knew better than to touch anything. My eyes would have to do the work. I glanced at the two wine glasses stationed on the countertop. One was empty, no doubt awaiting my arrival. The second was a little over half full. I used my phone to take a picture of the glasses, following it with a shot of the hors d'oeuvres waiting to be baked.

And of course, that little blue flower.

Next, I bent low and scanned the white marbled floor. No signs of a struggle, no wet footprints—except my own.

But crumpled beneath one of the barstools, I saw something that made my heart skip a beat. A red, knitted scarf was wedged against the bottom of the island. It was a scarf I'd seen before, hours earlier. Wrapped around Sam Petrie's neck.

Before I could decide what to think, I heard the ambulance pull up in front of the house, sirens blaring. I hurried to unlock the front door. A pair of officers stormed in, guns drawn, and began searching the premises. Behind them, two paramedics hurried up the walk with a folded stretcher and a bag of medical supplies. I led them to the unconscious woman, explaining that I'd found her in the hot tub and dragged her inside. The woman nodded curtly, and they set to work, taking Kimberly's blood pressure, checking her eyes, and inserting an IV line into the crook of her arm. "Pupils dilated," the woman barked. Then she turned to me. "Do you know if she's ingested any drugs?"

I shook my head. "Not sure. She was unconscious when I found her." I pointed to the wine glasses. "I assume she'd had some wine, but I don't know about drugs."

Footsteps thundered down the hall then, and I turned to see Sanchez striding into the kitchen, his lips tight. He looked at me—glared, actually—and stood over Kimberly, watching the paramedics work. They told him their patient was stable but unconscious. The officers entered the kitchen, guns holstered, and reported that the house was clear. He indicated that they should go to the backyard and check the scene. Without a word to me or even another glance, he stormed out the back door after them.

Though I wasn't exactly sure why, I was clearly in the doghouse.

39

From the kitchen window, I watched the officers prowl across the backyard, flashlight beams cutting through the darkness. Sanchez worked in the sleet, examining the deck and the rim of the hot tub. He took out his phone and snapped a few pictures. I hadn't been able to get back out there and shoot any myself. I wondered if he'd share.

I heard my father shout from the front entry. "Callie?"

"In the kitchen," I yelled.

He rushed in, his face creased with worry, and grasped my shoulders. His eyes scanned every inch of me, looking for injuries. "Are you all right? Are you hurt?"

"I'm fine, Dad. It's Kimberly who's hurt."

He pulled me into a bear hug and looked over at the paramedics tending to the still-unconscious woman. "What have you gotten yourself into, Sundance?" he said, his voice catching. "Two crime scenes in, what, three days? Your mother is a basket case."

"I doubt that, Dad. All those years as a cop's wife—she's as steady as they come. All she needs is another one of those meditation sessions. Or maybe a spin on her inversion table."

"Callahan Maureen Cassidy, this is not a joking matter. What your mother needs is to lay eyes on you. Just as soon as we can get out of here."

Frank Laramie lumber into sight then, his coat shining with melting ice pellets and his hood pulled over his head. His eyes darted around the room. "Glad you're okay, Callie. Where's Sanchez?" I pointed at the back window, and Frank nodded, heading toward the door. "Stay put. We'll talk in a bit."

I cringed. When the chief of police says we'll talk, it doesn't mean a pleasant chat over coffee.

But it wouldn't compare to the ferocity of the interrogation I was about to receive from my father. He started pacing, his hands clenched. I waited. When he finally spoke, his voice was stern.

"Why did you come here, Callie? Why couldn't you just stay out of it like I asked? Like we all asked?"

"Dad, it's lucky I did come. Kimberly was in danger. It was my responsibility—"

"No. It's not your responsibility. None of this is your responsibility. Your responsibility is to stay out of harm's way. Why is that such a difficult concept?"

Had my father forgotten I was forty-three years old? That I had been an investigative journalist for *The Washington Sentinel?* That I had taken photos in war zones and interviewed serial killers?

I sighed. Any attempts to remind him of those facts would only exacerbate the tension. I decided to try for a redirection. "What are you doing here anyway, Dad? How did you know where I was?"

He sighed. His face was still creased in frustration, but at least he'd stopped pacing. "After you called Sanchez, Frank called me. He swung by the lodge and picked me up while Sanchez hightailed it over here."

Adult as I claimed to be, professional as I considered myself, my father's presence here filled me with a feeling of safety. Despite his lecture, I was glad he'd come.

The back door opened, and the four men reentered the kitchen, stamping their feet on the mat and brushing the sleet from their shoulders. Pellets of ice clung to Raul's hair, and when he shook his head, droplets flew as if from a sprinkler.

Raul moved beside the paramedics and stared down at Kimberly's inert form. "Is she going to make it?"

"Vitals are steady," the paramedic responded. "That's a good sign. Can't say anything for sure, not until we get more tests." He pointed at her neck. "Looks like someone tried to choke her. But there's no evidence she resisted. With her dilated pupils, it's possible she was under the influence—or drugged."

My eyes widened, and I turned to Frank. "Drugged?"

He nodded.

"You don't seem surprised."

"I'm not. Victoria's tox screen came back positive for zolpidem tartrate. She'd been drugged too, before she was stabbed. We assume it was used to subdue her, reduce her ability to fight back."

Zolpidem tartrate. I searched the data files in my memory and came up with Ambien, a common sleep aid. Though it was a prescription drug, it would be relatively easy for someone to get their hands on a supply, if they didn't already have it on hand.

"Kimberly contacted me less than an hour ago," I said. "Her text didn't sound like she was impaired."

There was a flurry of activity as the paramedics pulled a handle to raise the gurney on its wheels. "We're outta here," one of them said. I watched as they rolled the stretcher across the kitchen. Kimberly's eyes were closed, her expression almost serene. I sent her a silent message of strength.

Raul nodded to the officers. "You two head over to the hospital and keep an eye on things there. Crime scene techs are on their way, should be here within the hour. I'll join you then."

When the group had departed, Raul leaned a hip against the breakfast bar and crossed his ankles. His eyes bored into me. Outside, sirens blared as the ambulance squealed away.

I looked from Raul to Dad. Frank's eyes were on me too. I glanced at the floor, to the red scarf, and quickly averted my eyes. They'd see it soon enough, I realized, but I just couldn't bring myself to point it out.

This couldn't possibly be Sam's doing. My mind raced to find an alternative. "It has to be Parker who did this," I said. "He told me today that Victoria had been blackmailing him. She'd threatened his precious reputation, his financial status. He must have killed her to shut her up. He framed Kimberly so she couldn't divorce him and take all their assets. When it looked like Kimberly might get off, he tried to kill her too."

"Not possible," Raul said.

"What do you mean? It's not only possible, it's probable. The man is a weasel. He—"

In a tight, barely controlled voice, Raul said, "Stop, Callie. I'm telling you, it's not Parker."

Dad moved to my side, standing beside me like a bodyguard. Frank cleared his throat. "Callie, we've had Parker at the station for the past couple of hours. Can't say for certain he didn't kill Victoria, but he has a rock-solid alibi for this attack." He pointed from Raul to himself. "Us."

My brain struggled to process the information. "When did you release him? This just happened—he could have rushed over here from the station…"

A thick silence blanketed the room, as threatening and ominous as the storm clouds outside. No one believed Parker had left the police station and hurried home to commit murder. Not even me now, really. But there was something else rumbling beneath the surface here. Raul and Frank knew something, and I wasn't going to like hearing it. "What is it?" I said, my voice low.

Raul glanced at Frank, who gave him a small nod. "Parker told us about Sam. That he's not Elyse's father."

The blood drained from my face. I glanced again toward the scarf crumpled beneath the barstool. "You can't think Sam did this," I said, my voice quavering. "Kimberly's the mother of his child. He'd never hurt her."

"Sam told you, didn't he? That's why he was there last night when I happened by. And you didn't see fit to let me know."

My father looked at me, his disappointment palpable. "Is he right, Callie? Did you know about Sam?"

I hesitated, then nodded. "I did. But Dad, he told me in confidence. If I'd believed it had anything to do with Victoria's murder, I'd have told you. And them. Besides, Sam was planning to go to the police himself, after he told Elyse."

"I see." My father dropped his arm and drew a deep breath. "Callahan, if you know anything else, it's time for you to tell us. Everything."

I bit my bottom lip. There weren't too many more secrets I was holding on to, but Dad was right. It was time to spill the ones I still had.

I looked squarely at Raul. "You're right. I knew about Sam. I didn't—and still don't—believe that information led him to kill Victoria, or to assault Kimberly." He opened his mouth to respond, but I held up a hand. "Please, just let me finish. Sam would never break into my cabin. He'd never scare me that way. He'd never have made those threatening phone calls. It's not in his character."

Raul shook his head. "We can discuss your insights into human nature another time. For now, finish telling us what you know."

His attitude stung, but I'd earned it. I'd relished my earlier notion that Raul had grown to trust me, to respect me. But the way he saw it, I hadn't returned the favor.

I owed him the truth. All of it.

40

"A ll right," I said, taking a deep breath. "First, I need to show you this." I pointed at the scarf, and Raul crouched down, studying it without touching it. He looked up at me, a question in his eyes. "It's…well, I'm pretty sure it's Sam's. I know that looks bad, but I'm sure there's an innocent explanation. He and Kimberly share a daughter, after all. It's not that strange that he'd be here to talk about Elyse. She and Kimberly aren't speaking right now, and I know he was concerned about their rift."

Raul grew very still. "Okay. Crime scene techs will process the scarf. Is there more?"

I pointed at the flower on the counter. "It's just like the one in Victoria's office, and in my cabin the night of the break-in." I lifted my eyes to Raul's. "And in Sophie's notebook."

"What are you talking about?"

I went to my purse and pulled out Sophie's pink notebook. After a brief hesitation, I held it out to him and told him about the visit Tonya and I had made to Sophie's house—the search of her desk, the photo, the notes she'd written. "I haven't figured out yet what they all mean. Maybe you can."

Another long silence as the trio contemplated this new piece of evidence. Frank wore surprised expression. Raul's face conveyed simmering frustration.

But Dad's response was the worst. Disappointment.

After Raul flipped through the notebook, he closed the cover and slapped it against an open palm. "It would have been nice to have this a couple of days ago," he said. "I don't know what's in here, but it might have saved Kimberly Lyon from being attacked."

"I tried to give it to you this morning," I said, talking so fast my words tripped over each other. "You weren't in. Did Betsy tell you I stopped by the station? I asked for Frank, too, but he was at a county meeting…"

But Raul wasn't interested in my excuses. He was furious. "We could charge you with tampering with evidence. Or breaking and entering." Then he looked at my father. "Did you know about this?"

Dad took a step forward, shoulders squared. "I don't know what you're implying, but you should remember who you're talking to."

Frank stepped between them. "That's enough," he said. "Everyone calm down. No one's charging anyone with anything."

The detective's jaw clenched and then relaxed. He took a deep breath and lifted his hands in a peace-making gesture. "I apologize. I let my temper get away from me. There's no excuse for that." He turned to me, and his eyes were hard. "Callie, you can go home. But you need to come to the station tomorrow to make a statement. As for Sam—"

"I'm telling you, Sam didn't do this. I know him. He couldn't—"

I'd pushed too hard. The dam burst. "You *know* him? You expect me to trust your judgment? Your judgment didn't serve you too well when it came to Jameson Jarrett, did it?"

I reared back as if he'd slapped me. Tears sprang to my eyes. Dad looked as if he was barely subduing his fury. Raul's expression quickly changed from anger to contrition. "Callie, I'm… that was uncalled for. But I warned you to stay out of this."

Dad's glare never wavered, and his voice didn't soften. "Gentlemen. My daughter and I are leaving now. She told you what she knows. Unless you are officially charging her with something, I'm taking her home."

Frank stood with his arms crossed in front of his chest. He heaved a deep sigh. "That's fine, Butch. But Callie," he said, looking my direction, "we do need you at the station tomorrow morning."

"Make it afternoon," my father snapped. "We'll arrange for her attorney to be present."

Attorney? Dad was either making an aggressive bluff, or he believed I was in real trouble.

Frank nodded. "One o'clock then. Callie, do we have your word you won't leave the village?"

"Yes," I said. "I want to help you find out who did this."

Dad held up a hand to silence me. "No more talking. Let's go."

Without another word between us, Dad and I buckled into my Honda, with Dad behind the wheel. We skidded in silence across the slick streets. I knew him well enough not to attempt conversation. We both needed time to process what had happened.

The sleet had turned to snow, and fat flakes floated hypnotically in the air. The image of Kimberly in the hot tub filled my head, followed by Victoria on the floor of her office. My thoughts turned to Sam's scarf, and the tiny flower on the counter. It was overwhelming. Tears came then, and I cried silently until my nose ran.

When my emotions had run their course, I wiped my cheeks with the heels of my hands. My feelings needed to take second place to rational thought. Raul had made it clear that Sam was now his primary suspect. Sam needed me. And I felt intuitively that I was close to figuring things out. I held all the pieces of the puzzle—I just needed to assemble them.

With Kimberly out of the running as a suspect, only a few

alternatives remained. Brian Ratliff was still viable. He had a motive against both women. He supposedly had an alibi, at least for the night of Victoria's murder, but I still wasn't convinced it was unbreakable.

And Parker? Timing was everything where he was concerned. I didn't dispute that he was at the police station, but he could have left there, rushed to their home, and strangled his wife before I arrived. She hadn't been in the hot tub very long... I shook my head. Even I had to admit that scenario was a longshot.

Then my mind went to an even darker place. Could Sam really be responsible? Could the kind, gentle man I'd known have snapped under the weight of Kimberly's secret? I tried to picture him ramming a letter opener into Victoria's chest. His strong fingers squeezing Kimberly's neck.

No. It couldn't be true.

Raul had accused me of an inability to be objective. Maybe so, but as hard as I tried, I just couldn't envision it.

In fact, I didn't believe the crimes had anything to do with the facts surrounding Elyse's conception. The root of these attacks stretched further into the past. As Mrs. Finney had remarked, "The answers lie where the end began." The image of Bethany Weller cowering in the locker room screamed for my attention. That piece, I felt sure, would somehow complete the picture.

The parking lot in front of the lodge was unusually full, considering the unoccupied status of most of the rooms and cabins. "What's going on?" I asked, as Dad pulled into a space.

He shrugged. "No idea."

I took his arm and stepped gingerly across the icy parking lot toward the lodge. Mom's silhouette filled the glass entrance as the door slid open. Out dashed my exuberant dog, bounding toward me. Then his doggie telepathy kicked in. He skidded to a halt and approached slowly, ears flat and tail limp, gently placing his muzzle in my hand.

I crouched and let him lick my face in a display of compassion. Carl watched from the door. No compassion from that canny creature.

Mom stepped into the night, her forehead creased with worry. She reached a hand to my cheek, then folded me into her arms. "Oh, Angelface. You must be a wreck. Tonight, I will sanction a glass of wine. Just one, though." She waggled a finger at me as if I'd already tried to defy her.

After she released me from her grasp, another figure approached—the woman who had become my ferocious protector. "Mrs. Finney," I said.

To my surprise, she also pulled me into an embrace. I hadn't pegged her as a hugger. She whispered in my ear, "One mustn't search a field of daisies for a solution that lies in the weeds at the side of the road."

"No, one mustn't." I puffed my cheeks, with no idea what she meant. Nor did I have the mental reserves to decipher it now.

Dad kissed Mom on the cheek. "What's with all the cars?"

With an enigmatic expression, she pointed at the lobby. "Come see."

Inside, we saw four people assembled near the stone fireplace in the Great Room. One by one, they turned as we entered. Tonya stood behind the couch, holding two mugs. She smiled, though her eyes reflected her fear. On the couch, Jessica Fannon ran a hand through her short red hair. Summer Simmons sat cross-legged next to her.

And the last person in the group? I knew who it was before he even turned around. Sam's soft smile was cloaked in a haze of pain and worry.

41

Dad, Mom, and Mrs. Finney settled onto a facing couch. I took off my coat and draped it across the back of a chair, feeling a little otherworldly, like my brain had reverted to a slow-motion setting.

Tonya glided toward me, a vision in a long-sleeved tangerine caftan. Once I took the mug of mulled wine she offered, she led me around the couch and seated me next to Sam. She then sat on the other side of me so I was nestled between the two of them. I understood her point—I was surrounded by friends.

But I knew it was Sam, more than I, who needed the comfort of friends.

"I guess you heard about Kimberly," I said to the group, trying to project a strength I didn't actually feel.

Tonya patted my leg. "We did. That's why we're here."

"Does Elyse know?" I asked Sam.

He nodded, his eyes clouded and mouth set in a firm line. "She's at the hospital with her mother." When I lifted an eyebrow in an unspoken question, he added, "She thought it best that I not be there. Given the circumstances."

"The detectives…Sam, they think you might've hurt Kimberly. And Victoria."

He wasn't surprised. No one in the group seemed surprised.

"Were you at the cafe tonight? Can anyone alibi you?" I

held my breath, hoping he'd say yes.

But he shook his head. "The place was dead." He closed his eyes and rephrased. "Empty, I mean, because of the storm. I was beat anyway, so we closed early. I went home and passed out in front of the TV."

"With Elyse?" I said, my fingers crossed.

Another shake of the head. "She was at a friend's house. As soon as I got the news, I picked her up and took her to the hospital."

"This is so ridiculous!" Jessica said, her voice filled with outrage. "None of us believe Sam is capable of those acts. It's that goon Sanchez, wanting to get the first feather in his cap. I'd like to kick him in the rear!"

"Breathe, darling," Summer said, placing a calming hand on her partner's knee. "Anger does not serve us. We must send positive thoughts into the universe."

"Humph. Right now, I'm more likely to send my middle finger to the universe than a positive thought."

A nervous titter went through the group. Summer sighed.

Tonya looked past me at Sam. "Tell her the rest," she said.

He took a deep breath. "I went to Kimberly's house this afternoon. It was just for a few minutes. Elyse has been so upset since all this happened, practically inconsolable. I thought Kimberly and I needed to talk about it. And we did. That's all. I can promise you Kimberly was perfectly fine at the time I left." He glanced at my father. "I need to let Sanchez know I was there."

"He already knows," I said. "You left your scarf behind. It was crumpled up behind a barstool in the kitchen."

His hand went to his neck. "Ah. I thought I'd left it in the cafe."

"And it gets worse," I said. "Parker told Raul and Frank about Elyse."

I paused, glancing at Jessica and Summer. "It's okay," Sam said. "I told them a few minutes ago. Everyone here knows all the crucial information."

I nodded, relieved that all the secrets were out in the open.

"So what now?" Tonya turned to my father. "You know how this works, Butch. What do you suggest?"

Dad leaned forward, his hands on his knees. When he spoke, his voice rumbled with authority. "First, I need to remind you that Detective Sanchez and Chief Laramie are skilled and honest officers of the law. I hired them both myself, and I have complete confidence in them. Let me reassure you that they aren't out to falsely accuse anyone, least of all Sam."

He walked to the fireplace and watched the flames leap. As always, he weighed his words. The group waited quietly. "You're probably not going to like this," he said, turning to rest his eyes on Sam. "But I think you should let me take you to the station. It's my opinion they'll be coming to talk to you first thing tomorrow, if not sooner. It will look better for you if you go to them. I can arrange to have Sanchez and Frank meet us there. I think you need to get ahead of this."

"No way, Dad," I protested. "That's tantamount to turning himself in. He can't—"

I felt Sam's hand press gently on my shoulder, and I stopped. It was his fight, after all. His decision.

"Butch is right," he said. "I didn't hurt Kimberly. I didn't kill Victoria. But I need to meet with the detectives, answer their questions." He clasped his hands in his lap. "The only hitch is Elyse. She's alone at the hospital with her mother. I know they say Kimberly is stable, but she's still unconscious. If something happens, if Elyse needed me and couldn't get in touch with me…I don't want her there by herself."

Jessica's hand shot into the air. "Summer and I will go." She glanced at her wife, who nodded her assent. "Elyse is my student, and we get along well. I think she'd be okay with us being there. We can go right now."

Sam exhaled deeply, his relief evident. "Thank you. That makes this so much easier." The three of them stood, and

Sam wrapped his arms around the two women. Then Jessica and Summer gathered their coats and hurried to the door, exiting into a cold gust of air.

My father went to the corner of the room and made a call. Then he walked back to Sam. "They'll meet us at the station. You ready?" he asked.

"Butch, you don't need to go with me. I can handle this."

Dad clapped him on the shoulder. "I know you can, Sam. But it won't hurt to have someone in your corner. Someone who knows the routine. It would be my honor."

Sam nodded with gratitude. Then Tonya rose, her expression fierce. "I'm going too. Power in numbers, you know."

"Me too," I said, jumping to my feet.

"Oh no you don't," Dad said, pointing at me. "If you recall, Sundance, you were ordered to report to the station tomorrow afternoon yourself. You need to sit this one out. Tonya and I will keep you updated."

"But Dad—"

Sam put his hands on my shoulders. "Callie, I already have Elyse to worry about. If you go to the station, I'll be so nervous I'll look guilty. I'd rather you didn't come."

I bit my lip.

"Sugarplum," Tonya said, "your skills are needed elsewhere. Go back to your cabin and solve these crimes."

Teardrops quivered on my lashes, and I wiped them away with the back of my hand. "All right. I can do that. By the time you get to the station, I intend to have this figured out."

"That's my girl," Dad said. "But call me when you do. No chasing off after leads on your own."

He looked at me sternly, and behind him, my mother nodded.

"Okay if I take a few minutes to walk Callie home, Butch?" Sam asked. "After that break-in, and what just happened to Kimberly, I don't like the idea of her walking through the dark by herself."

If I had internal eyes, I'd have rolled them. It was a sweet gesture, of course, but I could take care of myself. There was a newly installed alarm, after all. And I had the creatures for protection, as well as my pepper spray. But I kept quiet, knowing Sam needed to feel like he was helping.

My father looked pleased. "Absolutely," he said.

Sam and I walked to the lodge entrance. As the glass door slid open, I heard Mrs. Finney's voice from behind us. "Remember what I told you, dear. If you do, I expect this will be over soon."

Woody and Carl led the way down the path. I breathed in the crisp air and gazed at our surroundings. It was as if the four of us had entered a snow globe. The clouds had lifted, and the moon hung plump and bright in the sky. Stars sparkled around it like accent diamonds. I wished Sam and I were simply on a stroll through the winter night.

On a whim, I looped my arm though his and saw him smile in the dark. He was such a good person, kind and generous, loving and forgiving. With the added bonus of being one of the best-looking men I'd ever laid eyes on. How had I let him slip away? I couldn't let that happen again. Especially not like this.

I unlocked the cabin door and disarmed the alarm system, flicking on the soft light on the nightstand. The creatures, uncharacteristically subdued, jumped onto the bed and curled up together. I lifted my eyes to Sam's. "Sam, I have something I need to tell you. When I left all those years ago…I want you to know how sorry I am for the way I handled things."

"None of that," he said, laying a finger across my lips. "We were kids." He studied my face, his eyes resting on my lips. His breathing quickened. "I know this isn't the greatest timing…"

His fingers wove into my hair, and his hand cupped the back of my head as he leaned toward me. The kiss was gentle, his lips warm and soft against mine. The memories came flooding back. I wrapped my arms around his neck.

It was a quick kiss, both a hint of the future and a remembrance of the past. "I've wanted to do that since Monday night," he said. "Well, since long before that, if I'm being honest."

"I'm glad you did." I smiled and pulled his face toward mine for another. Then Woody's head nudged between our thighs and Carl zigzagged through our ankles.

"Guess they know when it's time for a guy to go." Sam touched my cheek, and then he walked to the door. "I'll call you as soon as I can."

"Sam, be careful," I said. "Don't underestimate the power of circumstantial evidence."

He touched his lips to mine once more. "I'm not worried, Callie. I didn't do anything wrong, and I have an army on my side."

As I closed the door, I put my fingers to my lips and smiled. Then my rush of happiness turned into a wave of anxiety. Did I truly have feelings for Sam again, or was I simply responding to fear by reaching back toward a simpler time? Was this a stupid mistake he or I—or both of us— would regret? Was he already regretting it?

I sighed. Tonya would tell me to stop overanalyzing. Dr. Lowell would advise me to allow joy into my life.

Whatever those kisses were, whatever they meant, I needed to put them out of my head for now and focus on crime solving. That was the best thing I could do for Sam— and for myself. It was time to get back to work.

42

I brewed a pot of coffee and planted myself in front of the computer, determined to stay put until I'd identified the real killer.

In front of me lay the crumpled suspect list I'd created at the start of this whole mess. I scratched off Kimberly's name. She hadn't choked herself, after all. From what Sanchez had said, Brian Ratliff was a long shot, at least for Victoria's murder, since he had been rollicking around with a mistress in Denver that afternoon. Yes, two different people could have committed the two different attacks, but the idea seemed so preposterous that I wouldn't waste time on it.

Jessica and Summer? No way. I'd already eliminated them in my mind, and their genuine concern for Sam and Elyse earlier sealed the deal.

My pen hovered above Parker Lyon's name. Crossing him off the list was tough—I'd come to believe he was my major suspect. But his presence at the police station so close to the time of Kimberly's attack constituted an alibi I couldn't ignore. Sanchez claimed there was no way Parker could have had enough time to get to Kimberly's after the detectives released him. But still. The line I drew through his name was lighter than the others.

Then there was Sophie Demler. Since no one had seen her in days, I hadn't given her much thought as a suspect.

But she had motive for wanting to hurt both women. They'd stolen her shop, betrayed her friendship. The photo in her notebook with the two women's faces slashed indicated rage and might have foreshadowed an act of physical violence. And the fact that no one had seen her didn't necessarily mean she'd left town. She could simply be in hiding.

On the other hand, Sophie could be a victim herself. If these crimes were indeed rooted in the past, Sophie's high school alliance with the Vixens might have made her yet another target. Perhaps Sophie wasn't missing. Perhaps she was dead.

But since there wasn't really any evidence to suggest that was the case, I put the idea aside.

Moving to the last name, I tapped my pen against the page, unwilling to even consider it.

My heart knew Sam was no murderer. But as Raul had already made clear, the knowledge of my heart did not constitute evidence. To save Sam, I needed to uncover the identity of the real killer.

Problem was, my meager suspect list offered no answers. I tossed my pen across the table. What was I missing?

Pushing the list aside, I opened my laptop and pulled up the photos I'd shot in Victoria's office. The yearbooks on her desk. The lavender notecard. The photos hanging on the wall. On the floor, her lifeless body. The letter opener. The tiny blue flower.

That flower.

My mind flashed to the flower on Kimberly's kitchen counter. The one hidden in Sophie's notebook. The flower dropped on my bed during the break-in. It had to mean something. But what?

No epiphany.

My bladder insisted on a break. It was eleven o'clock, two hours since Sam had left, and I still had no answers. I felt the solution percolating in the back of my mind, but I couldn't grab hold of it.

After I visited my tiny bathroom, I let Woody out for one last late-night bathroom visit of his own. The falling snow twinkled in the porch light as I stood in the doorway. I rested my arms on the deck railing and waited for the solution to leap into my brain. So close. I was so close.

Woody hopped across the snowdrifts back into the warmth of the cabin, and I followed him, locking the door while he curled up beside the fire. Before I turned the bolt, he had fallen asleep, and for a moment I envied him the freedom from worry that a well-tended dog's life offered.

Of course, he'd just had to pee in the snow, so there was that.

As I returned to my chair, my phone buzzed with a text: an update from Jessica. Kimberly hadn't regained consciousness, but doctors said she was stable. Elyse was emotional but hanging in there.

I texted my thanks and dialed Tonya's number. After four rings, she answered, her voice barely above a whisper. "Hey. Not much to tell. Your dad is in the interview room, but they won't let me in. He came out a few minutes ago and said Sam will probably be released tonight, but it's only temporary. He'll need to go back tomorrow with an attorney."

I caught my breath. "They're going to arrest him?"

"If nothing new breaks, it looks that way. Try not to worry. If you're going to solve this, do it fast."

An hour later, I was no closer to a solution. Frustration and exhaustion clouded my ability to think straight. I threw myself face down on the bed, willing my mind to reboot. Woody stretched across the quilt and licked my face. I felt Carl perched on my back. At least, I hoped it was Carl.

I closed my eyes for a moment, letting my brain rest. I must have drifted off, because my cell phone's ringtone nearly knocked me off the bed. When I saw the name on the screen, I answered immediately.

"Sam? Where are you?"

"I'm home." His voice held a note of despair, though I could tell he was trying to disguise it. "I have to go back tomorrow morning, but my lawyer will be with me."

"Any word from the hospital? When Kimberly regains consciousness, she'll be able to tell us who did this and clear you."

There was a long stretch of silence. "The doctors say she's in a coma. They're not sure what's causing it, so they can't predict when she'll come out of it. We just have to hope for the best."

My hand flew to my mouth. "Oh, Sam. That's…I'm so sorry. How is Elyse?"

"Jessica and Summer took her to their house and gave her a Tylenol PM. She's asleep in their guest room." He sighed. "I'm going to get some sleep myself. You should, too. There's nothing more to be done tonight. Tomorrow is another day, and we'll get it all figured out then."

I told him I'd talk to him tomorrow, and we hung up. But I wasn't planning to sleep. I was determined to get to the bottom of this before morning.

43

C arl's yowl caused adrenaline to shoot through my veins. My eyes shot open, and I looked around, disoriented. I realized I'd fallen asleep in the chair beside my bed, a yearbook open on my lap.

The clock read six a.m. I must have been asleep for three or four hours. I felt a wave of panic on top of the adrenaline. Time was ticking away, and I was no closer to figuring out who had murdered Victoria and attacked Kimberly.

Carl stood on the bed, watching me with a sage expression. His tail swished, and he reached out a paw and batted the yearbook.

It was open to Bethany Weller's sorrowful portrait.

The cat leapt onto my shoulder, wrapping himself around the back of my neck. He mewed in my ear.

I lifted the book and ran a finger across Bethany's name. Suddenly, my mind clicked onto Sophie's notebook and a set of initials she'd jotted inside. BW. Could it be Bethany Weller?

Here it was again—a connection in my mind between the murder and the girl from my past. I jumped up and went over to the computer. I googled Bethany Weller's name, a move I should have made two days ago. Carl pranced across the desk, his tail held high. I clicked on four Bethany Wellers before landing on a link belonging to my old classmate.

It was her obituary, dated three years ago.

A feeling of sadness pulsed through me as I studied the screen. In the center of the page, a youthful Bethany beamed out at me from happier days—pre-sophomore year in high school. Beneath the picture, these words: We Will Never Forget. The phrase was surrounded with tiny blue flowers, just like the ones deposited in all the locations the murderer had recently visited.

Forget-me-nots.

I skimmed the accompanying paragraph, details about a life that ended much too soon. When I read the survivors' names, the answer flashed into my brain as if it had been hidden there the entire time, crouching in an unexplored nook. I remembered where I'd seen Bethany Weller this week. And I suddenly understood the reference in Sophie's notebook: *BW SIS.*

I scooped the cat from the table and held his face inches from mine, staring into his eyes as if he could confirm my hunch. He meowed at the indignity and squirmed from my arms.

But I knew I had to be right.

No cause of death was listed in the obituary, so I kept digging. I hit pay dirt when I found a newspaper article detailing the circumstances surrounding Bethany's death. With that, the last puzzle piece fell into place. I now realized exactly why these crimes had been committed. And by whom.

Ultimately, though, my case was circumstantial. Though in my heart of hearts I knew it to be true, I couldn't prove it.

I leaned back and draped an arm across my forehead. Should I take the information to the detectives? With the paltry evidence I'd uncovered, I didn't think it would do much good. And I didn't want to face Raul again without an iron-clad case.

What I needed was a confession.

I tapped my fingers on the table. To confront the killer alone reeked of stupidity. If I even suggested the possibility to family or friends, they'd lace me up in a straightjacket. But if I took someone with me, I knew I'd never get what I needed.

If I went in alone, I believed the person would tell me what I wanted to know.

Yes. Alone was the best way, the only way, to get the killer to admit to murder. Without that confession, Sam's fate hung in the balance.

So which path should I take? The stupid yet necessary one? Or the safe yet uncertain one?

Not surprisingly, I chose stupid and necessary.

Dad called to tell me he no longer felt it was necessary that I be accompanied by an attorney when I went to the police station in the afternoon. But, he added, it was absolutely necessary that I be accompanied by him. We agreed to meet at noon for a quick lunch beforehand.

I didn't mention the plans I already had in mind for the morning.

I peeked through the blinds and saw that the snow had intensified, falling like a curtain over the resort. Woody and I swaddled up and took a quick, brisk walk, returning to the cabin for a hot shower (just me, not Woody) and kibble (just Woody, not me). Carl paced around the room, moody and distracted. I felt much the same way.

At eight forty-five, I slid my phone into one pants pocket and my pepper spray into the other. After setting the security alarm, I crouched down and pulled Woody into a long hug. "Wish me luck, big guy." He responded with a wag and a slurp. Carl ignored my attempts at an affectionate goodbye. Instead, he arched his back and hissed at me. Very supportive.

When I opened the door to leave, he leapt in front of me, blocking my exit. I lifted him, snarling, and walked over to set him on the bed. He swiped at my arm. If I hadn't been wearing a thick coat, his claws would have left scratches.

"What's gotten into you?" I asked. He stared at me, ears plastered back, and a trickle of foreboding passed through me. Then he jumped off the bed, darting out the door and into the trees, just as he had the evening of the break-in. Woody appeared behind me and whined. I stroked his head and murmured a few reassurances before nudging him back into the cabin and closing the door. I stood for a moment in the falling snow. The cat's antics had gotten under my skin.

But still. Sam's freedom hung in the balance. I had no choice.

I stepped off the porch and, not wanting my parents—or the ever-alert Mrs. Finney—to catch sight of me, left the path to take the shortcut. Snowdrifts swallowed my feet and ankles as I plodded through the woods. After a few rough minutes, I emerged onto Evergreen Way. My heart pounded. Perspiration dotted my upper lip, despite the cold. A mantra choruses through my head: Stupid. Necessary. Stupid. Necessary.

I glanced at the empty storefront and remembered my ten o'clock appointment with Call Me Willie. I doubted I'd be able to keep it. Anyway, the fate of my future photo gallery was in limbo. If I couldn't get this confession, if I couldn't prove Sam's innocence, I didn't think I'd be able to stay in Rock Creek Village. I'd never feel at home here again.

Deep, calming breaths inspired by the nearby yoga studio only made me woozy, so I concentrated on simply putting one foot in front of the other. When I neared my destination, I pulled out my phone and placed a call, fingers crossed that it would go straight to voicemail. I'd never been particularly superstitious, but I did ascribe to the scientific fingers-crossed theory, and it worked for me now. I left my message and climbed the snow-crusted flight of stairs, holding tight to the railing.

When I arrived at the landing, I texted Tonya, outlining as briefly as possible what I'd discovered. The call and the text would serve as my insurance policy. What I was about to do might seem stupid, but I wasn't an idiot, after all.

Don't do anything stupid!!! she responded, mimicking my thoughts. Urgency conveyed via three exclamation points.

I texted back: *I'm there now. PLEASE give me 15 minutes before you send anyone.* Urgency conveyed via caps lock.

My phone buzzed with another text, no doubt Tonya trying to deter me, but I put the device in my pocket without reading it.

I sucked a breath of frigid air into my lungs. As I exhaled a smoky cloud, I turned the knob and entered the waiting room.

44

D
r. Lowell opened the inner door immediately, as if she'd been hovering inside the door. I shrugged off my coat and sat on the couch. She took her regular spot. Worry lines creased her face.

"Callie. I'm so glad you kept your appointment. I wasn't sure you would. Last night must have been so traumatic. Finding Kimberly that way... I still can't believe it..."

"Did you hear Sam might be arrested?"

"The whole thing—it's just dreadful. Let's talk it through."

I hesitated. Though I'd rehearsed how I wanted this to go, I was as nervous right now as a stage actress who hadn't memorized her lines. I took a breath and plunged ahead. "I've been thinking a lot about the past. How everything that happens in the present is the result of something that came before it."

She tilted her head. "You mean like fate?"

I considered. "Not exactly. Not like there's some big book that has every event mapped out in advance. More—karma, I guess. What goes around, comes around. Like that."

She gave me a quizzical look. "Can you give me an example?"

My heart pounded in my chest so hard I thought she must be able to see the movement in the fabric of my shirt. This was the decisive moment. I could choose right now to move forward—or to back off and let the police handle it.

But if I chose the safe route, Sam might be the one to pay the price.

The moment's pause stretched into two, then three. Dr. Lowell shifted in her chair. Finally, she spoke. "Callie, you seem distraught. Perhaps we should put this topic aside for later, when you're less upset. Diving into a subject too quickly, before your mind is ready, can be psychologically damaging—"

"No, I'm ready. I want—need—to tell you what's on my mind."

I stood and moved across the room, standing beside Dr. Lowell's desk. "I want to talk about a girl I knew in high school. This girl…" I lifted the framed photo, the one I'd noticed when I was snooping on my first visit. The photo that showed Dr. Lowell in a cap and gown, posing with her mother and a young woman I now knew to be her half-sister.

Bethany Weller.

Dr. Lowell's face paled, and her lips tightened. She rose warily to her feet. "Callie, that's enough," she said. As I witnessed her change in demeanor, my fight-or-flight reflex peaked. But flight was not an option.

I turned the photo toward Dr. Lowell and pointed at Bethany. "This girl was a sophomore in high school the last time I saw her. She was half naked in the locker room, surrounded by a group of mean girls. Bullies. They were led by Victoria, who is now dead, and Kimberly, who nearly met the same fate last night." My eyes filled with tears. A wave of grief washed through me. "I failed her in high school. I wish I could tell her how sorry I am for that. But I can't, so I'm telling you instead."

She snatched the frame from my hands. "Beth was my sister," she said, her gaze dropping to the photo. "She told me about you. Said you made the other girls leave her alone. She was grateful for that. Why do you consider that a failure?"

"I should have reached out to her after that, checked on her," I said. "I should have helped her through a rough time. But in typical fashion, I was absorbed in my own pursuits—*my* photography, *my* writing, *my* boyfriend. No time for a girl who needed a friend. And what's even worse? I later became a bully myself, when I became judge and jury to an innocent man just because I thought he was a jerk."

Dr. Lowell tossed the photo onto her desk. "Stop being a martyr. You're not as important as you think."

Ouch. Gone was my compassion-filled therapist. In her place stood a cold, suffering survivor of her own trauma.

"You didn't send that man to jail," she went on, "and you didn't cause Beth to spiral out of control. If anyone failed her, it was me." She shook her head angrily. "To be honest, everyone failed her. Her father dumped her and our mother refused to see that anything was wrong."

She moved to the window and stared outside. "You know what ultimately happened to Beth, I assume."

I had learned the key parts of the story. The newspaper articles and the obituary had provided the facts, and I'd surmised the details. But I needed to hear them from Dr. Lowell's lips. It was the easiest way to free Sam.

"The basics," I said.

Dr. Lowell was silent. For a moment I thought we had come to an impasse. But then she began to fill in the blanks of Bethany's story.

"After her sophomore year, when it became obvious those vicious girls would never let up and that no one at the school could—or would—help her, Mom and Beth moved away. A fresh start, they thought. But nothing was ever fresh for my sister again. One thing I've learned is that, once people have become prey, they often find it difficult to erase that odor from themselves. It takes insight. But insight requires support, but Beth didn't get that. Not from our mother, and not from me."

"Did she see a counselor?" I asked.

"Of course," Dr. Lowell snapped. "I was in college to be a psychologist, remember? Beth attended two sessions with a therapist and refused to return. I remember feeling irritated that she had rejected her wise older sister's suggestions, so I essentially left her to fend for herself. I figured if things got bad enough, she'd end up taking my advice."

Another interlude of silence followed. I glanced at the clock, then the door, feeling my window of opportunity slipping away. But then she continued in a monotone voice. "But Beth found her own way to ease the pain. Escape through alcohol, then painkillers, then cocaine—whatever she could get her hands on. You can guess the rest of the story. Addiction, just a different form of torture. Toward the end, I started to panic. Got her a top-notch drug counselor. Checked her into rehab after rehab. None of it worked. She was just too damaged."

The rage in Dr. Lowell's voice diminished. In its place, I heard sadness and regret. "Two years ago, her spiral ended when her car crashed through a side rail and plummeted off a mountain."

I'd read the newspaper accounts. Bethany was thrown from the car. Police found her body in a gorge, twisted and broken. Though investigators had ruled the crash an accident, I had my doubts. I imagined Dr. Lowell did too. The girl had wrecked her car on purpose.

"You were years older, off at college when this whole chain of events began," I said. "You did everything you could for her. Some people can't be saved."

"And when exactly did you earn your counseling degree?" she asked, her voice infused with sarcasm. I tensed, fearing her rage might be returning.

"I didn't," I said. "A wise woman has been teaching me the importance of forgiving myself. I'm wondering if she can take her own advice."

She narrowed her eyes. "Oh, please. Don't you think I've tried? It's not like I want to live with this grief and anger for the rest of my life. My degree, my license, my whole career was devoted to fixing my sister. I dedicated my entire adult life to taking care of her and my mother. Mom got sick and died five years ago. Another casualty of my sister's problems, no doubt in my mind. All my training and I couldn't help the only two people in the world I loved. It all began because of two horrible sociopaths and their gang of recruits…"

"And now you're intent on making them pay," I said.

She glared at me for a beat. Then her mouth wreathed into a twisted smile that was scarier than the glare. I instinctively reached into my pocket to grip the pepper spray. But she one-upped me, pulling a sleek steel gray 9 mm pistol from the oversized pocket of her sweater.

I had brought pepper spray to a gun fight.

45

T ake out whatever is in your pocket and put it on the desk," she said.

I did as she commanded, placing the pink canister next to the framed photo.

"What's in your other pocket?"

"Just my phone." I held it up in my left hand, and she gestured for me to lay it beside the pepper spray.

"I should have guessed you'd figure it out. Too bad. I tried to warn you off. I liked you, Callie, even admired you. I truly hoped I could help you."

Past tense? That was worrisome. Positioned as she was between me and the door, she blocked any chance I had at escape—assuming I could pull off a miracle and zigzagged out of the path of a bullet fired at close range.

If only I'd brought my Wonder Woman bracelets.

I needed to keep her talking. That's what they did in those cop shows I watched.

"You *are* helping me. You're showing me how to forgive myself. I'm making progress, too." I tried to brighten my tone. "I haven't told you my good news. I'm going to lease the empty shop downstairs. I'm opening a photo gallery. A fresh start."

Dr. Lowell barked a laugh. "Keep her talking, huh? That's your strategy? A last-ditch effort to prevent the inevitable. I guess I can indulge you for a few minutes, but only because

I'm curious. How did you figure out it was me?"

"Does it matter?"

"I suppose not. But I think you'll want to humor me. What was my mistake? I thought I was so careful. So clever."

I nodded. "Your plan was solid. Nearly foolproof, in fact. Framing Kimberly for Victoria's murder—that was brilliant. Two birds with one stone, as the saying goes."

"My master stroke," she said, her eyes lighting up. "What I really wanted was to see Kimberly go to prison, to suffer there for the rest of her life. Can you imagine that stuck-up snob in an oversized orange jumpsuit, trapped behind bars for eternity? Can you just picture her in those disgusting crusty showers? In the mess hall eating bologna sandwiches? The carbs alone would drive her insane. And she'd be penned up with women she despised—or better yet, women who despised her. The sweetest revenge." Insanity flashed in her eyes.

"Then why did you go to her house last night? Why did you try to kill her?"

"Because of you. Your infernal snooping. Even after my warnings—the calls I made, the break-in—you kept pushing. I was afraid you might end up proving she didn't murder Victoria. I couldn't have that. Kimberly's freedom, when my sister is dead for eternity?"

"How fitting that you used drugs to subdue them both," I prompted.

"I enjoyed that angle too. A tribute to my sister," she said, her lips twisting. "Getting to Victoria was a breeze. She was a client, after all. She trusted me. And she was delighted to share all the dirty details about her affair with Parker, including how she rigged the back door of the event center for their little trysts. She called to tell me about her fight with Kimberly on Saturday. I asked if she wanted me to come by for a session. Attention was Victoria's drug of choice, so I gave her mine. I crushed three Ambien before I went, laced her wine with them, and she was out like a light. Then I used her phone to text Kimberly, bided my time, and stabbed Victoria with her own letter opener." A smile creased her face. "Victoria's eyes opened just as the blade went in, and I whispered my sister's name. That gave me joy. I wanted her to know who was responsible for her death, and why."

I shuddered, but tried to keep the repulsion out of my voice. "And you did the same with Kimberly last night?"

"No sense reinventing the wheel," Dr. Lowell said with a shrug. "My plan was to knock her out with the drugs and drown her in the hot tub. Simple. I was actually hoping that loser husband of hers would find her and be implicated. She didn't succumb as easily to the sedative, though. Higher tolerance, I suppose. The Ambien in her wine made her loopy but never completely knocked her out. So I had to resort to more... physical methods." I glanced at her muscular hands, picturing them around Kimberly's neck.

"You put her in the hot tub," I said. "To destroy evidence?"

She pointed her gun at me. "Bingo. Kimberly told me she'd asked you to come over, so I knew I had to hurry. I really thought she was dead when I tossed her over the edge. Her blood pressure must have dropped and slowed her breathing. Guess I got a little careless." She shook her head. "I'll just have to hope she never comes out of the coma."

Her academic tone, her nonchalance, gave me a chill. She was so calm, even though one woman was dead, another debilitated, and a man I cared about was about to be arrested.

I knew my own future hung in the balance.

Then I thought about another potential victim. "What about Sophie Demler?" I asked.

Dr. Lowell cocked her head. "What about her?"

"She was one of Victoria's Vixens. One of the girls in the locker room that day. And now she's gone missing. Did you kill her too? Dispose of her body?"

"Wouldn't that be a nice twist?" she said. "But no. I toyed

with her a bit. Sent her a threatening note. She was smarter than Victoria and Kimberly, though. Hightailed it out of town. She was a minor player anyway. I wanted the two big fish."

She lifted the gun again. "Now you've heard the whole sordid story. It's your turn. Tell me what I want to know. How did you figure it out?"

I stole a glance at the clock. I'd gotten the confession I wanted. Where was the cavalry? Now all I could do was stall for time. "The answers lie where the end began," I said.

She looked annoyed. "No riddles. I want an explanation."

"That is the explanation. Everything fell into place once I figured out that the murders had their genesis in the past. Any number of people in this town hated Victoria and Kimberly, but these attacks didn't feel impulsive. That made me believe they had nothing to do with present circumstances. The rage that exploded in these acts had simmered for a long time. When I looked through my old yearbooks, I saw your sister's photo, and it stirred a memory. It took a while to latch onto it, but when I remembered that day in the locker room, I understood how this began."

She frowned. "I worried about those yearbooks. It's the reason I took them when I saw them on your bed."

"Is that why you broke into my cabin? To steal the books?"

"No. I just wanted to leave the note. I wanted to scare you, to keep you from pursuing your little investigation. As I told you earlier, I wanted to protect you."

While her purported benevolence didn't overwhelm me with gratitude, it did give me a smidgen of hope that I might yet get out of this alive.

"Even when you remembered that locker room scene, you didn't realize Beth was my sister, did you? Or that she was dead?"

I shook my head. "I didn't put it all together until this morning. I remembered seeing Bethany's face recently, but

I couldn't pinpoint where. For a while, I even speculated she might have grown up and murdered Victoria."

"If only she'd had the pleasure," Dr. Lowell said. "I wish. You remembered her picture on my desk, though, right? I wondered if you recognized her. But you never mentioned Beth, never seemed to connect the two of us."

"Not right away, no. But Carl kept drawing my attention to her yearbook picture."

"Carl?"

"It doesn't matter," I said. "I could feel myself moving closer, and finally it just clicked. I remembered the graduation photo on your desk and realized you and Bethany were sisters. An internet search confirmed it and explained the details of Bethany's... accident. Her death. You moved to the village not long after she died, didn't you? You've been planning this for years."

She rubbed her forehead with her free hand, the gun wavering. I considered making a move toward the door, but she regained her focus and steadied the gun.

"The flowers," I said, my voice soft. "Forget-me-nots. You couldn't forget her, couldn't let her death go unpunished."

"I was probably the only person in the world who remembered Bethany." Her voice hitched. "I moved here two years ago, after Mom died. I had the silly notion that it might help me feel closer to my lost sister. Before she got to high school, Beth had loved it here, had been so happy. I lived with my father in Utah and wasn't around much. I guess I hoped by moving here I might recapture some of Beth's joy. Turned out being around Victoria and Kimberly had the opposite effect on me. It was as if they were standing beside my sister and my mother's graves, laughing. It consumed me. They faced no consequences, exhibited no remorse, while my sister and my mother lay in the ground."

"I can't even imagine your pain," I said.

Dr. Lowell waved, flicking away my empathy. "We all have our crosses to bear, don't we?" She smiled.

"Abandoning everyone you loved? Sending an innocent man to jail? Your life hasn't been a picnic, Callie. The difference is, I am a victim of someone else's actions. You've done it to yourself."

My mouth dropped open. I already understood that Dr. Lowell was extremely dangerous, but the cruelty in her words convinced me there was no talking my way out of this. Now I had to rely on the help of others. I hoped Raul had listened to his voicemail, or that Tonya had contacted him and sent him to my rescue.

And I had one other trick up my sleeve. I crossed my fingers.

46

D r. Lowell, Bethany wouldn't want this." My one last ditch effort—an appeal to the memory of her sister. My breathing came in shallow bursts.

The anger in her eyes turned to pain. Her expression became that of a wounded wild animal—one whose agony would cause it to attack. "No. She wouldn't have wanted any of this. She didn't want what happened to her in high school either. But she got it anyway, didn't she?"

Her face suddenly crumpled, and her shoulders shook with silent sobs. Maybe those tears were a sign she was ready to end this. I moved toward her, thinking I might comfort her into surrender.

When she saw me in motion, she took a step backwards and raised the gun, her finger just above the trigger. I stopped short and lifted my hands in surrender, convinced I had only seconds to live.

Still, hope never dies. Until the body does.

"You're trembling," she said. Her eyes widened in comprehension. "You think I'm going to shoot you."

"Well, you are aiming a gun at me," I pointed out.

Her laugh held no humor. "Oh, Callie. Like you, I'm very good at my job. So permit me to deliver one last diagnosis. We only had two sessions, but they were enough. Sit, if you'd like. Or perhaps now is a good time to lie on the couch."

"I'm fine here."

She nodded. "In my professional opinion, you suffer from maladaptive perfectionism. It's easily treatable if the patient has the capacity for insight and the willingness to implement a few cognitive strategies, such as the ones we've already discussed."

She watched me for a response, but I only blinked. "You also vacillate in and out of minor depression. Again, awareness should be enough to get you through any future bouts, but keep an eye on it. I suggest you listen to your mother and cut back on your alcohol consumption." She tilted her free hand toward her mouth, miming a drinker tossing one down. "Alcohol is a depressant. Best to leave it alone. Lastly, you battle low self-esteem, as most women do. You compensate with a hefty dose of self-centeredness."

She shrugged. "And that's it. Everything that makes you unhappy is reparable with lifestyle changes and good relationship choices, which you appear to be making. Keep doing what you're doing. Consider regular attendance at meditation class. You'll be fine."

Meditation class? Good relationship choices? What kind of sick game was Dr. Lowell playing?

She smiled at me, confident in her expert role. The gun never wavered.

"My self-diagnosis is a bit more complicated," she said. "I've been severely depressed most of my adult life. I suffer from post-traumatic stress disorder, and I'm on the OCD scale. And now that I have achieved at least part of my quest by killing Victoria, I find myself succumbing to suicidal ideation."

She trained the gun on me. "I like you, Callie. But I don't feel the same about myself."

Slowly, she raised the gun toward her temple.

Just as I finally grasped her intention, the door edged open behind her. A small ray of hope bloomed in my chest. My rescuer had arrived. If I could distract Dr. Lowell for just one more moment, Raul might still save the day.

I kept my eyes on her and spoke in a low, gentle voice.

"Please don't do this. Bethany needs you here, telling people what happened to her. You can help keep it from happening to anyone else. I'll stand by you." And then I was crying, realizing how much I wanted to save her.

The gun dropped an inch. "I'm sorry, Callie. I truly am. I didn't plan to do this in front of you. But you'll be fine. And so will Sam and Elyse. So many people love you all. I have no one."

As she lifted the gun again, the door flew the rest of the way open, crashing against the wall and startling Dr. Lowell, who turned toward the noise.

But it wasn't Raul. Instead, my rescuer took the form of a tall, stocky woman clad in purple yoga pants.

Mrs. Finney's entrance provided me with the distraction I needed. I leapt toward Dr. Lowell and thrust my palm into her nose. She bobbled the gun. Mrs. Finney followed with a smooth martial arts motion, landing a kick to the back of Dr. Lowell's knees. The weapon flew from her hand, and the therapist fell face first onto the floor. The purple dervish pounced on the doctor's back and shoved a forearm across her neck, pinning her to the ground.

I stared at her in shock. "Mrs. Finney?" I asked.

"Yes, dear, it's me," she said. "Now be a love and retrieve that gun. The bobbies aren't far behind, but until they arrive, we need to keep this killer in our sights."

As I tried to make sense of everything, I was shocked to see Carl peeking around the door jamb. "How did you get here?" I asked him. He sashayed toward me and rubbed against my calf.

Dr. Lowell lay motionless on the floor, her eyes vacant. Perched on the woman's back, Mrs. Finney smiled up at me. "My dear, you owe this lovely feline a very nice spot of catnip. He jumped out at me as I was taking my morning hike, screaming and yowling as if his fur was on fire. When he was certain he had my attention, he sprinted down Evergreen Way. He led me straight here."

I shook my head. "Of course he did. And you just happened to be out hiking? Without even wearing a coat?"

She granted me another of her enigmatic smiles. "The soul's warmth is rarely enhanced by outer garments."

At least that one I understood.

Moments later, footsteps pounded up the stairs and Raul rushed into the office, gun drawn, followed by Frank, also wielding his firearm. Like cartoon characters, they both skidded to a halt, jaws dropping at the sight of Mrs. Finney atop Dr. Lowell and me aiming a gun at the therapist's prone figure.

To his credit, Raul recovered instantly, holstering his weapon before relieving Mrs. Finney from her position and then crouching next to Dr. Lowell, handcuffs poised. Frank pried the gun from my fingers. "It's okay, Callie. You've done your job. We've got this now."

After he had cuffed Dr. Lowell, Raul rose and pulled her to her feet, settling her onto the couch. She appeared confused and disheveled, her eyes focused on some distant reality only she could see. Then my father showed up, scanned the scene and hurried toward me. "You are grounded," he muttered, lifting my chin and studying my face. "For the rest of your life."

Over his shoulder, I saw an uncharacteristically frazzled Tonya enter the room. Sam rushed in right behind her, his eyes filled first with terror and then relief. Dad released me and moved away to call Mom.

Tonya pulled me into a hug. Sam wrapped his arms around us both.

"That was the longest fifteen minutes of my life," Tonya said. "But when you're blood sisters, you have a pact."

I squeezed her so hard she gasped. "Enough, girlfriend," she said, wriggling from my grasp. "People will start to talk."

I laughed and turned to Sam. "And how did you get roped into this dramatic moment?"

"Tonya called me and told me to pick her up right away," he said. "Refused to tell me why until we pulled up to the curb."

I opened my mouth to respond, but Raul's voice boomed from behind me. "All right, everyone out. Except you." He pointed at me, and then to Mrs. Finney, his expression incredulous. "And you."

After a few tut-tuts and cooing noises, Tonya and Sam filed out of the room. Dad lifted a protesting Carl into his arms and promised to check on Woody. When everyone else was gone, Frank took a position by the door, his eyes on Dr. Lowell. Raul stared at Mrs. Finney and me, his arms crossed. "Who wants to tell me what happened here?"

Without answering, I moved toward the desk.

"Where do you think you're going?" he asked.

"To get my phone. I think you'll want it, since I turned on the audio recorder before I entered the room." I gave him a wink. "All in a day's work."

47

I didn't make it to my appointment with Call Me Willie at ten.

But I was at his office the next day.

And now, just one week later, the papers had been signed and notarized, the deposit check cashed. I'd called Preston, my former boss, and explained unequivocally that I wouldn't be back. And here I sat at a table in the center of the cavernous space that would soon become my photo gallery: Sundance Studio.

For now, though, it served as Party Central. My family and friends had decorated—folding chairs, tables covered with paper cloths, and strings of sparkling white lights suspended from the ceiling. Everyone who entered received a plastic flute filled with sparkling champagne as they entered. A huge sheet cake rested on a table.

Its message? "Congratulations, Callie. Welcome Home."

I wasn't sure who had planned this little shindig, but it wasn't much of a surprise, given Mrs. Finney's demand this morning for the gallery's keys.

But still. It was a lovely gesture, and I was touched.

As I sat at the table of honor, I looked around the room, watching people clustered in small groups, talking and laughing. Raul, with whom I had kissed and made up—minus the kiss—caught my eye and gave me a wink as he and Frank conversed with two other officers who had worked the case. Jessica and Summer were there, laughing with Fran from Quicker Liquor, who had supplied the champagne—in bottles rather than boxes. Selena Sanchez, Raul's mother and the woman at the helm of the high school, talked with Mrs. Barney, the librarian, who never even so much as waggled a finger at me for those overdue yearbooks. Anyway, she'd have them back as soon as they were released from evidence.

Even Parker had shown up. He lifted his glass to me, a pompous smile on his face. I lifted my own glass in return. He wasn't an evil guy after all, just shallow and self-absorbed. But he'd been beside Kimberly's bed nonstop until she'd finally awakened, and word had it they were going to give their marriage another try.

I watched my parents listening to Mrs. Finney, who was no doubt regaling them with yet another axiom. Mom reached down to pet Woody and Carl, who stood at her feet wearing the burgundy sweaters she'd knitted for them. Woody looked pleased, as if he belonged on the cover of Doggie GQ. But I swore Carl rolled his eyes.

Strangest of all, Sophie Demler had made an appearance, tanned and self-satisfied following a week-long Caribbean cruise with her mother. It seemed she'd taken the threat to heart and left for sunnier climes, neglecting to inform her boss—or anyone else, for that matter. She was chatting in a…was I imagining it?…flirtatious manner with Dan the Bartender.

The eminent editor of *The Gazette* and my dearest friend in the world, glided into a chair next to mine, draping one arm over my shoulder and gesturing with the other. "This is all for you, sweet potato," she said. "What do you think of that?"

I took a moment to rein in my emotions. "To tell you the truth, I feel undeserving. It's hard to believe all these people came here for me."

"Wait until the grand opening. We'll do that event up big. It'll make this little fête look like a garage sale."

Though I smiled, Tonya saw right through it. "Why the melancholy clouds in those beautiful eyes?"

"Just thinking about everything. A woman is dead. Two, if you count Bethany Weller. Kimberly was nearly killed—"

"She's out of the hospital, you know. Tucked home in bed and ordering everyone around like royalty, from what I hear. I'm told she'll make a full recovery. No memory of what happened, but otherwise, none the worse for wear."

"That's good," I said. "But there's just so much fallout. Brian uprooted the twins and moved to Denver. Elyse is left to deal with the whole new experience of having two dads. And Dr. Lowell…"

"I heard you visited her yesterday. Any improvement?"

I shook my head. "She's still catatonic, unless she's faking it. They say she'll stay in the psychiatric facility until they declare her fit to stand trial. If that ever happens. So many lives forever altered. It almost seems inappropriate to be celebrating my good fortune."

Tonya flicked my arm with one of her sculpted nails. "Get over yourself, sugar lamb. Life is all about change and loss and struggle. That's what creates room for joy. And when joy comes, as it always does, we have to embrace it."

She leaned over and whispered in my ear. "Plus, that nasty boutique has closed for good. That's a silver lining worth celebrating."

Laughing, I blotted my eyes and looked toward the front door as it swung open. Sam walked in, taking my breath away yet again. Elyse followed, ducking her head with an uncharacteristic shyness. I felt bad for her, worried that Sam had forced his daughter to attend this little gala. When he stopped to say hello to my parents, Elyse headed over to my table.

"Can I talk to you, Ms. Cassidy?" she said, barely meeting my eyes.

"Sure. But only if you call me Callie." Tonya rose, mumbling something about refilling her glass, and I motioned Elyse into the empty chair.

"Okay. Callie." A tentative smile. "When my dad told me where he was going, I asked if I could come along. I want to apologize for how horrible I've acted. You've been nothing but kind to me. You even stood up for me at school that day. Thing is, I saw how my dad looked at you. I guess I was scared of losing him. It's been…hard."

She hesitated, her eyes glistening. Though they weren't related biologically, the expression on her face looked so much like Sam that she couldn't possibly be anyone else's daughter. I touched her hand. "There's no need to apologize, Elyse, but I appreciate it. I expect you'll have a rough time for a while. But you're a strong young woman. Whatever I can do to help you, please just ask. Maybe we can even be friends."

A mischievous smile played on her face, and she nudged me with her elbow. "I'll bet you'd like that. It'd make it easier when you date my dad."

Butterflies fluttered in my chest, and I felt the deer-in-the-headlights expression on my face. Elyse responded with a bigger grin. "I'm just messing with you. I hope the two of you do hook up. He's been alone for a long time, and… well, you're cool."

I blushed as Sam sauntered up to the table, looking from me to Elyse with narrowed eyes. "What's going on here, ladies?"

"Girl talk, Dad. I'm going back to the cafe. This party is for the old folks." She kissed him on the cheek and walked toward the door.

"Want to tell me what that was about?" He dropped down beside me.

"Nope," I said, smiling. "Suffice it to say you have a very mature daughter."

He chuckled. "Yeah, well, you haven't been around when I catch her coming in after curfew. But I'll admit, she has her moments."

He squeezed my hand. I squeezed back, and we made googly eyes at each other like the teenagers we'd been not so long ago.

Tonya returned with a fresh glass of champagne for each of us and shook her head. "Oh, for heaven's sake, get a room, you two."

Sam snickered, and I blushed. Tonya turned serious. "So, sweetie pie, I've heard most of the details, almost everything," she said. "In fact, as you know, I've written a series of award-caliber stories about the incidents in question, good enough to get me my own Felden Prize, I suspect. There's just one thing I don't know…"

I laughed. "If you don't know, it's doubtful I do either."

"Oh, I think you do." She raised a carefully plucked eyebrow. "What's the deal with Mrs. Finney?"

All three of us looked in the stately woman's direction, and she glanced up and wiggled her fingers. Almost in unison, we wiggled ours back. I leaned in, my voice low. "I'll tell you, but it has to be off the record. You're both sworn to secrecy."

Sam nodded immediately, but Tonya hesitated, pouting. "Off the record? That's not fair."

"It's the only way I'll divulge."

"What if I confirm the information on my own?"

I shook my head. "Nope. This has to be our secret."

She considered her options and relented. "Okay, then. Spill. It better be worth it."

I whispered the whole story, everything I had learned at the close of the investigation. It included the letters C, I, A.

"Mrs. Finney?" they said together, eyes wide.

I shushed them. "Yes, dears. Her."

"She's an operative?" Tonya whispered. "What's she doing in Rock Creek Village?"

"Former operative," I corrected. "Seriously, though, you should have seen her in action. The woman is highly trained. And she came here with specific instructions to watch over me."

"Instructions? From whom?" Tonya asked.

"None other than Preston Garrison, my former boss.

After the email Jameson Jarrett sent me, I knew Preston was worried, but I had no idea the extent of his concern. Mrs. Finney had been a regular guest lecturer for an investigative journalism class Preston taught at Georgetown. She'd mentioned wanting a change of scenery, so the two of them put their heads together, and here she is."

For once, Tonya was speechless.

"By the way," I added, "she's not British. The accent is fake. But I suspect she'll hang onto it as long as she stays in the village."

"Bloody hell." Sam whistled through puffed cheeks. "I can see how she made a good agent though. Who'd suspect her of being a spy?"

My mother called me over to the serving table. "Time to cut the cake, sweetheart. Say something profound to all these people here to celebrate you."

I'd figured I should say something in gratitude to my family and friends, so I had chosen my words ahead of time. The question was, could I make it through my little speech without becoming emotional?

The windows of the shop framed the mountain range, and the afternoon sun poured across their peaks, seeping into the gallery and touching the walls with a shimmer I interpreted as hope.

I looked around the room at the smiling, expectant faces and accepted that I would cry. So be it.

My voice quivered. "Robert Frost wrote, 'Home is where, when you have to go there, they have to take you in.' And you people have taken me in with generosity, love, friendship, warmth, and unconditional acceptance. Not to mention a heavy dose of intrigue and drama."

Everyone laughed, and I smiled through my tears. "I wish I had the words to express how grateful I am to you all. This place, this village, is where I belong."

I wiped the tears away as my audience clapped and cheered.

I was finally home.

*Read on for a sneak peek at the next book in the
Callie Cassidy Mysteries series.*

Double Exposure

Coming May 2021

1

"**G**ood news, Callie. You don't suck. At least, not today."

The baritone voice proclaiming my non-sucky status belonged to Ethan Paterson, the business teacher at the local high school. I'd hired him this summer to help promote my newborn photography gallery, Sundance Studio. He was standing in front of the shop, arm extended like a *Price is Right* model toward the spotless display windows and the immaculate stoop.

Hands on my hips, I inspected every inch of the facade and felt my anxiety begin to dissipate. "They left us alone last night," I said.

"Maybe they're done for good. Bored with their stupid pranks." His blue eyes twinkled beneath short-cropped red hair, and his smile radiated from his scruffy beard and mustache. At twenty-eight years old, he was the definition of a Scottish ginger. Every time I looked at him, broad shouldered and stocky, I half expected to find him clad in a kilt.

His smile was infectious, and I grinned back at him as I ran my finger across the inscription etched on the front door's glass insert. *Sundance Studio, Callahan Cassidy, Photographer.* Sometimes I still had trouble believing I was back in Rock Creek Village and that this gallery belonged to me. I turned my gaze to the mountains, awash in the buttery early morning light. A soft breeze carried the scent of wildflowers. Another gorgeous June day in the Rocky Mountains. This place didn't suck. And neither, apparently did I.

For now, anyway.

"I hope you're right. I don't know how much more I could take without going ballistic."

The vandalism had started on Monday, though I didn't realize at the time that's what it was. That morning, I'd found the wooden sign normally hanging above the gallery's entrance on the ground, propped against my front door. I figured it had simply fallen, victim of a faulty screw perhaps, and some Good Samaritan moved it to my doorway. I got out my ladder, reattached the sign to its iron bracket, and went about my day.

On Tuesday, I arrived to the sight of puckered tomatoes, peeled onions, and wilted lettuce littering my stoop, as if a passing zombie suddenly remembered he was a carnivore and disposed of his rotting salad at my door. A glance down Evergreen Way confirmed that the salad shooter had not victimized anyone else. I experienced my first twinge of concern.

Yesterday, that twinge blossomed into full-blown paranoia. A would-be graffiti artist had scrawled the B word in red spray paint across the studio's box window, followed by the poetic words: *You suck, Callie.*

Once I'd recovered from the jolt, and the wave of embarrassment that accompanied it, I first snapped a few pictures and then filled a bucket with soapy water. After scrubbing the offensive words from the glass, I quizzed neighboring shop owners. No one had witnessed the event, nor had they experienced any vandalism of their own. My father Butch, the former Rock Creek Village police chief, insisted I file a police report. I did as instructed, but I knew the police couldn't do much about it. I just had to hope the pranksters didn't escalate.

Though my realistic—okay, cynical—nature warned me against premature relief, I was grateful that today provided, if not an end, a reprieve. It couldn't have come at a better time.

"Thank goodness," I said. "We have so much to do. No time to pick up garbage or clean windows." I flashed him a grateful smile. "Thanks again for coming in so early."

"Will Alexis be joining us?"

I glanced at my watch, choosing to ignore his sarcasm. "She should be here any time now." At twenty-two years old, Alexis Butler, the assistant I'd hired a month ago, hadn't yet developed the same preoccupation with punctuality as Ethan, but she'd proven reliable. She wouldn't let us down.

"Happy hour starts at five, right?" Ethan asked.

I nodded and dug into my pocket for the door key. "We'll close the gallery at one and set up. Shouldn't take more than an hour to put out a few tables and string some lights from the ceiling. Then we can all go home and change. I'll come back by four so Sam can set up catering, but I won't need you and Alexis until four thirty."

I extracted the key from my pocket, fumbled it, and watched as it clattered to the sidewalk. Ethan stooped to retrieve it. "Nervous much?" he asked with a gentle smile.

"Is it obvious?"

"Shoulders up to your ears, ragged breath, can't hang onto a key. I'd say so." With a steady hand, he inserted the key into the lock and pulled the door open. "Take a breath. It's only a bunch of *Washington Sentinel* reporters coming to see your new digs. It's not like you'll be hosting Ironman and Thor."

That elicited an actual laugh, my first in days. Ethan was right. I was getting riled up trying to impress my former boss and some ex-colleagues, most of whom I hadn't even liked much.

"I'll try to relax," I said, taking one of the meditative breaths I'd learned at Yoga Delight down the street.

But I couldn't reach my inner Zen. My guests were fancy

Sentinel journalists, after all, and I'd left their ranks to become a semi-obscure landscape photographer, catering to tourists. I kept imagining all those judgmental eyes scrutinizing my gallery with an air of superiority.

You would have been exactly the same way a year ago, I thought regretfully.

Still, I yearned to impress them. My mind raced with everything I needed to accomplish before they arrived. Finish the photojournalism display, reorganize the portrait section, change out a few of the winter landscapes to highlight summer shots. Only a few hours to complete the tasks—while dealing with what I hoped was a steady flow of morning shoppers.

Ethan snapped his fingers in front of my face. "Earth to Callie. Listen, my friend, the only thing that's going to calm you down is scratching items off your to-do list. Let's get started."

I nodded and hurried into the studio, flicking on the light. Biting my lip, I paused to scan the walls, trying to see my photos as a newcomer might. First, my eye rested on the gallery's focal point: a huge panoramic shot of the majestic Rockies soaring heavenward from a meadow filled with wildflowers. A colorful array of wildlife photos surrounded this centerpiece—shots of elk, mountain goats, deer, marmots, and chipmunks. Beside the door, a rack held postcard-sized prints of original Callie Cassidy landscape photos. I felt pride well up inside me. Even my snooty ex-coworkers would have to admit the studio was stunning.

Smiling, I headed toward the sales counter. Then my nose twitched as I detected a foul odor wafting through the usually pine-scented space. The smell was unpleasant but familiar, pungent but organic—and it was an odor I'd experienced a hundred times in my back yard.

Behind me, Ethan called out, his tone urgent. "Callie, stop. Watch your step."

I turned to look at him, my right foot hovering mid-air. But momentum partnered with gravity, and my beige canvas shoe descended with a squish.

Into a huge brown pile of poop.

I leapt backwards and squealed like a schoolgirl. I'd covered wars and murders and gruesome accidents. I'd seen more dead bodies than I cared to remember—people who'd been shot and bludgeoned and stabbed—including a resident of our own village just a few months ago. All those scenes I'd handled with fortitude and aplomb.

But poop was my kryptonite.

How ironic that I had chosen two four-legged poop machines as my roommates.

Just then, the bell above the door jingled and Alexis entered, pulling her frizzy brown hair into a ponytail. Her brown eyes narrowed. She wrinkled her nose and then pinched it. "Ugh. What reeks?" Her eyes landed on the squished mound of poop. "Eww. Is that Woody's doing? Where's that bad dog hiding?"

If he had been privy to Alexis' comment, my Golden Retriever, who at this moment was likely snuggled up with his feline brother Carl at our new townhome, would have lifted his snout in haughty disdain. Since he wasn't here to defend himself, I did it for him. "Woody hasn't pooped inside since his puppy days. This pile was already on the floor when Ethan and I walked in."

She pursed her lips. "More vandalism? But how did they get inside?"

"Good question," I said. "I'm sure I locked the doors before I left last night." I tried to replay the events in my mind, but my memory was hazy. Yesterday had been a long and hectic day, and I'd been exhausted by the end of it. "Well, I'm almost sure…"

"Who could be doing this?" Alexis asked.

"I know who gets my vote," Ethan said. "Those twits Baden and Banner Ratliff. Juvenile pranks are just their speed." He scowled and stalked off to the tiny kitchen behind the back wall of the gallery.

"Tweedledee and Tweedledum," I murmured, remembering my private nickname for the boys. I understood Ethan's suspicions. After the events that occurred a few months ago, the twins had reason to hate me—at least in their own minds. They'd moved to Denver in February to escape village gossip but had returned to Rock Creek Village a couple of weeks ago, just before the incidents began. It made sense that they were responsible. The question was, how would we prove it?

Alexis took a deep breath and followed it with a gagging noise. "Well, I'm not cleaning up this mess." She tiptoed around the pile and went behind the sales desk, the ever-present frown lining her face.

Ethan emerged from the back with a bucket of soapy water, a dustpan, and a plastic ruler he'd use for a scoop. "Don't worry, you delicate little flower," he said. "Your knight in shining armor is here to take care of the mess. As usual."

She shot him an angry glare and lifted her hand, middle finger extended. I suppressed a smile. "Now, now. You two play nice. We have too much to do to indulge in faux sibling squabbles." I wrangled out of my soiled shoe and hobbled toward the front door. "Thanks for cleaning up, Ethan. After he's done, Alexis, please figure out how to get rid of the odor. I'd rather not open to the public with the odor of feces hanging in the air."

When I reached out to relock the door, I glanced through the window in the door and did a quick double take.

Across the street, on a bench in front of the Peak Inn, sat two boys, laughing and elbowing one another. I leaned closer to the glass and peered out at them. They looked straight at me, smirks on their faces. Then one of them pinched his nose, while the other flapped his hand in front of his face, as if waving away a stench.

It was the Ratliff twins. I yanked open the door, but before I could cross the street to confront them, they jumped off the bench and took off down the street.

As I stood on the sidewalk and watched them sprint away, I wondered what other evil plots they had in store for me.

About the Author

Lori Roberts Herbst lives in Dallas, Texas, but spends a lot of time when she should be writing staring out the window and wishing she owned a home in Colorado mountains, too. She is a wife, mother, grandmother (gasp!), cozy mystery author, former counselor, and former journalism teacher. Lori serves as secretary of the Sisters in Crime North Dallas chapter and is a proud member of the SinC Guppies and the Mystery Writers of America. You can (and should!) follow Lori on Facebook and Instagram. Subscribe to her newsletter at www.lorirobertsherbst.com for updates and freebies.

Made in the USA
Coppell, TX
02 April 2021

52877489R00173